GOING, GOING, GANACHE

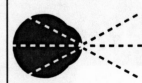

This Large Print Book carries the
Seal of Approval of N.A.V.H.

GOING, GOING, GANACHE

JENN MCKINLAY

WHEELER PUBLISHING
A part of Gale, Cengage Learning

Detroit • New York • San Francisco • New Haven, Conn • Waterville, Maine • London

GALE
CENGAGE Learning®

LIBRARY OF CONGRESS CATALOGING-IN-PUBLICATION DATA

McKinlay, Jenn.
  Going, Going, Ganache / By Jenn McKinlay. — Large Print edition.
    pages cm. — (A Cupcake Bakery Mystery) (Wheeler Publishing Large
  Print Cozy Mystery)
  ISBN-13: 978-1-4104-6238-1 (softcover)
  ISBN-10: 1-4104-6238-2 (softcover)
  1. Cooper, Melanie (Fictitious character)—Fiction. 2. DeLaura, Angie
(Fictitious character)—Fiction. 3. Bakeries—Fiction. 4. Bakers—Fiction.
5. Baking—Fiction. 6. Murder—Investigation—Fiction. 7. Large type books.
I. Title.
PS3612.A948G65 2014
813'.6—dc23   2013033683

Published in 2014 by arrangement with The Berkley Publishing Group,
a member of Penguin Group (USA) LLC, a Penguin Random House
Company

Printed in the United States of America
1 2 3 4 5   18 17 16 15 14

For Annette (Nettie) Amaturo, the Mel to my Angie or the Angie to my Mel depending upon the day, your friendship is one of my greatest joys. Thank you for being the sister of my heart and for giving this book such a cool title. And, of course, to the rest of the Amaturo crew, Fonz, Dom, Mike, Andrew, and Alyssa, you inspire me in so many ways and are without a doubt the coolest family ever! I love you all!

ACKNOWLEDGMENTS

Without my readers, I am nothing. So I want to give a big, sloppy thank you to all of the readers who have been on this journey with Mel and Angie since the beginning. Thank you for all of your kind words and encouragement. It is so very appreciated.

An extra heaping of thank-yous to Kate Seaver, my amazing editor who makes my books sparkle and shine; Katherine Pelz, her fabulous assistant editor; Andy Ball, a truly gifted copyeditor; and Kayleigh Clark, public relations guru. Also thank you to Jeff Fitz-Maurice, the artist who creates these spectacular covers. Truly, I am in awe of your talent. Much gratitude to Jessica Faust, my wonderful agent, I feel so very lucky to have you in my corner.

And as always, hugs and kisses to Chris, Beckett, and Wyatt, there simply are no words to express how grateful I am to have my Hub and the Hooligans in my life. You are everything to me.

ONE

"No, I'm not feeling it," Amy Pierson said. "Do it again, and this time try to give it that southwestern city-girl flare. This photo shoot is for *Southwest Style* magazine, after all."

Angie DeLaura looked at Melanie Cooper as if to ask if she could please hurl a cupcake at the bossy butt in the couture suit. Mel gave a slight shake of her blond head in the negative. She didn't want to move too much and have Amy yell at her again.

It was mid-October in Scottsdale, Arizona, and although the sun was hot the breeze was cool, keeping the inordinate amount of makeup Mel had on from melting off her face. She and Angie were outside their bakery in the small patio area, posing for a picture to run alongside the piece that had been written about them for an upcoming issue of *Southwest Style,* the premiere magazine about urban living in the desert.

What Mel had assumed would be a staff photographer snapping a picture of them behind the counter in the bakery had turned into a full-on spread, featuring Mel and Angie in poofy retro-fifties skirts, with crinolines, and starched cotton blouses with pearls.

Because Scottsdale's heyday had been the fifties and because the bakery was decorated in a retro-fifties style, Amy Pierson, the magazine's art director, had decided to run with the fifties theme, and thus Mel and Angie found themselves outfitted like June Cleaver in stilettos.

The makeup artist had teased Angie's long brown hair into an updo á la Audrey Hepburn, while Mel's short blond locks had been styled in lush waves reminiscent of Marilyn Monroe. They were tricked out in an ultra-feminine chic style that made them positively unrecognizable.

"My head itches," Angie whispered.

"My feet hurt," Mel returned. The high heels they had been put in were arch-crampers, and Mel longed for her beat-up Keds, her comfy jeans, and a simple T-shirt.

"Okay, ladies, let's see those smiles," the photographer said. He was a young guy named Chad, who happily snapped away while Mel and Angie stood frozen, surrounded by tiers and trays of cupcakes, trying to look like they were having the time of their lives.

Fairy Tale Cupcakes, their bakery in Old Town Scottsdale, was in the heart of the tourist district, which was one of the many reasons for their success. They did loads of special orders, but their walk-in traffic kept them steadily busy with drop-ins who wanted to fortify themselves with a cupcake or two before, during, and after a day of doing the tourist thing.

Mel observed the crowd gathering to watch and hoped that Marty Zelaznik and Oz Ruiz, their two bakery employees, were inside preparing for the crush once the magazine people departed.

The magazine had asked Mel to design cupcakes that would reflect the Southwest, so she had used bright fondant to create cupcakes devoted to cactus-flower blossoms. Each cupcake sported a flower, so magenta prickly-pear blooms blended with white and yellow saguaro flowers in several tiers of cupcakes that were festive and lovely and very southwestern.

Mel wasn't entirely comfortable with the dolled-up-babe look she and Angie were using to represent the bakery. But given that the magazine had a national subscription

11

base of several hundred thousand, she was determined to do whatever it took to get in print. The coverage would go a long way towards making Fairy Tale Cupcakes the place to buy cupcakes in the Valley of the Sun.

Chad's camera clicked repeatedly as he moved, stepping closer and then backing away, dropping to one knee and then climbing onto a chair, all to get the shots he wanted. Mel smiled until her face hurt and her eyes began to cross. Angie was making small whimpering noises in the back of her throat as Chad paused in front of them. *Snap. Snap. Snap.*

"No!" Amy said, peering over his shoulder to study them. "I'm still not feeling it. Chad, let's discuss. Maybe it's the lighting."

"Relax, ladies, but don't move too far," Chad said as he went to confer with Amy.

" 'Every girl on every page of *Quality* has grace, elegance, and pizzazz. Now, what's wrong with bringing out a girl who has character, spirit, and intelligence?' " Angie muttered to Mel.

Classic movie buffs, they had played this game with their friend Tate Harper since they were kids. Mel was about to identify the movie when a voice from nearby said, " 'That certainly would be novel in a fashion magazine.' "

Mel and Angie both turned to look at the man who had spoken.

"*Funny Face* with Audrey Hepburn and Fred Astaire," he said. "Good one."

"Looks like we found a new member of our tribe," Mel said. She held out her hand to him. "Melanie Cooper."

"Angie DeLaura," Angie said as she did the same.

The tall, red-haired man smiled as he shook each of their hands. He was dressed in all black and had the chiseled good looks of a male model. Mel noticed that his hand was soft to the touch and his fingernails were neatly trimmed and buffed. She sighed. She couldn't remember the last time she'd had a professional manicure.

"Justin Freehold," he said. "Creative director for *SWS.*"

"Is it just me, Justin," Angie asked, "or do there seem to be an awful lot of chefs in this photo-shoot kitchen?"

"Nice mixed metaphor," Mel said. "But she's right. Who are all of these people?"

Justin scanned the crowd.

"Good question," he said. "Pretty much anyone with their name on the masthead of the magazine is here, and that's why."

He jerked his head in the direction of a

man standing apart. He was tall and fit but looked to be somewhere in his fifties as his dark hair was giving way to silver. He had laugh lines that creased the corners of his eyes, but he also sported a hard jaw that made Mel think he was accustomed to making tough decisions.

"That would be our new leader, Ian Hannigan," Justin said. "He just bought the magazine and saved it from an untimely death. Everyone is determined to shine under his ever-watchful gaze."

"So that's why this went from a 'say cheese' to a 'strike a pose' layout," Angie said. "I suppose in the end it will be better for the bakery, but when we get done, I may just shave my head. Honestly, feel this."

She raised her right hand and patted her head. It didn't move. Curious, Mel touched the loaf of hair on Angie's head. Yep, it was as crusty on the outside as a baguette.

"Wow," she said.

"More like *ow*," Angie retorted.

Justin squinted into the crowd. "I know most everyone here, except for her. Does she work for you?"

Mel followed the line of his gaze. Striding through the crowd with her stocky frame wedged into a polka dot blouse and a black poodle skirt with a pink poodle on it, and

14

wearing black-and-white saddle shoes, was Olivia Puckett. She was also hoisting a tray of brightly colored cupcakes over her head.

"Please tell me I'm hallucinating," Angie said.

"Okay, but you have to do the same for me," Mel said.

Olivia owned the rival bakery Confections and, for reasons unknown to Mel, she had developed a pathological competitiveness with Mel and Angie. It seemed if there was baking attention to be had, Olivia wanted all of it.

"Oh, yoo-hoo, magazine people," Olivia called. "If you're having a hard time photographing these two, I'd be happy to fill in."

"Is she for real?" Angie snapped. "I did not let them do this to me" — she pointed to her head — "so that woman could march in here in that ridiculous skirt and take over our photo shoot."

"I'll take care of this," Justin said. "I can't imagine Amy would do a switch-up like this at the eleventh hour."

Mel watched as Justin approached Amy and Chad and the silver-haired Ian Hannigan, along with several other intimidatingly well-coifed people. They huddled together like players on a football team, and Mel was alarmed when she saw Amy's head break

15

out of the circle and stare at Olivia with a considering look.

"This is unbelievable," Angie said.

"What's the holdup?" a cranky voice asked from behind Mel. "How long does it take to snap a few pictures?"

Mel turned to find that Marty and Oz had slipped out the front door of the bakery to join them.

"What's she doing here?" Oz asked. He did not have to specify that he was talking about Olivia.

"Trying to horn in on our photo shoot," Mel said. "Apparently, Angie and I are so un-photogenic that they're actually considering it."

"Aw, what's the matter, princess?" Olivia sneered as she ambled over to the patio. "You don't really think you're model material do you?"

Mel heaved a sigh. She was pretty sure she was developing a bunion on her right foot, and the last thing she needed was a battle with Olivia.

"How did you find out about this?" she asked.

Olivia shrugged. "I have my ways."

Her eyes shifted away, however, and the piercing truth hit Mel like a dart in a bull's-eye.

"You have a spy!"

"What? No, I don't!"

"Oh my god, look at her face!" Oz said. "She's totally lying."

"I am not," Olivia huffed.

"Then how did you know to dress in that getup?" Marty asked as he moved in front of Mel and Angie, as if to protect them. "Someone tipped you off that they were doing a fifties theme."

"Listen, old man," Olivia said —

"Who are you calling old, gray beard?" Marty interrupted.

"Ah!" Olivia took one hand off the tray of cupcakes she was still holding to feel her chin for errant whiskers.

Feeling none, she snarled at Marty, grabbed a vivid pink cupcake off her tray and lobbed it at him.

Marty ducked, and it landed in Angie's hair and got wedged there like a bird in a nest. Angie wobbled on her feet; obviously the weight of the cupcake in her already heavy hair had knocked her off balance.

"Ha! How'd you like that, princess?" Olivia cackled. "I've got one with your name on it, too."

"Stop calling me princess!" Mel snapped, trying to steady Angie as she listed to one side.

17

"No?" Olivia asked. "How about I call you b— ?"

A white cactus flower cupcake landed with smack-dab precision right in Olivia's pie-hole. Mel whipped her head around and saw Marty looking at her with an innocent expression.

"What?" he asked. "I slipped."

"Nice," Oz said, and the two exchanged a knuckle bump. "Pitcher?"

"All-American," Marty said. "You know, back in the day."

Mel propped Angie against the table. Angie gave Marty an impressed thumbs-up, but Mel knew retaliation —

Smack! A cupcake slammed into the side of her head. The cake thudded to the ground, but she could feel the frosting ooze down her face as it slid out of her short blond hair and landed on her shoulder.

Now she was mad. Mel forgot about Ian Hannigan, the owner of the magazine. She forgot that they were supposed to be here to showcase their shop with a happy, peppy photo shoot. Without thinking of the consequences of her actions, Mel snatched up the spotlighted extra large cupcake in the center of the table and charged at Olivia with a roar reminiscent of Mel Gibson's character in *Braveheart*.

18

TWO

"What do you have to say for yourselves?" Tate asked. "Do you have any idea how much trouble you're in?"

Mel, Angie, Marty, and Oz sat slumped in a booth in the bakery. They were covered head to toe in frosting and chunks of cake. They looked like they were the lone survivors of a cupcake massacre.

"But it wasn't —" Angie protested, but Tate held up his hand.

"Don't! I don't want to hear it," he said. "This thing with Olivia is out of control. It's a turf war over cupcakes. Now I want you to figure out how you're going to make peace with her once and for all."

"What?" Mel hopped out of the booth she'd been sitting in. "But she's got a spy. She practically admitted it. She's infiltrated the ranks."

Tate looked at her as if to say, *So what?*

"Everyone should take a lie detector test,"

Marty said. "Mel, I'm sure your uncle can hook us up with one from the Scottsdale PD."

They all stared at him.

"What?" he asked. "I'll go first."

"Marty, I think it's safe to say that we all dislike Olivia as much as you," Angie said, "but you're kind of going around the bend on this one."

"But he's right," Mel said. "We have a leak, and I want to know who is giving out our secrets. If Olivia hadn't shown up today, none of this would have happened."

"She has a point there," Angie said to Tate.

He pushed back the sleeve on his Brooks Brothers suit and reached into her hair to pull out a chunk of cupcake.

"Saving this for later?" he asked.

"Funny," she said.

The door to the bakery was pushed open with a jangle of bells. Tate glanced up and saw Ian Hannigan stride into the bakery.

"Let me handle this," he said. "Do not move so much as a sprinkle."

"Heh-heh," Oz laughed. "T-man is on a roll today."

Mel gave him a sour look. "That's because he doesn't have gobs of frosting in his underpants."

Oz wriggled in his seat, and Mel knew

she'd made her point.

"What do you think is going to happen to us?" Angie asked. "That Hannigan guy looks very unhappy."

"Who cares?" Marty asked. "I say it was worth it to chase off that harpy once and for all."

"Too bad she unloaded her tray on us first," Angie said, flicking a chunk of icing off her forearm.

"She did look pretty funny running down the street with Mel chasing after her with the ginormous cupcake," Oz said. Then he snorted.

"I would have caught her, too, if it wasn't for those stupid high heels. Honestly, platform high heels! I'm tall already; didn't the wardrobe people realize that heels on me are redundant?" Mel asked.

"He was a dude," Angie said. "They don't get it."

"Still, we got Olivia good," Marty said.

Mel and Angie exchanged a glance. It was true. Between Marty, Oz, and Angie, Olivia had been pelted with a rainbow of cupcakes until she was slip-sliding her way out of Old Town, around the corner, and out of sight.

"She looked like a B-movie monster," Angie said. "The Abominable Frosting Monster."

21

Angie let out an uncharacteristic giggle, which made Mel chuckle and set off Marty and Oz as well.

Mel tried to stop, knowing that it was bad form to laugh in front of the magazine people. Still, the harder she tried to block the mental picture of Olivia blinking bright yellow frosting out of her eyes, the more it tickled her funny bone and the harder she laughed.

She saw Tate whip around from his conversation and glower at them. She clamped her lips together, trying to rein in her giggles. But then Marty let out a sound like a cork popping before he started wheeze-laughing, which set off Mel and the others again.

The giggle fit was contagious and, to Mel, it was the best therapy in the world. Her sides actually hurt from laughter spasms and, when she finally wound down, she felt relaxed for the first time since putting on those stupid heels.

Tate crossed the room towards them. He was loosening his tie as if it were strangling him.

"Having a good time?" he asked. It was clear that he was not. "Because you are looking at a major snafu here."

"Buzz-kill," Angie said.

Tate glowered.

"Are you finished?" he asked.

He was looming over the booth where they sat as if they were a line of kids outside the principal's office.

"Do you have any idea how much money you have cost the magazine in staff time, equipment, wardrobe, and so forth?" Tate asked.

"A lot," Mel said, trying to sound reasonable.

"Thousands," Tate corrected her. "Mr. Hannigan could easily sue us right down to our last paper cupcake thingy."

"Liner," Oz said.

"Whatever," Tate snapped. He was tugging on his ear, never a good sign, and his breathing was coming and going in sharp bursts, as if he'd run a race.

"Well, that seems a bit over-the-top," Angie said. "I mean, yeah, we made a mess —"

"A mess?" Tate said. His eyes practically bugged out of his head. "One or two dropped cupcakes are a mess, but what you four did was like cupcake napalm. There is frosting all over the sidewalk, other storefronts, cars. You're damn lucky you didn't hit any pedestrians."

Mel hung her head. A quick glance at the

others, and she saw that they did the same. Tate paced back and forth in front of them like a military commander disciplining the troops. Mel tried not to be annoyed, since it was his large financial investment in the bakery that was the sole reason it existed. Oh, business was good and they were turning a tidy profit, but without Tate's start-up scratch, Fairy Tale Cupcakes would have remained just that — a fairy tale.

"We'll take care of the cleanup," Oz said.

"Yes, you will," Tate agreed. "In fact, you and Marty need to get outside and get going on that. Now!"

Both Marty and Oz scuttled out of the booth and headed out the door. Mel had a sneaking suspicion that they were relieved to have been excused from the firing squad, but she didn't say as much.

"We should go help, too," Angie said.

"No. You two, being the faces of the bakery, are going to go over to Mr. Hannigan right now and commence groveling," Tate said.

"Ooh," Angie said. "You know that's not my gift."

"Well, it had better start to be," Tate said.

"When did you get all alpha male?" Angie asked. She stood in front of him, glaring up at him. "I'm not sure I like it."

"Really?" Tate asked. "How would you feel if I told you I don't care."

Angie gasped, and Mel echoed her. This was a heretofore unseen side of Tate, and she wasn't sure she liked it either.

"Do you have any idea who Ian Hannigan is?" Tate asked.

Mel and Angie exchanged a look and then looked back at Tate. Mel knew that Angie was thinking the same thing she was — that they'd show Tate they did, too, know who Hannigan was.

"He owns the magazine *SWS*," Angie said.

"And he saved it from ruin," Mel added.

Mel felt that, despite being covered in frosting they both could be quite smug about their knowledge base in regard to Ian Hannigan.

"Ian Hannigan is one of the richest men in the world," Tate said. "He is a media mogul. He doesn't just own *SWS* magazine. That's nothing to him. That's a plaything, a shiny new toy for the moment. He owns Hannigan Inc. Heck, he *is* Hannigan Inc."

"Never heard of it," Angie said.

"Really?" Tate asked. "Well, maybe you've heard of the It Channel?"

"Oh, I love that channel," Mel said. "It's very cutting edge, lots of shows about technology and new inventions."

"And maybe you've heard of Gan Productions? As in HanniGan?" Tate asked.

"Oh, they produce a lot of good movies," Angie said. "I particularly liked —"

"I'm sorry," Tate said. "I hate to interrupt, but there are about fifty more companies under the Hannigan Inc. umbrella that I have yet to mention."

Mel raised her eyebrows.

"Now do you see?" Tate asked. "This isn't just some chump who owns a magazine. This is one of the world's media giants, and you two have really ticked him off."

"Uh-oh," Angie said.

"So it's all coming into focus now," Tate said. "Great. My work here is done."

"You know, the sarcasm thing that you've got going," Mel said. "I'm not really enjoying it."

Tate just stared at her, doing a fair impression of a brick wall.

"It's just a guess," Angie said. "But I don't think he cares."

"Go. Make. Nice," Tate said each word as if he'd ripped it off a bone with his teeth.

Mel pushed the frosting-sodden bangs off of her forehead and rose out of the booth to stand beside Angie.

"I hope you're feeling charming," she said to Angie.

26

"With this hair?" Angie asked. "I look like a troll doll. All I need to do is show some belly."

"Don't!" Tate ordered.

Angie heaved a sigh. "As if I would. Unless . . . do you think it would work?"

Tate glared at them through eyes that were lowered into mere slits. His face was forbidding enough that Mel was actually happy to go and face the media mogul. Surely he couldn't be much worse than Tate at the moment, could he?

Together Angie, Mel, and Tate crossed the bakery to where Ian stood in the corner. He had a group around him about three deep, so Mel and Angie stood patiently, waiting for the smack-down that they had no doubt would be delivered in short order.

A woman with blunt-cut gray hair and wearing pointy-toed heels, sheer black hose, and a form-fitting black chemise with a red bolero jacket over it, stood beside Hannigan. He was talking to her, but she had her body turned half away from him and looked to be refusing to make eye contact, which Mel found fascinating. The woman projected an aura of contempt and disdain that was palpable, and Mel felt infinitely more afraid of her than of Ian Hannigan.

Justin stood in front of Mel, so she

grabbed his sleeve and tugged. He turned, and she whispered, "Who is the scary woman?"

A small smile played on Justin's lips; he didn't have to ask who she was talking about.

"That's Brigit MacLeod," Justin said. "Editor in chief."

"That's bad," Angie whispered.

"Really bad," Mel agreed.

"Do you hear me, Brigit?" Ian barked over their whispered conversation.

Brigit went rigid, crossed her arms over her chest, and studiously ignored him.

Ian turned and seemed to take notice of Mel and Angie for the first time.

"Ah, here they are," he said. He rubbed his hands together as if in anticipation. "Everyone, I'd like you to meet your new bosses for the next week."

THREE

Mel looked behind her to see if he was introducing someone she hadn't seen. But no, when she turned back around, Ian Hannigan had his laser-like scrutiny centered right on her.

Once upon a time, Mel had been a corporate minion. She had been a dynamo in the world of marketing in Los Angeles and had been scrupulously working her way up the food chain. When she realized that the only happy moments in her life were her daily stops at her local bakery, she had ditched it all to go to culinary school.

She had dealt with people like Ian Hannigan back in LA. They were cunning and ruthless and had the singular ability to bend people to their wills. But Mel wasn't in that world anymore, and Ian Hannigan was standing on her black-and-white tiles in her bakery. This was Mel's turf, and she called the shots here.

"Mr. Hannigan," Mel said. "I don't think we've been introduced. I'm Melanie Cooper, one of the owners of the bakery."

She extended her hand, pleased to see it was clean of frosting.

Hannigan studied her for a moment and then clasped her hand in his. Mel was surprised to feel callus-toughened skin along his palms, and his fingers were large and strong as if he actually used them for more than holding his cell phone to his ear.

"This is my partner, Angie DeLaura," Mel said, and they shook hands as well. "And you've already met Tate Harper."

Hannigan nodded and continued to study them. His gray eyes were like chips of steel, and he held his jaw out in a stubborn pose as if he's made up his mind about something and was determined to see it through.

"Ladies," he said. "This photo shoot turned into quite a production."

A chuckle sounded in the corner of the room, and Chad, the photographer, looked up from where he was working on his laptop.

"Oh, sorry," he said. "I was just reviewing some of the day's takes."

Under Hannigan's unwavering stare, Chad cleared his throat and looked back down as if hoping his laptop had an escape-hatch option.

"I came to this photo shoot to see how my staff worked as a team," Hannigan said. He looked at Mel. "You own a business. You understand the importance of teamwork."

"I do." Mel nodded.

And she did. She had only hired people to work in the bakery who fit in with the irreverent outlook she and Angie maintained. Her team was a ragtag band of misfits bound only by a mutual love of cupcakes; still it was a criteria of sorts, and it seemed to be working.

"That fiasco out there showed me one thing," Hannigan said. "While my people did a lot of pushing and shoving, throwing one another into the line of fire, your people rallied around you and neutralized the threat."

"True," Mel said. "But it helps to have a common enemy. Olivia Puckett, the poodle skirt, has been a thorn in our backsides since we opened."

"I think we can certainly agree on a common enemy," Brigit said. Her voice was gritty and low-pitched, just as Mel would have expected it to be. Her venom-filled glance at Hannigan left no doubt as to whom she felt the enemy was.

Hannigan gave Brigit a look that Mel was

sure would have frozen the blood in her veins. Brigit, however, merely shrugged and gave him a closed-mouth smile that carried more of a threat in it than a knife pointing at his chest.

Mel felt Angie lean against her, and she knew it was Angie's way of communicating that she saw what was happening as well. Obviously, there was tension at *SWS*, namely that Brigit MacLeod hated Ian Hannigan, and she didn't care if he knew it.

"Although a common enemy can be an excellent bond," Hannigan said, turning back to Mel, "a common goal can be an even stronger bond, because it requires a commitment to a desired outcome."

Mel glanced at Angie and saw her own confusion reflected back at her in Angie's warm brown eyes. What the hell was Ian Hannigan talking about?

"It is to that end, that my staff will be coming to work for you, Ms. Cooper," he said.

"I'm sorry," Mel said. "I must have misheard you. Did you say your staff was coming to work here?"

"Correct," Hannigan said. "These people need a common goal, something to work towards together, so I have decided that they will learn how to bake cupcakes together."

"So, like a corporate cupcake boot camp?" Mel asked.

"Exactly," Hannigan said. "The magazine's annual community outreach gala is this Saturday night. I think one thousand cupcakes ought to do it, and then we can consider the damage done to this photo shoot paid in full."

Mel glanced over her shoulder at Tate. He was standing in the corner with his arms crossed over his chest in a fair imitation of Hannigan. He gave her one small bob of his head.

"Well, when you put it like that, how can we refuse?" she asked.

Mel and Angie had taught classes before, so it wasn't the idea of teaching the staff of *SWS* magazine how to make cupcakes that had Mel in her bakery at two o'clock in the morning with her cat, Captain Jack, at her side.

A white cat with a black patch over one eye, Captain Jack looked and acted every inch the pirate he was named for. While he batted a paper cupcake liner across the floor, Mel scoured the tables and chairs and neatened and restocked the display cases that lined one wall.

No, the teaching part was easy, and the

one thousand edible cupcakes by the end of the week was doable as well. It was having several unwilling participants underfoot for a week that was giving her pause. She had no doubt that Brigit MacLeod would rather chew off her left foot than spend a week in a kitchen.

Mel wasn't much for confrontation. Her adolescent years had been spent on the plus side of plump, making her the target of bullies and mean girls. Typically, the head cheerleader in her high school, Cassidy Havers, had been the nastiest of the lot and had followed Mel in the hallways and chanting, "Give me an *M*. Give me an *E*. Give me a *L*. Give me an *E*. Give me a *P-H-A-N-T*. What does it spell? Melephant! Hey, want a peanut, Melephant?"

Then Cassidy would pretend to hold out a peanut to her. Truly, the act was a work of cheerleader genius that made the entire student body laugh at Mel. And, of course, Cassidy was a tall, thin redhead, whose parents had given her a boob job for her sweet sixteen.

Mel found it a cold comfort that her own family loved her for what was on the inside and not for the size of her bra cup.

They loved her so much, in fact, that when Mel's brother, Charlie, spent a Saturday writing odes to Cassidy's faux front on all of the walls in all of the public men's bathrooms in South Scottsdale, including Cassidy's phone number in his poetry, and Mel's father caught him red-handed, or rather with marker in hand, Charlie was given a raise in his allowance, and the matter was never spoken of again.

On the upside, Cassidy was so busy dealing with her crop of new admirers, she had quite forgotten to torment Mel anymore.

Brigit MacLeod, editor in chief, reminded Mel of Cassidy. Brigit was the sort of woman who knew what sort of response she wanted from people and exactly how to get it. Mel had a feeling Brigit was going to resent Mel for this situation, which was not unwarranted, and that she was going to make Mel miserable for it.

The kitchen door swung open and in stepped Joe DeLaura. He was wearing his gray T-shirt and plaid pajama bottoms. He looked sleepy, and he scratched his head as he watched Captain Jack race across the floor in front of him.

"I had a feeling I'd find you down here," he said. "Couldn't sleep?"

"No, I —" Mel began, but he interrupted her.

"I was talking to Jack," he said.

"Oh," she said.

She watched as Joe crouched down and made kissie noises and wiggled his fingers. Captain Jack did not even try for typical cat aloofness. Instead, he abandoned the cupcake liner and ran at Joe, who scooped him up with one hand and cradled him to his chest. Lucky cat.

"What's the matter, buddy?" Joe asked as he scratched Jack's chin, eliciting a purr that sounded like an idling racecar engine. "Are you worried about the mean magazine people coming tomorrow?"

Jack's purr got louder.

"You know it will be fine," Joe said. "They will be so impressed with your culinary brilliance that they will be just as captured by your spell as I am."

Mel felt her heart do that ridiculous fluttery thing that it did whenever Joe was around. He was the middle of Angie's seven older brothers, and Mel had pined for him from afar from the first time she'd seen him when she was twelve and he was sixteen.

It had taken twenty years for him to notice her in *that* way — not his fault, since law school and being an assistant district attorney had kept his calendar full. But they'd been dating for a year now, and Joe had seen Mel through several scary times. He was her rock. He'd recently asked her to marry him, and Mel had said yes.

She had asked him to keep their engagement a secret, however. It was silly, she supposed, but she wanted to keep it just for them for a while. Through her work at the bakery, she'd seen enough engagements and weddings to know that once the intention to marry became public knowledge, the engaged couple no longer owned it.

Mel loved her mother to pieces; truly, there was no finer woman alive than Joyce Cooper. But if Joyce had one wish to make in this life, it would be that Mel marry dear Joe — Joyce always called him "dear Joe" — and settle down, preferably on the same street as Joyce, and commence with the baby making. Mel wasn't ready yet.

"Come here, Cupcake," Joe said. He held out his available arm, and Mel stepped into his embrace. He planted a kiss on her lips, and asked, "Do you want to talk about it?"

Mel thought about it. Would it help to blather on about her fat childhood and low self-esteem and how Brigit terrified her and brought it all back in its full Technicolor glory? No.

"Nah," she said. "But I appreciate the offer."

"What I said was true, you know." Joe

37

squeezed her tight. "I am completely under your spell, and they will be, too."

Captain Jack worked his way across Joe's chest and into Mel's arms.

"And I'm not the only one," Joe said.

Captain Jack tucked his head under Mel's chin while she held him close, and started to snore.

Joe checked the lock on the front door and shut off the lights. He ushered Mel through the kitchen and out the back door, locking up as they went. They climbed the stairs to her apartment above the bakery, and Mel turned to face Joe on the landing.

"I'm so glad I have you two in my life," she said.

His brown eyes were like melted chocolate and his smile was crooked as he asked, "So, when are you going to make an honest man out of me and marry me?"

Four

Mel stepped into her tiny apartment, letting Joe shut and lock the door behind her. She put Jack down in his cat bed and turned to face Joe.

"Soon," she said. "We'll announce it soon."

Joe rubbed a hand over his eyes, and Mel could see that he was tired.

"You know there's been talk about me going for the district attorney position when my boss retires," he said.

"You'd make a great one," Mel said.

"I'd like you by my side when I do it," he said.

"I will be," Mel promised. "Every step of the way. I'll even bake cupcakes."

He gave her a small smile. "I'd like you there as my wife."

"Because it's politically advantageous?" Mel asked. She knew as soon as the words left her mouth that it was the wrong thing to say.

"Is that what you think?" he asked.

He spoke in the same reasonable tone he always used when mediating a dispute amongst his siblings. Mel was not sure how she felt about being on the receiving end of his negotiating skills.

"No," she conceded. Although, deep down she wondered if there was a part of Joe that had decided a cupcake baker was a pretty inoffensive political ally.

"Listen, I won't rush you," he said. "But I want to be sure that this is still what you want."

"Yes," she said. She wondered if he had noticed her slight hesitation. If he had, he didn't show it. "I just don't want to share it with anyone yet."

He looked like he wanted to say something but thought better of it. For the first time in their relationship, Mel felt as if there was a chasm between them, a rift rent by words not spoken, and she knew it wasn't just Joe who was holding back, it was her, too. And yet she didn't know how to say what she was feeling, so she said nothing.

They climbed back into Mel's futon. Joe lay flat on his back and Mel curled up on her side, facing away from him. Joe reached out and put his hand on her hip, as if trying to bridge the gap between them. Still, Mel said nothing.

There was a quiet little voice inside her head telling her that there was more holding her back than not wanting to share their good news with the world, but she refused to hear it.

For now, she had the cupcake boot camp to get through, and she couldn't be distracted by a handsome man with soft brown eyes who wanted to make her his wife.

Mel sighed and fell into a doze with Joe's hand still warm upon her and Captain Jack snuggled up on the pillow between their heads.

Boot camp started at seven in the morning. Despite being a baker, Mel was not a morning person. Per usual, a hot cup of coffee had been left on her nightstand by Joe, who had already left to start his day.

Mel scratched Jack's head and took her coffee into the bathroom, where she prepped for her day. Given the scouring she'd had to give herself yesterday to get all of the frosting off, today's shower was more of a repeat rinse, and she was on her way in minutes.

Captain Jack ate a hearty breakfast, and she left him to return to his sweet dreams with a pang of envy. After her midnight cleaning bender, she really would have loved to get some more shut-eye.

Angie was just walking through the front door when Mel arrived. Mel stared at her for a second, and Angie held up her hand, indicating that she did not want to hear it.

"Your —" Mel said, but Angie shook her head and interrupted. "I am aware of my hair. Thank you."

"But —" Mel began, but Angie said, "Uh-huh. Not open for discussion. Rest assured, I have tried everything and let it go."

"Oh, okay," Mel said.

"I'm going to go and make coffee now," Angie said, and she disappeared into the kitchen, taking her loaf of hair with her.

While Angie put on the big pot of coffee, Mel gathered the books they used to show customers who wanted special orders. She figured Brigit and company would want to choose what sort of cupcakes they would make, so if she gave them the books to peruse, they could pick how they were going to spend their week.

She stacked the books on the steel table in the kitchen, as it was the largest space to have a meeting in the bakery. She then went out to open the front door and await their boot-camp attendees.

Justin Freehold was the first to arrive. Mel

noted that he was again dressed in all black, but a decidedly more casual version, in jeans and a T-shirt.

He and Mel exchanged good mornings, and then Angie came through the kitchen door bearing a tray full of coffee with sugars and creamers.

"Angie, your ha—" Justin said, but Mel shook her head, and his voice trailed off.

"What?" Angie asked. There was no good morning for Justin from her.

"You're a goddess to have fresh brewed coffee at the ready," he said.

"Yes, I am," she agreed.

The door opened again, and in strode Amy Pierson in a gray pinstripe jacket and matching pencil skirt — not exactly baking wear. She was chatting on her phone and sat down in the corner booth of the bakery without so much as nodding at the rest of them.

The door opened again, and in strolled Sylvia Lucci, the woman in charge of the fashion portion of the magazine. Yes, it had been her people who'd dressed Mel and Angie up in the retro fifties outfits. Sylvia was a stunner with exotic features, almond-shaped eyes, and thick, glossy dark brown hair that hung past her shoulders, framing her heart-shaped face, giving her a fragile look. Her figure was a perfect hourglass, and she wore a form-fitting knit dress that showed it off to perfection.

"Justin, I might have known you'd be here first," she said. "You suck-up."

Mel glanced between the two, but Justin was smiling, so she knew it was good-natured teasing.

"Mel, Angie, you know Sylvia Lucci, our fashion director," Justin said.

They shook hands, and Sylvia pursed her lips when she looked at Angie.

"Are you fond of that hairdo?" she asked. "Or did my wardrobe people cause a malfunction with your follicles?"

"Would you like this?" Angie asked and pointed to her head. "My brothers have been teasing me nonstop."

"The brothers saw it?" Mel asked.

"I went over to my parents to see if mom could undo it, and Tony took a picture of it with his phone. I believe it has gone viral among the seven of them and will probably land on the Internet any day. Sal has started calling me 'The Loaf.' "

"You have brothers?" Sylvia asked.

"Seven Italian older brothers," Angie sighed.

"Oh, honey," Sylvia said. *"Sono Italiana con molti fratelli."*

44

The two women embraced, and Justin looked at Mel and said, "I didn't know we were having an Italian daughters' meeting. I would have worn my Venetian Carnevale costume and dressed the part."

"I can fix your hair," Sylvia said. "You know Christine's Salon? It's just around the corner from here."

"The one owned by Mean Christine?" Angie asked warily.

Sylvia laughed and it chimed in the air like bells.

"She's actually a friend of mine. She's nice to me because she likes favorable reviews in the magazine. She'll let us use one of her sinks."

"Are they open yet?" Mel asked.

"She will be for me," Sylvia said as she scrolled through the numbers on her phone.

"Is it all right if I go?" Angie asked. "Can you manage?"

"Are you kidding? Go!" Mel said. "Anything to get that lump of hair off your head."

As Angie and Sylvia left, a man came in. He was skinny and had a waxy complexion, as if he didn't see enough daylight. He wore a dress shirt and a tie, which was loose around his neck. His thinning gray hair was combed back from his forehead in a hairline that looked as if it were suffering from erosion and was now a few inches from where it had originally begun.

"Coffee," he ordered, and snapped his fingers at Mel.

Mel raised her eyebrows in surprise. One of the many reasons she had never gone into the restaurant biz was because of customer attitudes like this one. She had never responded well to a snap of the fingers or a "come here" whistle.

"Sam, where are your manners?" Justin asked. "Melanie Cooper, this is Sam Kelleher. Sam is our features director."

"Nice to meet you," Mel said.

"Did you know I won a Pulitzer?" Sam asked. "It was for real news, hard news, back when I worked for the *Los Angeles Times*. Now look at me. I'm in cupcake frigging boot camp. If I had a gun, I'd eat it."

"If I had a gun, I'd loan it to you," Mel said.

Sam stared at her as if noticing her for the first time. His eyes were almost black and tucked behind fleshy pockets that sagged as if his skin had given up after too many hours spent in smoke-filled rooms subsisting on meals of cold coffee and Twinkies.

"You've got a backbone, Melanie Cooper. Good thing, because you're going to need it," he said and he barked out a laugh. Then he left them to get a coffee from where Angie had left the fixings.

Mel turned wide eyes to Justin. He grinned at her.

"I'd say you have a new fan," he said. "Sam hates everyone, except Brigit. He and Brigit go way back. She used to be hard news, too."

"Really?" Mel asked. "She seems so —"

"Hip? Trendy? Edgy?" Justin suggested.

"Yeah, all that," Mel said. "But I was thinking more along the lines of scary."

"Oh, she's that, too," Justin said. "Terrifying in fact."

The front door banged open, and in strode Brigit as if by talking about her they had summoned her. Mel felt herself stand a little taller and noticed that Justin did the same.

Like Sam, Brigit was not dressed for a day of cupcake baking but more for a day at the office. She wore a linen sheath dress with a wide dark brown belt and matching dark brown Alexander McQueen pumps. Her silver hair was twisted up on the back of her head in a delicate twist, she had large pearls on her earlobes, and her makeup was flawless.

Brigit stood in the doorway and looked around her, scanning the room. She and

Sam exchanged nods and she winked at Justin, and then her gaze settled on Mel. She crooked her finger at her, beckoning Mel forward while she glanced at the smartphone in her other hand.

Mel glanced at Justin, who nodded.

"Molly, be a dear and show me your office," Brigit said.

"It's Mel. M-E-L," Mel said.

"That sounds like a man's name," Brigit said. "Is it short for something?"

She tapped the screen of her smartphone, and Mel had the feeling that the woman wasn't even listening to her, but when she hesitated, Brigit's head snapped up and her blue eyes hit Mel like two laser pointers.

"Well?"

"Melanie," she said. "It's short for Melanie."

Brigit tipped her head. "You should use it. A woman should not squelch her femininity just to survive in a man's world. We are not liberated if we are poor imitations of them wearing bad suits, nor are we equal if we take our fashion cues from strippers and whores and use our breasts instead of our brains to achieve our goals."

Mel felt her mouth slide open and she struggled for a response. "It's just a nickname."

"Rethink it," Brigit said. "Now, your office?"

Mel glanced at Justin, who looked as though he was trying not to laugh, and then said, "Please follow me."

Mel's office was a converted broom closet in the corner of the kitchen. She pushed the door open and cringed at the mess. She had no doubt that Brigit would have another lecture at the ready about her filing system, which was a stack of papers and catalogs piled one on top of another until they threatened the spill off the desk.

To her surprise, Brigit glanced around her, and said, "This will do."

"Do?" Mel asked.

"I have a magazine to put out," Brigit said. "No matter what Hannigan is trying to prove, I can't take a week off to bake cupcakes, as I have subscribers and advertisers to answer to. Now, I've put Bonnie, our food director, in charge of selecting the cupcakes, subject to my approval of course. She should be here shortly."

Brigit moved forward, leaving Mel no choice but to back out of her own office or risk being run over by the shorter woman. Then Brigit shut the door in Mel's face. Before she turned away, Mel heard the distinct sound of a thump on the floor and suspected that Brigit had just cleared off her desk with all the tact, diplomacy, and finesse of a backhoe.

FIVE

Mel was just about to barge into her office and give Brigit a piece of her mind when the kitchen door opened and in came Justin with another woman, who looked the complete antithesis of Brigit MacLeod. She had a sturdy build with generous curves, she wore no makeup on her freckled face, and her curly red hair was held back by a wide black hair band. Instead of a snappy business suit, she wore jeans and a T-shirt. Mel liked her immediately.

"Melanie Cooper," the woman said with her hand outstretched. "I'm Bonnie Hummecker, the food director for *SWS,* and I'm a huge fan of your work. In fact, I'm the one who recommended you to Amy Pierson for the magazine."

"Oh, hi," Mel said, and shook Bonnie's hand. Her relief at finally meeting someone who wasn't scary, mean, or impossibly gorgeous made her want to reach out and hug the woman. "It's a pleasure, a real pleasure to meet you."

Bonnie smiled and her entire face lit up. Then she gave Mel a knowing look.

"Let me guess," she said. "Amy ignored you, Sam was mean to you, Brigit scared you and took over your office, Justin has been charming, and Sylvia isn't here yet."

"Close," Justin said. "You're off by one."

"Wait," Bonnie said. "Let me revise. Okay, Sylvia found a mirror somewhere and got lost in it."

"Actually, she's trying to help my partner get her hair back," Mel said.

"Did it go somewhere?" Bonnie asked.

"More like it's in lockdown on her head," Mel said.

"That's pretty nice of the beautiful one," Bonnie said.

"They have an Italian-sisterhood thing going," Justin clarified.

"Ah," Bonnie said as if it all made sense now. "Well, since Brigit put me in charge of choosing the cupcakes, let's check out your kitchen and see what we're working with."

Bonnie put her purse on the steel table, then walked the room, taking in the walk-in refrigerator and the double sinks.

"Oh, you have a Blodgett convection oven," she cried, and clasped her hands in front of her. Then she checked out the steel counter that ran along the wall. "Oh, and a Hobart mixer! This is perfect. I named my two corgi dogs Blodgett and Hobart."

"You did not," Mel said.

"I did, too," Bonnie said. "Look."

She pulled out her smartphone and, sure enough, the wallpaper on the phone's display window showed two corgis with the tags Blodgett and Hobart.

"That's awesome!" Mel laughed. She had a feeling that she and Bonnie Hummecker were going to get along just fine.

"Blodgett and Hobart are named for an oven and a mixer?" Justin asked. "Huh. And all this time I thought they were named for some unfortunate relatives."

Bonnie laughed and swatted his arm. "Justin, your knowledge base in the culinary arts is pitiful. Good thing you have a week to get up to scratch. Get it? Up to *scratch*?"

Justin rolled his eyes, but Mel laughed. For the first time, cupcake boot camp looked like it might actually be a pleasure.

The door to Mel's office popped open, and Brigit stuck her perfectly coiffed head out. Her reading glasses were lowered on her nose, and she looked over the top of them at them.

"Bonnie, have you planned our cupcakes yet?"

"Working on it," Bonnie said, completely unruffled by the censure in Brigit's voice.

"I want to hear your plan in thirty minutes. Justin, send Sam in to me." The door banged shut.

To Mel it felt as if she'd been slapped across the face, but Bonnie and Justin didn't seem fazed in the least. Mel wondered if maybe she'd been her own boss too long and she just wasn't adjusting well to being ordered around. Or maybe Brigit was just a rude shrew who could use some lessons in manners.

Justin left the kitchen to get Sam while Bonnie sat down at the steel table and pulled a notepad and pen out of her voluminous purse.

"Okay," Bonnie said. "I guess we should start planning. We'll come up with five flavors and designs that we don't like very much, and then we'll come up with five that we do like."

Mel sat beside her and gave her a questioning look.

"Why do we need five that we don't like?" she asked.

"I've worked with Brigit for four years now, and I have come to learn that she

54

always rejects the first few ideas offered, even if they are the best, because she wants her people to dig deeper and be more creative. So we will offer up the mediocre ones first and then hit her with our favorites after she's rejected us. Win-win."

"I'm so glad you're here," Mel said. "I don't think I could navigate all of this without you."

"Sure you could," Bonnie said. "You'd just spend more time stressed out and crying than you will because I'm here."

"Is that how it was for you when you started at the magazine?" Mel asked.

"Yep," Bonnie said. "But I'm a lot tougher than my dimples and freckles would have you believe, and Sam actually coached me in how to handle Brigit."

"Sam?" Mel asked.

"I know he doesn't seem the type to help out anyone, but he was kind to me," Bonnie said. "And then I paid it forward to Justin, who did the same for Sylvia."

"Who did the same for Amy?" Mel asked.

A guilty look passed over Bonnie's face and she let out a sigh.

"No one. None of us can stand Amy," Bonnie confessed. "That girl would prostitute her own grandmother for a promotion. She's on her own."

Justin and Sam entered the kitchen. Sam went right into Mel's tiny office while Justin joined them at the table.

"Don't forget," Justin said. "We need to make gluten-free cupcakes for Margery Firestone."

"Who is Margery Firestone?" Mel asked.

"She owns the next largest chunk of the magazine after Ian Hannigan," Bonnie said. "She's old money from New York and a real b—"

"And she can only eat gluten-free food," Justin interrupted, giving Bonnie a look.

"What?" Bonnie asked. "I was going to say she is a real belle of the ball type."

"Oh," Justin said. "Sorry to interrupt."

"I'm so sure," Bonnie said. She gave him an annoyed look, but Mel saw a teasing twinkle in her eye. "Well, let's get started before Brigit pitches a complete hissy fit."

"I have no idea what you want to do, but here are some of my books," Mel said. She put the albums of special-order cupcakes in front of Bonnie, who dove into them with the sort of glee only another baker would show.

"Okay, for the gluten-free, I think we should go with a simple chocolate cupcake recipe with a ganache icing," Brigit said. "If we make it moist with an intense burst of chocolate in the cupcake, no one will care if it's gluten-free or not."

"I use almond flour when I bake gluten-free. Will Margery Firestone be okay with that?" Mel asked.

"Are you kidding? She has a chocolate weakness. If she can stuff four or five of those into her mouth, she'll be thrilled," Justin said.

Mel wrote down *gluten-free chocolate with ganache* on the pad she'd put on the table earlier. Next she would break the list down into ingredients to see what she had and what they needed.

"You know, while ganache is a delicious frosting, especially when you use dark chocolate, it's the ugly stepsister in the decorating department," Mel said. "It just doesn't have any wow factor."

Bonnie nodded in agreement and Justin frowned.

"Well, it's autumn," Justin said. "The obvious throw-away ideas are autumn leaves or pumpkins."

"Yes, so we'll offer those first," Bonnie said. "Just so Brigit can have her initial rejections."

"How about scarecrows and haystacks," Mel said. "Those are overdone and we can throw those away, too."

"Nice to see you getting into the spirit of things," Justin said.

"Still, we need a theme, to bring all of our cupcakes together," Bonnie said. "That will make it easier to choose flavors."

"Harvest," Mel said.

Both Justin and Bonnie shook their heads.

"No, hear me out," Mel said. "I'm not proposing cupcakes with mini John Deere tractors on them, although for a kid's birthday —"

Both Justin and Bonnie stared at her.

"Sorry, losing focus," she said. "No, what I'm thinking is a real harvest of cupcakes. So, we'll have a gluten-free chocolate cupcakes with ganache and top them with chocolate-dipped strawberries or pomegranate seeds. Then we can have an apple pie cupcake, so it could be a spice cake with apple pie filling in the middle and on the top we can pipe buttercream icing to look like a pie crust lattice."

"And what about pumpkin?" Justin asked. "If we're doing a harvest, we have to have pumpkin something."

"A pumpkin pie cupcake with a dollop of whipped cream and sprinkled with nutmeg," Bonnie said.

"I like it," Mel said, and she wrote it down. "Now, I'd like to do something unusual, too."

"Like what?" Justin asked warily.

"Not everyone has a sweet tooth," Mel said.

"Shocking," Bonnie joked.

"I know. I really don't know how they get up in the morning," Mel said. "But I'm thinking corn, and also fig."

"Fig?" Justin asked and pursed his lips. "As in Fig Newton fig?"

"Not exactly," Mel said. "I was thinking more of a fig-and-pistachio cupcake."

"With a cream cheese frosting," Bonnie added.

"What about corn?" Justin asked. "I thought you said you wanted to do something with corn."

"How about a sweet corn cupcake with brown butter and honey icing?" Bonnie asked.

"Oh, man, I think I just drooled on myself," Justin said.

Mel laughed and looked over her pad. "That's five. I think we've got it."

"Excellent," Bonnie said. "Let's make up an ingredient list. I can have my assistant go to the store."

As Mel started to jot down the ingredients to make two hundred of each type of cupcake, the back door opened. Angie was back

59

with Sylvia, and her hair was no longer a hard lump on her head but rather trailed down her back in a riot of lustrous black curls, very much like Sylvia's, in fact.

"Well?" Angie asked as she pointed to her head and spun around. "Go ahead. Lay the compliments on me."

"You are a vision," Justin said.

"Gorgeous," Mel said.

"Fabulous," Bonnie said. "But I missed the before look."

"It was a total hair emergency," Sylvia said. "Trust me."

"Ah," Bonnie nodded.

"Time's up!" a voice called from the office.

Mel's office door banged open and Sam all but fell out of the room with Brigit right behind him.

Six

"How do you work in there?" Brigit demanded. "It's like trying to work in a bathroom stall."

Mel opened her mouth to answer, but Sam gave her a sharp look and said, "She's not really interested."

Mel and Angie exchanged a look, but no one else seemed taken aback by his rudeness.

"So, what have you come up with that will dazzle me?" Brigit asked. "Wait, where's Amy?"

"She was on the phone out front," Justin said.

"Get her in here," Brigit said to Sam. "This is an all-staff meeting. No excuses."

"Will do." Sam disappeared through the swinging door.

Angie and Sylvia took places at the large table. Brigit remained standing, and started paging through Mel's books with a frown.

Mel felt her hands get damp with sweat. Good grief. She realized she was actually nervous. How could this woman who really had nothing to do with her, except having taken over her office and her bakery for the next week, have such an effect upon her?

Of course, there was the little problem of having Ian Hannigan expecting Mel to lead this ragtag band of prima donnas through a cupcake boot camp in the hopes that they would have more of teamlike mentality at the end of it. Yeah, from what Mel had seen, these people were the type to eat their own and were not likely to form any bonds of friendship, be it for a charity event or not.

"What?" Amy snapped as she slammed through the kitchen door with Sam hot on her heels.

"Oh, I'm sorry," Brigit said. "Did we interrupt your very busy morning of kissing Hannigan's behind?"

The hot red flush that suffused Amy's face gave away the fact that she had been doing exactly what Brigit suspected, talking to Ian Hannigan.

Amy yanked on the lapels of her gray suit and tossed her straight dark brown hair over her shoulder. She looked as if she was eager for a confrontation.

"I merely like to be in touch with my

superiors," she said.

Bonnie and Justin immediately broke out in giggles.

"Something funny?" Brigit asked.

"Ahem." Justin cleared his throat. "Sorry. Her word choice was amusing."

Brigit frowned. "Because she said 'in touch'? Really? How old are you — twelve?"

"That depends, are we talking actual years accrued or emotionally?" he asked.

Brigit scowled.

"I'd say twelve's about right," Justin said.

"Listen," Brigit said. "I am not in a good mood. I have a magazine to turn out, and spending a week as a cupcake baker is not on my itinerary."

"Now, let's hear your ideas," she said. She consulted the delicate gold Le Vian watch on her wrist. "You have five minutes."

"We were thinking cupcakes with falling leaves," Bonnie said.

"No," Brigit said.

"A huge cupcake haystack," Justin offered. Mel noticed that his lips twitched; thankfully, Brigit had begun pacing and didn't see him almost smile.

"No," Brigit said. "Honestly, people, could you be more trite?"

"Cupcakes in Halloween costumes," Amy said.

"Apparently, you can," Brigit said.

"How about the cactus blossoms they were going to use for the photo shoot?" Sam asked.

"At least those were original," Brigit said. "But no."

Justin and Bonnie looked at Mel and nodded. Brigit had rejected at least five. Now was their chance to get her to like their idea.

"A harvest theme," Mel said. Her voice cracked, and she cleared her throat. She was not going to let Brigit's laser-like scrutiny freak her out. Brigit knew her magazine, fine; Mel knew her cupcakes.

"Explain," Brigit said.

"I see a large cornucopia with cupcakes made from ingredients that are just coming into season right now, such as pomegranate, fig, and pumpkin."

Brigit tapped her lips with her index finger while she considered. "Colors. What will they look like?"

"Dark chocolate ganache with pomegranate, apple pie with a buttercream piped like a lattice pie crust, pumpkin with whipped cream sprinkled with nutmeg," Mel said.

"What else?" Brigit asked.

"Fig and pistachio with cream cheese icing," Bonnie said.

"Corn with brown butter and honey frosting," Justin added.

"Sketch me what they'll look like," Brigit said to Bonnie. To Justin, she said, "Figure out how to make an enormous cornucopia to display them on. Sylvia can help you."

"Sam and I will be in the office," she said, and then looked at Mel and Angie and added, "I'm assuming you two can coordinate the baking?"

They both nodded. Mel was surprised to find that Brigit's powers of intimidation apparently worked on Angie as well. As far as she knew, she'd never seen Angie take orders so quietly before. Then again, maybe her new hairdo had mellowed her.

"What about me?" Amy asked. "What am I supposed to do?"

Brigit looked as her as if she were a gnat that was too quick to be killed.

"Well, dear, why don't you help the girls with the baking?"

"What?" Amy argued. "I'm not some chunky foodie who dreams of being in a kitchen, stuffing her face."

"Really?" Brigit asked. She scanned Amy's tight suit with a look that told everyone she was sure the girl was hiding a Twinkie somewhere. Then she turned and walked away.

"I hate her!" Amy growled. "I absolutely

hate her!"

She stomped around the kitchen in her spiky heels, texting furiously on her phone. Mel had no doubt that she was tattling on Brigit to Ian Hannigan.

Justin, Bonnie, and Sylvia hopped up from their seats and headed towards the bakery side of the shop where they could work at the tables.

"We'll just go work in there," Bonnie said, "while you get your shopping list together, and then, you know, I'll be happy to go and get supplies. No need to pester my assistant for this."

"Yeah, and I'll come with you," Justin said.

"Count me in," Sylvia said.

"We'll just see what she has to say when Ian gets here and sees that she's assigned me to the kitchen," Amy muttered under her breath. "Ha!"

Amy continued to rant under her breath, and the rest of the cupcake boot campers cleared out as if an impending storm was about to blow the door down.

"And they criticized our cupcake war with Olivia as being immature?" Angie asked Mel as they watched the magazine staffers scatter like cowardly roaches.

"I know, right?" Mel asked. "Come on, let's make a supply list, and then we have to get to work. We have one thousand cupcakes to bake and only four days to get this done."

Angie followed Mel with paper and pencil while Mel checked their supplies. This was going to seriously deplete their reserves, and she certainly hoped that Tate had made it clear to Ian Hannigan that they were not paying for the ingredients. She was still going to have to bake for the shop, and she had several special orders due that weekend. She felt her stress level ratchet up, and she had to force herself to close her eyes, calm down, take a deep breath, and find her baker Zen.

Angie stood beside her, tapping her pencil against the pad in her hand. "Better now?"

"Much," Mel said.

"I'd be a better editor in chief than that shriveled-up old hag," Amy was muttering to herself.

She was slouched on a stool at the recently vacated steel table, looking like the whiny kid on the playground who no one wanted to play with.

Mel would have felt sorry for her, but she found she couldn't feel sympathy for someone who seemed intent upon bringing about her own misery.

Mel had done the corporate thing, and the simple fact was that Amy wasn't helping herself by going over Brigit's head to Hannigan. Brigit was obviously unhappy with her, and it was apparent that no one else on the staff had the warm fuzzies for her either. Even as an outsider, it was painful to watch someone so young committing career suicide.

"Pistachios," Mel said to Angie. "We'll need at least sixteen cups of shelled nuts."

"Wow," Angie said. "Should I plan to buy in bulk at Sprouts?"

Mel gave her a look. "You're going with the others?"

"Yes, and preferably before the boss man gets here," she said. "Much as I love a good butt-chewing, I think I still have scars on my rear from the last time he let us have it."

"Fine," Mel said. They finished the inventory, and Angie went into the front of the bakery to gather the troops.

Mel was left alone with Amy while Brigit and Sam were still holed up in her office. She wasn't sure what to do with herself, and suddenly the bakery which had always been her sanctuary was feeling overly crowded and a bit claustrophobic.

It was a relief when the bakery opened to the public and Marty arrived for the morning shift and Tate followed him shortly thereafter. Marty headed straight out to the front to unlock the door and fire up the jukebox, while Tate lingered in the kitchen, perusing the cupcakes in the walk-in cooler.

Tate considered one of the perks of being the chief investor in Fairy Tale Cupcakes to be that he could help himself to the goods whenever the need arose. Judging by the three cupcakes he'd stacked on his plate, his need was greater today than usual.

He took a seat at the farthest end of the table, away from Amy, and bit into one of Mel's signature cupcakes, the Blonde Bombshell, an almond cupcake with almond buttercream.

"Where is everyone?" he asked through a mouthful. "I thought you'd all be elbow deep in cupcake batter by now."

"I. Don't. Cook!" Amy said as if he'd been talking to her. "I'm going outside to meet Ian."

With a toss of her long dark hair, she strode out of the kitchen to the front. Tate blinked after her.

"Ian Hannigan is coming here?" he asked. "Why?"

"As far as I can tell, because Amy tattled on Brigit, who has taken over my office with Sam Kelleher, the features guy, while everyone else ran out of here to go buy supplies, including Angie, in a lame attempt to hide

69

from Ian Hannigan, who is probably going to go ballistic. In fact, I am expecting everything to blow up on me any moment now."

"Hannigan is definitely on his way?" Tate asked as he reached for a napkin and wiped his mouth. He actually sounded nervous.

"I suppose. Unless he doesn't get any of the numerous messages from Amy or he has something better to do. Tate, are you scared of Ian Hannigan?" she asked.

"No. Maybe. Not exactly," he said.

Mel studied him and realized he wasn't wearing his usual superhero investment-guy power suit with his matching platinum cuff links of wealth. Instead, he was in jeans and a charcoal gray Henley, looking very much Saturday-night-movie casual instead of Tuesday-morning power broker to the rich and richer.

"What's going on with you?" she asked. "Are you sick or something?"

"No, I'm fine," he said. "I just don't think I should be here snarfing down cupcakes when —"

The kitchen door swung open and in strode Ian Hannigan. His face was set in lines of seriously unhappy.

SEVEN

Marty was hot on his heels. "I told him not to come back here, but he said you were expecting him."

Mel nodded at Marty to let him know that it was okay and that Hannigan had told him the truth.

Marty glared at him from under his bushy gray eyebrows and stomped back into the front of the bakery, yelling, "If you need me to do some clean-up just holler."

"That's some feisty counter help you've got there," Hannigan said.

"The older ladies like him," Tate said.

"Good business." Hannigan nodded in understanding, and Tate sat up straighter, looking pleased.

Amy had followed Hannigan into the room and was standing beside him with a smirk on her lips, like she was the teacher's pet ratting out the kids who'd been smoking in the parking lot on lunch break.

Mel had never been a smoker, but she'd done her share of skipping school to hit the local convenience store for a candy bar fix between classes, and the same kind of tattle-pants had ratted her out to the principal back then. She did not like tattlers and snitches, and she was really beginning to dislike Amy Pierson.

"Brigit!" Hannigan barked.

Mel glanced at her office door. There was no sound coming from within. She wondered if Brigit would just ignore him. She felt her stress level rise while Amy looked even more smug.

"You have five seconds to come out or I'm coming in," Hannigan yelled.

"Good luck with that," Mel said under her breath to Tate, who shushed her.

The door banged open and out strode Brigit, looking like she was about to tear someone's head off. Mel backed up to stand behind Tate.

"What do you want?" Brigit asked.

She planted herself right in front of Ian with her hands on her hips, looking like she was more than willing to go toe-to-toe with him.

Ian leaned forward. "Cupcake boot camp means you learn how to make cupcakes. What did you not understand about that?"

72

"I am trying to turn out a magazine," she said. "Or, as the owner, do you not care about that?"

"I care," he said. "I also care that the staff on this magazine has zero morale, which affects the work that they do. You can't coax good stories out of your staff by browbeating them."

"I do not browbeat," Brigit argued. "I merely set my standards high and expect them to be met."

"You're a bully," Ian said.

"I can live with that if it means that this magazine survives while those around it slink off into obscurity," Brigit said. "What's the matter, is your little pet unhappy?"

She glared at Amy, who huffed in outrage. Hannigan ignored both of them.

"Amy is not my pet," Hannigan said. His voice was low as if he was trying to control his temper. "I am trying to build a stronger sense of team amongst —"

"Oh, stop!" Brigit snapped. "You are such a liar. This isn't about the magazine. You could give two hoots if this magazine lives or dies. This little boot camp whatever is about punishing me, and we both know it."

"My god, your ego is mythic!" Hannigan roared.

"*My* ego?" Brigit leaned forward, meeting

him glower for glower. "That's unbelievable coming from you. You are one of the richest men in the world. You could have bought any magazine you wanted, but you bought mine. Why?"

Hannigan didn't answer. He turned away, but Brigit wasn't about to let him escape her. Mel was riveted watching the two titans of the publishing world go after each other. She had a feeling the argument wouldn't be over until someone lay bleeding.

"I'll tell you why you did it," Brigit said. "You bought *SWS* so that you could destroy it. I've spent my life building this magazine into what it is, and nothing would make you happier than to see it fail. Well, let me tell you, it will be over my dead body."

"If need be," Hannigan said. His voice was low and lethal and made Mel want to hide under the kitchen table.

"Brigit, come on. Ian, be sensible," Sam said. He wedged himself in between them, forcing them to back up. "You two need to stop. There's more at stake here than an old score to settle."

"Really, Sam?" Hannigan asked. "It seems to me you chose whose side you were on a long time ago."

Sam looked pained, and Mel sensed that the history between the three of them was long and scarred.

"I'm sending out a camera crew," Hannigan said. "We're going to have still shots of the boot camp for the next issue of the magazine, and I'm sending out a video crew to put short spots up on our website. I expect to see everyone suited up and in the kitchen, or I'll start handing out pink slips. Am I clear?"

"As clear as cheap crystal," Brigit said. She cast him a look of such loathing that Mel was surprised Hannigan didn't drop dead on the floor right there.

"Cheap, yeah, that sounds about right coming from you," Hannigan said.

"Ian, there's no need —" Sam blustered, but Hannigan interrupted him.

"There's every need," Hannigan snapped. "I own the magazine. I call the shots. Not you, Brigit, and you'd better catch on to that fact, or I'll have to replace you with someone — oh, how do I say it? — *younger.*"

"I'm not replaceable," Brigit said. Her dark brows arched with a stone-cold confidence that left Mel awed. "You tried once before and failed. Are you really going to make that mistake again?"

Sam sucked in a breath, and Hannigan looked as if she'd just kneed him in the crotch. Brigit ignored them both, spun on her heel, and stormed out the back door to the alley, slamming the door behind her.

"Ian, I'm sorry, that was a low blow, even for Brigit," Sam said.

Hannigan held up a hand. He closed his eyes and shook his head as if trying shake loose whatever pained him.

"I'm going now," he said. "Make sure she does what I said. I'd hate to have to fire her."

"Would you really?" Sam asked. His voice was skeptical but not argumentative.

Hannigan didn't answer but strode back out into the bakery with Amy Pierson on his heels chattering like a squirrel in a nut war the entire way.

"Mr. Hannigan, Ian, I do have some ideas —" Mel heard her saying as the door swung shut.

"Ugh, he's created a monster with that one," Sam said.

"Sam, what is going on?" Mel asked. "It's pretty clear that the three of you have a history. Care to share?"

Sam looked at her. His sallow skin and wiry build were accentuated by the overhead lighting of the kitchen. He looked like someone who could use a cupcake.

"Sit," she said.

To her surprise, Sam did.

She went to the cooler and pulled out a tray of her favorite, Strawberry Surprise Cupcakes. She put two on a plate and poured a cold glass of milk. She plopped them down in front of Sam.

"Eat," she said.

He gave her a small smile. "You sound like my mother."

"Did you like your mother?" she asked.

"Loved her," he said. "Fabulous woman."

"Okay, then," Mel said. "So, tell us about the three of you while you eat."

Sam took a nibble of the pink buttercream and asked, "Strawberry?"

Mel nodded.

"That's my favorite," he said. "How did you know?"

"Hunch," Mel said. Actually, she had just thought the man needed a boost of pink in his life; maybe it would help even out his jaundiced skin tone.

Sam took a bite, and when he smiled Mel saw the happy little boy he must have been some sixty-odd years before.

"You were going to tell us about the history between the three of you," Tate said.

"Not mine to tell," Sam said. He pointed to the back door. "Go ask her."

"Rock, paper, scissors," Mel said to Tate.

"No."

"Oh, come on. One of us has to find out why Hannigan and Brigit are at each other's throats, or this is going to be a very frustrating and possibly catastrophic week," she said.

"Yeah, and that would be you," Tate said. He picked up one of his remaining cupcakes and took a big bite.

"Why me?" Mel asked. "You're the one who got us into this boot-camp thing."

Tate swallowed and then said, "No, technically you and Angie created the situation that required me to save you from having to pay back the thousands of dollars the magazine wasted on that fiasco of a photo shoot. You're in charge of the boot camp. You go deal with the diva."

"There's a reason she's a diva," Sam said around another bite of cupcake. "Every other magazine in the country is tanking but hers survives. She's brilliant. She's able to mix in real news about the world and keep it interesting. That's no small feat in a world where you are now expected to distill information in a hundred and forty characters or less."

Sam's tone left them no doubts about how he felt about new media. Mel had to admit that, although she found all sorts of things

78

on the Internet entertaining, sometimes she just wanted to unplug it and have peace.

"Fine, I'll go," she said. Then she glared at Tate, and added, "But if she bites me, you're taking me to the emergency room."

Mel opened the back door and cautiously stuck her head out. She half expected Brigit to kick the door shut in her face, but when she looked out, she saw Brigit pacing up and down the alley, smoking some sort of black cigarette with a gold tip and muttering.

"What?" she snapped when she saw Mel. "Am I not keeping my secondhand smoke twenty feet from the entrance?"

"No, you look to be at least forty," Mel said. She stepped out and closed the door behind her. She stood on the small landing. Three steps down and she'd be in the alley with Brigit, but if she took the staircase on her right that went up to the second floor, she could hide in her apartment and snuggle Captain Jack until all of the mean people went away.

Somehow, she figured that wasn't an option. She took the steps down into the alley, which had the usual alley stink of sour milk and rotten fruit, and stopped at the bottom to sit on the lowest step.

Brigit paced by her once, twice, three

times before she finally stopped and glared at her.

"What?" Brigit asked as she stubbed out her cigarette and threw the butt into the Dumpster.

Mel's inner adolescent chubster wanted to crawl under the steps and hide from the gorgeous haughty woman in front of her. Brigit MacLeod was everything Mel was not: She was strong, assertive and confident. When she walked into a room, no one could ignore her arrival. Mel was not like that. She wasn't confident, she was definitely not assertive, and she preferred coming in the back entrance so as not to be noticed.

"You scare me," Mel said.

EIGHT

Brigit blinked at her, obviously surprised at her candor. "Yes, I suppose I do."

"Why?" Mel asked. "Wouldn't it be easier to manage people if you didn't scare the bejeezus out of them?"

Brigit looked at her and studied her for a moment. "Not in my business. I'm not baking cupcakes. I'm fighting to survive in a world that is constantly changing, and every young, dewy-eyed little coed out of grad school thinks she can do my job better than me. There is no room for niceness in my world."

"I suppose not," Mel said.

They were both silent. Brigit leaned on the railing beside Mel.

"Why have you tied yourself to a bakery?" Brigit asked.

"What do you mean?" Mel asked.

She felt nervous having Brigit standing so close to her. The lingering scent of Brigit's cigarette mixing with the exotic perfume she wore wrapped around Mel like a heavy cloak.

"I knew Vic Mazzota," Brigit said.

"Oh." Mel nodded. She was surprised by the sudden constriction of her throat. Vic had been her mentor and had been murdered six months before. She still missed him. The hurt was still raw.

"He raved about you and your genius," Brigit said. "He wanted you to be a star. He was right. You and your partner could be stars on the Food Network."

"I'm stunned you think that after our less-than-stellar photo shoot."

"That was Amy's mistake," Brigit said. "I would never have dressed you up like two show ponies. It compromised the essence of who you really are. I would have done the shoot in the kitchen, in your regular clothes with you elbow deep in cupcake batter."

Mel felt herself warming to the editor in chief.

"Keeping it real," Mel said.

"Exactly," Brigit said. "But you didn't answer my question. Why not foodie stardom?"

"That's not for me," Mel said with a nervous laugh. "I'm happy right where I am."

"Slinging cupcakes?" Brigit asked. She sounded dubious.

"There's an artistry to it," Mel said. "And I get to be my own boss, make my own hours, and live an uncomplicated life."

"But you could be the boss of others," Brigit argued. "Hundreds of others."

"I don't think that's really in my DNA," Mel said.

Brigit studied her, and Mel hoped like hell there was nothing stuck in her teeth and no pimples were popping up on the horizon.

"What a waste," Brigit said with a shake of her head.

"We'll have to agree to disagree."

"If you change your mind, I can teach you how to be a leader, how to go after what you want and how not to take no for an answer."

"Forgive me for saying this, but that technique doesn't really seem to be working with your new boss," Mel said.

As if someone had slammed a window shut, Brigit's face grew stiff and closed. Mel couldn't read any emotion off of her. She wondered if she had gone too far, but figured if she had, she had nothing to lose.

"What is the history between you, Hannigan, and Sam?"

"Ask Sam," Brigit said.

"I did," Mel admitted. "He said it wasn't his story to tell."

The side of Brigit's mouth curved up for just a second in the tiniest of smiles. Mel realized she had never seen Brigit smile and had certainly never heard her laugh. For the first time, she felt sorry for Brigit, and her pity outweighed her fear. A life without laughter was unthinkable to Mel.

"That sounds like Sam, loyal to the end," she said. "We do have a history, a long one. But it isn't relevant now."

"Really?" Mel asked. She knew she sounded sarcastic, and she didn't even bother to lessen her tone. "You were nose-to-nose with Hannigan a few minutes ago in my kitchen, and you don't think your history is relevant? How are we supposed to pull this off if you people are in the middle of a power struggle?"

Brigit shrugged as if it was none of her concern.

"Oh, no," Mel said. "Now you're messing with my reputation. If we're doing this huge charity event with a video on *SWS*'s website and still pictures in the next issue, then you had better believe that you are going to figure out how you're going to get this done, and with a smile on your face, too."

"Excuse me?" Brigit's eyebrows pulled

together in one of the most menacing frowns Mel had ever seen, and if Mel hadn't been completely irritated, it might have given her pause. It did not.

"You heard me," Mel ground out.

Brigit put a hand over her heart in mock fear. "Stop, you're scaring me."

"Ooh, I did sound like a mean boss lady, didn't I?" Mel asked.

"When someone threatens something you love, it brings out the tiger mother in you."

Mel nodded. She got it now. Brigit was as fierce as she was because she loved her magazine as much as Mel loved her bakery.

"So, since you're in charge and seem to have connected with your inner boss lady, how do you suggest I deal with Hannigan? Meaning, how do I do this cupcake charity thing and manage to get out the next issue of my magazine?" Brigit asked.

Mel was quiet for a moment as she contemplated options. Then she tipped her head, and said, "Maybe we need to switch personalities for the week?"

Brigit gave her a hard stare, and then she laughed. She threw back her head and laughed loud and long. Her laugh sounded rusty, as if she didn't do it often enough.

"I like you, Melanie Cooper," she said as she wiped a tear away from one eye. "I think

85

you might be on to something. A mellower me and a tougher you; it might just work."

The back door banged open and Sam stuck his head out, followed by Tate. They must have dropped their cupcakes and run, because they both had dabs of frosting on their upper lips and in the corners of their mouths.

"Is everything okay out here?" Sam asked.

"Did you two go back for seconds?" Mel asked. They both looked guilty. "Sheesh, I leave my bakery for two seconds, and you just decide to help yourselves to the product. The cupcakes are for the customers, you know."

"What's gotten into you?" Tate asked. "You sound so —"

"Tough? Assertive? Mean?" Mel asked hopefully.

"Well, yeah," Tate said.

Mel spun around and exchanged an awkward high five with Brigit. They missed each other's hands on the first try and had to do it again.

"What's going on?" Tate asked. "You two look like you're up to something."

"Uh-oh, the Wicked Witch of the West and the Good Witch of the North have bonded," Sam said.

"You'll just have to see which is the

wicked witch," Mel said. "Now get back in there and get to work!"

She glanced over her shoulder and saw Brigit give her a very subtle nod.

Mel strode back into the bakery to find Angie, Justin, Bonnie, and Sylvia unpacking bags of supplies. There was no sign of Amy or of Hannigan, for which she was grateful.

"All right, people, listen up," Mel said. She was only a tad stunned when they actually did. "The stakes on this have been raised. We have a camera crew coming to film us while we work, and Hannigan plans to put it on the magazine's website. I, for one, am not going to allow my bakery to look anything other than professional. Got it?"

Angie was looking at Mel with wide eyes, as if she wasn't quite sure what to make of her.

"From now on you will dress appropriately, you will wear the bakery's aprons, you will participate, and you will work your butt off this week to make sure we have the finished cupcakes for the gala. Are you with me so far?"

Again, the group nodded as one.

"Excellent," Mel said. "Pull up a chair, everyone, we're going to work out a schedule."

The meeting went well. At the end of it, they had timed out the entire week. They were about to break for lunch when Amy came in through the swinging door.

"The camera crew is right behind me," she said. She gave Brigit a particularly thin smile. "Ian agreed that I should take the lead on the filming."

Brigit's left eyebrow rose, but Mel shook her head, and Brigit took a deep breath and said nothing. Sam gave her a look of concern, but he didn't say anything.

"How about a nice lunch at RA, the sushi place down the street?" Bonnie suggested. "Then we can come back and start baking."

"What about the filming?" Amy demanded. "I'm in charge of it, and I say we start now."

Brigit's lips were compressed into thin line, as if she were afraid that even the tiniest opening might allow a volley of harsh words to spew forth.

"Amy, you can set up the film crew while the others go eat," Mel said.

"What? You are not the boss!" Amy planted her hands on her hips and tossed her long, dark hair.

"Excuse me?" Mel asked. She stepped closer to Amy and raised one eyebrow, obviously daring her to repeat what she'd just said. "You're in *my* bakery and this little boot camp thing that we're doing, yeah, I'm in charge of it. So, I *am* the boss and you *will* do as I say, or you will be downgraded to dishwasher. You feeling me now?"

"You can't intimidate me. I'm going to call Ian right now!" Amy shrieked.

"And you just lost all of your personal power by threatening to go crying to the boss," Mel said. "Pitiful."

It was clear that Amy was furious at being called out in front of the others. She spun on her heel and slammed back through the kitchen to the bakery. They could hear her taking her foul mood out on the film crew.

"So, we're off for lunch?" Justin asked, rubbing his hands together.

"Be back in an hour," Mel said. "We have a lot of work to do."

Mel, Angie, and Tate didn't join the others. Mel wanted to use the lunch hour to do some prep work, and Angie had already been gone most of the morning. As the doors shut behind the magazine crew, Mel felt relieved to be left in peace with just Angie and Tate.

"Aren't you supposed to be at work?" Angie asked Tate.

"I took a personal day," he said.

Mel and Angie exchanged a look. Tate

never took personal days. He worked for his father's investment firm and was very, very good at making other people's money grow.

"Are you sure you're feeling all right?" Mel asked. "You don't look well."

"I'm fine," Tate said.

"Maybe you need fewer cupcakes and a little more cauliflower," Angie said.

Tate stood up and crossed the room. "I've got to go."

"What, no movie quote? Nothing? Not even, 'You see, Marcus. The ending is only the beginning'?" Angie asked.

"*The Human Comedy*," Mel and Tate identified the movie together.

"Oh, that was an easy one," Angie said. "Speaking of movies, are we on for our usual classic movie at your place on Saturday night, Tate? I'll bring the Sno-Caps."

"Uh, no," Tate said. "I'm not going to be able to make it this week. Gotta go."

He slipped through the kitchen doors and out the front without another word.

"Okay, what was that?" Angie asked Mel. "He is acting so weird."

"I have no idea," Mel said. "Hey, can you give me a hand setting up the kitchen like we're going to be teaching one of our classes? I think that's the best way to handle this bunch."

"Sure," Angie agreed. "Do you think Tate's sick?"

"He seems off but not ill," Mel said.

Angie began putting out bowls and whisks while Mel measured out ingredients. She noticed Angie was muttering under her breath and thumping the items down on the table harder than was necessary. When she slammed a glass bowl down, making the steel tabletop reverberate like a gong, Mel could no longer ignore her.

"Angie, stop banging the cookware!" she ordered. "Now, exactly what is your problem?"

NINE

"He didn't even notice my hair!" Angie said.

As if to emphasize her point, she did an elaborate hair toss that looked like it cricked her neck but, being Angie, she refused to show any pain.

"Clearly the man is losing his sense of priorities," Mel said. Her sarcasm went unnoticed by Angie, which was probably a good thing.

"Ah!" Angie gasped.

"What?" Mel asked, thinking Angie had hurt herself.

"You don't think he's seeing someone, do you?"

"Are you insane?"

"Hear me out," Angie said. "He called out of work, he looks terrible, and he doesn't want to get together on Saturday night, you know, the premiere date night of the week."

"So, he's under the weather," Mel said.

"Yeah, like lovesick under the weather,"

Angie said.

The kitchen door swung open, and Marty strode in. He was wiping his hands on his blue apron with the atomic Fairy Tale cupcake logo on it.

"I need backup out there," he said. "I've got a line five deep, and I'm out of Death by Chocolates."

"Angie will help you," Mel said.

Angie gave her a look that clearly stated she did not like being bossed around. Mel didn't care.

"If you'd rather be in charge of all this, be my guest." Mel held her arms out wide, gesturing to the cupcake boot camp preparations.

"Fine, I'll help."

"Well, thank you," Marty said, not sounding grateful in the least as the door closed behind him.

"You might want to see if Marty knows anything about what's going on with Tate," Mel suggested.

Angie looked at the door with a considering glance. "I'll try, but you know how men are. Marty will know every play Tate made in his last volleyball game, but Tate could get married and have two kids and Marty would never notice."

"You have a point," Mel said. "Good luck,

93

and report back."

Angie left through the swinging doors, and Mel sank gratefully into an empty seat. She could hear the faint sound of customers being helped on the other side of the doors, but the ticking of the kitchen clock was the dominant sound in the room, and she relaxed into the stillness.

She was not going to have a meltdown, or so she kept telling herself in the hope that it would keep her from bursting into tears and looking like a big sissy.

The truth was that being in charge did not come easily to her. She was a horrible delegator and generally preferred to do things herself, because that way she knew they would get done right. She really only trusted her bakery crew, and having this crop of strangers plus a camera crew was going to be a real test of her patience and nerves. Honestly, she didn't know if she was up to it.

It was an hour on the dot when she heard the bells on the front door jangle, signaling the return of the magazine crew. While they'd been gone, Amy had directed the camera crew to rig up cameras in the kitchen to cover all angles of the cupcake boot camp. Mel tried not to notice, but it felt as if there were a million watchful eyes on her.

Chad, the photographer, was there as well as Nick, a large man who had not spoken a word the entire time he'd been setting up the cameras and who had a very long red beard, undoubtedly to replace the hair he no longer had on his head.

Mel tried not to resent the cables and noise that the two brought with them, but she couldn't help feeling as if her sanctuary was being violated.

"*I* will go direct the staff," Amy said.

She looked as if she expected Mel to challenge her, but Mel really couldn't care less about the film portion of this venture, except that it not make her bakery look bad.

Mel glanced at the table to see that the chefs had all that they needed. She had decided to make the pumpkin cupcakes first. She figured they'd bake the different varieties and freeze them in batches, thawing them as each cupcake had a different type of frosting with different handling requirements.

A crash sounded from the front of the bakery, and Mel's head snapped up. Had someone dropped a tray of cupcakes? Not the end of the world, but it always hurt when one of her cupcakes went frosting-side down to its doom.

There was a shout — okay, more of a high-pitched screech — and then another one.

"Uh, Mel, we need you out here — now!" Marty said as he popped his head through the door.

Mel hurried through the doors into the main bakery. What she saw brought her up short, and she skidded into Justin, who stood gaping at the scene before him. Brigit had Amy in a headlock that any World Wrestling Entertainment champ would have given her props for.

Mel grunted as she caught her balance with Justin's help. "What's going on?"

"The smack-down of the century," he said. "Amy suggested to Brigit that she go have some quick Botox done since the magazine is trying to bring in a younger readership —"

"And she didn't think Brigit's wrinkles would go over well on camera," Sylvia interrupted.

"She said Brigit wouldn't want to scare away the young hipsters with her sagging skin, now, would she?" Bonnie relayed. Her eyes were huge, as if she couldn't believe Amy was still alive.

"She did not!" Mel gasped.

"Oh, yes, she did," Justin assured her.

"I didn't know Amy had a death wish," Sam said from Mel's other side. "And it looks like Brigit would be happy to grant it."

"Amy's mean and stupid," Bonnie said. "Deadly combination."

"True beauty lies within," Sylvia said.

Angie gave Sylvia a worshipful glance and Mel rolled her eyes and met Bonnie's chagrined look. It was easy for a knockout like Sylvia to say something like that, but perhaps if she looked like a mortal, she'd have a better understanding of how society really didn't give a hoot about inner beauty.

"Listen, you rubber-lipped, silicone-boobed, Spanx-wearing little tart, I was in this business before you were even born," Brigit said as she tightened her grip on Amy's head. "I wrote real news for real newspapers and I was traveling the world, being wined and dined by diplomats and celebrities while you hosted tea parties for your Malibu Barbies and anatomically challenged Kens. *SWS* thrives because of my commitment to excellence, not your fixation with drunken celebutantes. Now, you will respect me and what we do, or I will see you fired and on the dole with the hundred thousand other reporters who've been let go since newspapers were stupid enough to put their content online for free."

A blubbering sound came from the tangle of dark hair in Brigit's elbow. Mel didn't think Amy was in pain, but perhaps she was scared, which seemed a bit overdue in Mel's opinion.

"Well, fearless leader," Justin said out of the side of his mouth to Mel, "it's your call."

She glared at him. "No way! You're bigger than me. You can break this up much easier than I can."

"Bock bock bock!" Justin made clucking noises and flapped his arms.

"I am not chicken!" she protested. Justin continued to squawk and flap. "Fine!"

She stormed around the counter and faced Brigit.

"I thought you were supposed to be channeling me," Mel said. "Do you see me putting people in headlocks?"

"Did she say *you* needed Botox?" Brigit countered with a grunt.

"True," Mel conceded. "But I think you've made your point. You need to let her go."

Brigit met her gaze with a grin. "You have no idea how good this feels."

"Please. I took down my archenemy with a cupcake yesterday," Mel said. "I know exactly how it feels."

They exchanged a look of understanding.

"All right," Brigit said. Then she leaned close to Amy, and hissed, "Show some respect, or next time it will be worse. Got it?"

She let Amy go and stepped back. Amy came up in a surge of rage. Her face was red and streaked with tears, snot was leaking out of her nose, and her chin wobbled like a spoiled brat who had just realized she wasn't going to get her way.

In full temper, Amy struck out with a fist, but sadly her aim was lacking, and instead of popping Brigit, she punched Mel right in the eye, knocking her down and out.

TEN

Mel woke up, lying on a booth bench with Angie and Marty staring down at her on one side and Brigit and Justin on the other.

"Mel, are you all right?" Angie asked.

"Ooee, that's quite the shiner you've got sprouting," Marty said.

"A what? Why is my face frozen?" Mel sat up and a bag of ice dropped into her lap as the pink bakery spun around her in nauseating circles.

"Down you go," Angie said as she gently steered Mel back into the booth.

"Did someone punch me?"

"Amy," they all said together.

"Where is she?" Mel asked. She wasn't sure if she wanted to know so she could wallop Amy in return or because she was afraid of taking another hit.

"She's down there," Angie said.

Mel winced as she raised her head to glance at the floor. Amy was knotted up in an apron, and Sam was standing over her, looking like he'd happily jump on her if she fluttered so much as an eyelash.

"Customers," Mel said as she sank back down. "What happened to our customers?" No one said a word, and even through her rapidly swelling eye Mel could see that they were all actively avoiding her glance.

The front door banged open and Tate's concerned face appeared. "Mel, are you all right? Angie texted that you'd been punched in the face."

"I'm fine," Mel said, easing herself up into a seated position.

Ian Hannigan appeared beside Tate, and Mel removed the ice pack Marty had put on her eye so he could appreciate the damage.

Both Tate and Hannigan cringed and glanced away.

"Yeah, this boot-camp thing we've got going," Mel said. "It's not really working out for me."

"What happened?" Hannigan asked. He leaned back and glared at his staff.

"I'll tell you —" Brigit started, but Amy cut her off.

"Don't listen to her —" Amy said.

"Amy popped Mel right in the face!" Sam said.

101

"I was trying to hit *her!*" Amy protested, pointing at Brigit. "She had me in a head-lock."

"She deserved it," Brigit said.

The rest of the magazine staff nodded in agreement like a bunch of bobbleheads all in motion at the same time. Then they all started in at once. It turned into a chorus of yelling that made Mel's head pound.

Out of her good eye, Mel saw the door to the bakery open and the familiar faces of Mary and Rob Mitchell, with their children Danny and Emily, appeared. The family of four took one look at the melee in front of them, and quickly backed out of the bakery.

That ripped it. Mel threw her bag of ice onto the black-and-white tile floor like it was a hand grenade. The plastic bag popped open and ice flew everywhere.

"That's it!" she yelled. "You are driving away my regular customers and ruining my business. This insanity can't go on. Now, what are you people going to do about it?"

Everyone went silent and stared at her, but Mel didn't care.

"Well, I know what I'm going to do," Marty said with a glare at the magazine staff. "Go get a mop."

"Given that I'm not even sure of what's happening . . ." Tate began, but Hannigan

102

shook his head at him and his voice trailed off.

Hannigan jerked his head to the side, and he and Tate went and conferred in the corner.

"What's going on with them?" Marty asked Angie.

"No idea," she said.

"I didn't realize they were friends," Brigit said.

"As far as I know, they only met a few days ago," Angie said. She handed Mel a glass of water and an over-the-counter pain pill.

"Tell me the truth," Mel said. "How bad does it look?"

"Oh, why'd you have to say, 'Tell me the truth'?" Angie asked.

"You look like you've got a pumpkin sprouting out of your face," Marty said as he went by with the mop.

"Fabulous."

"Hey, there's a Halloween costume idea," Angie said. "We can paint it orange, and you can go as the Great Pumpkin."

"More like the great *lump*kin," Justin said.

"Shockingly, this is not making me feel any better," Mel said.

"Do you want to look in a mirror?" Sylvia asked. "I bet with some foundation we

103

could even it out, and it will hardly be noticeable."

"Pass on the mirror, but thanks," Mel said. "I'll let you know about the makeup when I have to go out in public."

Bonnie had gone into the kitchen with Marty, and she returned with another bag of ice and handed it to Mel. "Keep that on your eye. You're going to need it."

Tate and Hannigan left their corner, stepped around Marty, who was mopping up the ice, and approached the group.

"Listen up," Tate said. "There are going to be some changes."

"Well, this should be great," Brigit said. "What are you going to have us do next?"

Tate ignored her. "Ian — Mr. Hannigan — has agreed to disrupt his very full schedule in order to join the boot camp and oversee things."

"What?" Brigit asked. She turned to face Hannigan. "You wanted this all along, didn't you? You just want to —"

Mel popped up on shaky legs and stared over Hannigan's shoulder at Brigit. Mel shook her head very slowly, trying to get her message across to Brigit and not give herself a thumper of a headache.

Brigit looked as if she was going to shake her off like a pitcher on the mound refusing the catcher's signal. Mel shook her head again, and Brigit blew out an exasperated breath.

"Great," Brigit said through gritted teeth. "It will be just great to have you aboard."

"She's lying," Amy protested from the floor. "She doesn't want you here. She —"

Before she could get another word out, Mel stumbled into her, knocking her sideways with a knee to the back.

"Ow, hey!" Amy protested.

"Sorry, that sucker punch you hit me with is making me dizzy," Mel said. Then she gave Amy her best scary face to keep her quiet. It must have worked, because Amy swallowed hard and looked decidedly nervous. Mel figured her eye must look even worse than it felt, which was saying something.

"Well, this should be an . . . interesting experience, for the magazine staff to have you on board for the community service gala. Ian Hannigan decorating cupcakes. Who would have thought?" Brigit said. Her face gave away nothing. It was as smooth as ice and just as cold.

Ian glanced at her in surprise. "Well, would you look at that?" he asked. "Hanging out in a bakery has already begun to sweeten your disposition."

Brigit gave him a smile that was all teeth.

"Mel, I think you should have someone look at your eye," Tate said, bringing the attention back to Mel and her face. "Angie, will you go get her purse?"

"I can't leave. We don't have time," Mel protested. "If we're going to get these cupcakes baked and looking fabulous by Saturday, we have to start now. We've lost entirely too much time as it is."

She wasn't intentionally trying to rebuke the boot campers, but she knew it came out that way anyway. Frankly, her face hurt too much to care.

"Don't worry," Bonnie stepped forward. "I can get things started. You go get your face looked at."

"What are we going to do with her?" Sam asked as he pointed at Amy, who was still wrapped up in an apron.

"Ms. Pierson will be under my direct supervision from now on," Hannigan said.

Brigit gave out an undignified snort.

"You have a problem with that?" he asked her.

"None at all," she said. "Bonnie, dear, lead us to the kitchen."

"Don't worry," Angie said to Mel as she tucked her pocketbook under her arm. "Marty and I can handle this bunch."

"Come on." Tate ushered her out the front door. "Do you have your keys? My car is out of commission."

"Sure," Mel said. She rooted around in her bag, realizing that it was in desperate need of a cleaning, until she found her key ring. She handed the keys to Tate, and they made their way to her sporty little red-and-white Mini Cooper.

"What happened to your car?" she asked. Tate drove a silver Lexus and, as much as she loved her Mini Cooper, there was a certain luxury in his car's fine-grain leather seats that her face — okay, her whole body — could have wallowed in right now.

"Nothing is wrong exactly," he said. He opened the passenger door and helped her in. He came around the front and took the driver's seat, but said nothing more. Mel would have pressed him for more information, but her head hurt, so she rested back against the seat and let Tate take her to the nearby urgent-care office, where she really hoped they had better pain meds.

Mel returned in the afternoon to find that Bonnie had everything under control. The magazine crew had been baking all day, and the camera crew was busy at work, filming and snapping pictures. Mel had combed her short hair forward in an attempt to cover the darkening purple lump on her cheek. Unfortunately, it also impaired her vision on the one side.

Once the magazine people left, Marty, Oz, Angie, and Tate shooed her out of the bakery, promising to clean up the mess. Mel let them. Mercifully, Joe had texted her that he was working late, so she would be on her own for the evening.

Mel was fine with that, as it saved her from having to explain about her eye. She had a feeling that, no matter how she tried to tell the story, Joe was not going to be happy about it. She couldn't blame him, but she really didn't want to hear it.

The thought of resting her weary face on her pillow and snuggling with Captain Jack was about the only thing that was going to save this horrible day.

Mel woke up early. The lump on her face hadn't gone down, so she styled her hair once again in her new over-the-eye-socket manner. It made her look like one side of her head had been caught in a strong wind. It couldn't be helped.

She hurried down the steps of her apartment to the bakery below. She wanted to get the coffee started before the boot campers showed up, and to make sure that the bakery was tidy for another day of filming.

She turned on the landing with her keys in her fist to unlock the back door, when she saw something out of the corner of her good eye that drew her attention like a fly on frosting. It was a hand, palm up, just visible from around the corner of her building.

Mel sucked in a breath. She felt her heart hammer in her chest. She stood frozen for a split second while her brain processed what it saw.

Then she ran. She skirted the side of the building, hoping to find a drunk passed out from a night of partying at one of the clubs nearby.

No such luck. At a glance, she recognized Sam Kelleher, wearing his usual dress shirt and narrow tie, but now he lay in a pool of blood, his eyes were wide open and unblinking, staring up at the side of the building as if looking for help.

"Oh, no no no no," Mel whispered. She pressed her fingers to his neck, hoping for a pulse. His skin was cold and stiff to the touch. She shifted him slightly, hoping she was wrong, but one glance at the back of his crushed skull and she knew she wasn't wrong. He was dead.

Mel's body convulsed as if a huge fist were

squeezing her rib cage and forcing the air out of her lungs in gusts. She swallowed hard and bowed her head. A convulsion wracked her frame from the back of her neck all the way to her toes.

The sound of voices broke through the horror that enshrouded her, and Mel saw that some of the boot campers had arrived and were waiting out front. She tried to yell, but her throat was tight, making it impossible to get any sound out.

She gulped in some air and tried again. It was still a weak effort, more a puff of breath than a holler for help.

Someone glanced around the side of the building as if debating coming around the back because the front was locked up. He took a few steps in, and Mel recognized the outline of Justin.

"Mel?" he called as he walked towards her. "What's going on? The door is locked. Hey, who's . . . ?"

His voice trailed off as he stared down at his colleague, and the color drained from his face as he took in the sight of the blood and Sam's stiffened form.

"D-do you have your phone?" Mel asked, clearing her throat to make room for the words around the lump that was lodged in her larynx. "We need to call the police. Sam is dead."

ELEVEN

Justin fumbled with his phone while Mel stayed beside Sam. She felt as if she was guarding him from harm, even though whoever had done this to him was obviously long gone.

"No, stay back!" Justin said as he held his phone to his ear. He started walking up the narrow alley that separated Mel's bakery from the jewelry store next door.

"What the hell?" a voice asked from behind her, causing Mel to jump and spin around.

"Angie, you scared me," Mel said. She pressed her hand over her chest as if checking her own heart rate.

"Is that . . . ?" Angie's voice trailed off, and her brown eyes grew huge.

"Sam Kelleher," Mel said. "I just found him. Justin is calling the police."

"Don't tell me to stand aside, Justin!" Brigit's voice echoed against the brick walls.

"I want to know what's going on, and I want to know now."

"Brigit, don't," Justin ordered, but she pushed past him and strode towards Mel and Angie.

Mel thought about standing in front of the body but knew it would do no good. Brigit's gaze fastened on the scene before her, taking it in with a reporter's thorough scrutiny. She slowly sank to her knees beside Sam and smoothed the line of his tie with a tenderness that made Mel's heart hurt.

"Oh, Sam, no," she whispered. Her voice was drenched with grief, as if it were drowning under the onslaught of so much pain.

"What's going on?" Ian Hannigan strode down the alley. He was dressed casually in jeans and a T-shirt, but he still emanated authority.

He stopped beside Brigit and swore. Then he knelt down beside her and stared at Sam. His voice was choked when he asked, "Is he all right? What happened?"

"He's dead," Mel said. "I don't know what happened. I went to unlock the back door, and I saw his hand."

She swallowed the bile that lurched up her throat in an acidic rush.

"The police are on their way," Justin said.

Brigit leaned forward as if she might hug

Sam's inert body, but Hannigan held her back.

"No," he said. "The police will want him untouched."

A siren broke through the stillness of the morning. The other boot campers had come down the alley and stood in a cluster. Bonnie was weeping on Sylvia's shoulder while Amy stood with her arms crossed over her chest.

Hannigan and Brigit stayed with Sam's body as if keeping vigil while Justin moved to stand with Mel and Angie. He wrapped an arm around each of them, and Mel was happy to lean into his warmth. She noticed that Angie did the same, and for a moment it was like having Tate with them.

"Are you two all right?" he asked.

"No," they said together. Justin pulled them in closer, and it helped.

Mel heard the sound of several cars pulling up out front and figured the police had arrived. She wished she'd thought to have Justin ask for her Uncle Stan. He was a career detective on the Scottsdale PD, and she knew he'd want to know about this. She needn't have worried.

When she glanced down the alley, it was Uncle Stan in the lead, looking so much like her dad that her breath caught. In seconds she was enfolded in a bear hug that almost popped her eyes out of their sockets, which was particularly painful to her swollen eye.

"Can't breathe, Uncle Stan," she gasped. He eased his grip a little.

"Mel, when dispatch said there was a body here . . ." Uncle Stan's voice trailed off, and when she stepped back to study his face, Mel was pretty sure he'd just aged five years. Then he yelled, "What the hell happened to your eye? And why didn't you answer your cell phone?"

"I stepped into the middle of a girl fight and got clobbered. It looks worse than it is. As for my phone, I left it in my apartment," she said. "I'm sorry."

Uncle Stan nodded, then reached out and grabbed Angie with one meaty arm, hugging her in a spine crusher.

"You're my favorite DeLaura," he growled. "Don't scare me like that."

"Sorry, Uncle Stan," Angie said. She looked a little watery, and she hugged him back hard.

"Stan, we need to get these people out of here," a man's voice said.

Mel looked beyond Uncle Stan to see his partner standing behind him. Surprise made her mouth form a small O. The detective met her gaze.

"We meet again, Melanie Cooper," he said. "Nice eye. Girl fight, huh? Why don't *I* ever get those calls?"

Mel hadn't seen Detective Martinez in months. They'd met when he'd been investigating a murdered scam artist, who also happened to be the first man her mother had dated in over thirty years. It had made quite an impression upon him, no doubt.

"Detective Martinez," she said. "I thought you were with the Paradise Valley PD."

"Yeah, I transferred," he said. "More action in Scottsdale."

"Apparently," Mel said, and she glanced at Sam's body, where the uniforms were moving Hannigan and Brigit back from the body.

"Who found him?" Uncle Stan asked.

"I did," Mel said. Her voice sounded small, and she coughed as if to clear her throat.

"You okay?" Martinez asked, suddenly serious. His black eyes studied her face, looking for any sign that she was about to break down. Mel wasn't built that way.

She gave him a sharp nod, and said, "I'm good. No worries."

It was a complete lie and, judging by the way his right eyebrow lifted, he knew it.

"Mel, can you get everyone into the bakery?" Stan asked. "We need to clear the scene."

"Sure," she said. "Coffee?"

"By the gallon," Stan said.

Mel ushered everyone into the bakery. It did not appear that they would be opening today. She had Angie call Marty and Oz and tell them to take the day off. Angie then called Tate, but he didn't answer, so she left a message for him.

Bonnie took over brewing the coffee while the rest of the group sat at the steel table. Brigit and Hannigan both looked wrecked, and Mel realized that the history that ran between them and Sam wasn't just adversarial. Sam had meant a lot to both of them.

Mel glanced at Angie. She couldn't help but think that, if she ever found Tate or Angie's body bludgeoned in an alley, a part of her would die. Angie met her gaze, and Mel knew she was thinking the same thing.

"Tate's not answering his phone," Angie said.

"He could be in a meeting," Mel said. "Let's wait a bit, and if we don't hear from him, we'll call his office."

"Agreed."

The back door opened, and everyone turned as Detective Martinez glanced

117

around, scanning the room until he found Mel.

"Can I talk to you?" he asked.

"Sure," she said.

"Out here," he said.

"Oh, okay," Mel agreed.

She really didn't want to log more time in the alley with Sam's body, but then she felt horrible for even thinking that. The poor man was dead. She blew out a breath and strode out the door.

"Come on," Martinez said. He led the way up to her apartment. "We can talk up here if that's easier for you."

"Thanks," Mel said. She unlocked the door with the keys she had shoved into her pocket and pushed it open.

Captain Jack flew out from behind her futon and scaled Martinez's neatly pressed khakis like he was Jack's own personal palm tree.

"Jack!" Mel said. She reached out for him, but Martinez had already unhooked him from his pants and was cradling him like a football.

"It's all right," he said. "He's an excellent watch cat."

"Hmm," Mel said. She did a quick scan of her apartment, relieved that she'd made up the futon and that it was tidy — not up to her mother's standards, of course, but still pretty good for her.

"Can I get you anything?" she asked.

"No, thanks," he said. "Why don't you sit down before you fall down?"

Mel nodded and took a seat on her futon. There were no other chairs in the room, so Martinez sat beside her. Not too close, but close enough that she got the faint whiff of his aftershave.

She knew from their previous acquaintance that he had a weakness for lemon cupcakes, so she wasn't surprised at the scent of citrus that came off of him. Judging by the way Captain Jack sprawled in his lap, Jack liked it, too.

"Can you tell me what happened this morning, exactly as it happened?" he asked.

It wasn't a long story to tell, and Mel made quick work of it. Her voice only cracked a little as she recounted finding Sam's body.

Martinez made few notes. There wasn't much Mel was telling him that was terribly helpful. He frowned and asked her why Sam and the others were here at the bakery.

Mel blew out a breath and explained about the disaster of a photo shoot — Martinez's lips twitched in response, but he didn't interrupt — and how she and Angie had agreed to the boot camp as compensation for the money lost on the shoot.

He asked a lot of questions about Sam. Mel told him as much as she could.

"I'm sorry I don't have more information," Mel said. "I only knew him for one day."

"It's all right," he said. "You've given me some excellent starting points for when I question the rest of the *SWS* employees."

"He was murdered, wasn't he?" she asked.

"At first glance, I'd say so," he said. "The back of his skull was crushed. There's no sign of a weapon yet. If it was a hit-and-run from a car, he'd have been in the street and there'd have been damage done to his body. This looks to be a single blow to the head, a deadly one."

Mel stared at the floor. How could such a thing have happened, and right below her apartment?

"I didn't hear anything," she said. "Shouldn't I have heard something?"

"Were you on pain meds for the eye last night?" he asked.

Mel nodded.

"Then a train could have rumbled through here and you wouldn't have heard it," he said.

"Damn," Mel sighed. "Of all the nights to

sleep like the dead."

"Nice." Martinez looked at her.

"Oh, sorry, bad choice of words." Mel shook her head, which made her eye throb.

"About your eye, how exactly did that happen?" Martinez asked.

"Ugh, it's embarrassing," she said.

"For you?" he asked. "This has to be good."

"No, it's just stupid," she said. "Amy Pierson and Brigit MacLeod were having a scuffle over some crack Amy had made about Brigit. They do not get along at all, by the way, and I stepped in right when Amy took a swing at Brigit, and POW!"

"I'll say," he said. "She clocked you good."

He leaned close to her and studied the lump. Mel heard herself swallow and wondered if he did, too. If he did, he didn't show it. Instead, he very gently used the tips of his fingers to move the hair she'd brushed over her eye back from her face. Then he cupped her chin with one hand and tilted her head so he could see the injury in the light.

"Did you go to the doctor?" he asked.

"Yes," she said.

"No fracture?"

"No, he said it'd be normal in a week or two," she said.

"What did your boyfriend have to say about it?" he asked.

He leaned back a smidge to meet her gaze, but he was still within extremely close proximity, and Mel was finding it hard to keep her thoughts focused on anything other than the heat he was generating, the feel of his callused fingers against her skin, and the incredible length of his long black eyelashes.

"Uh . . ." she stammered.

"You still have a boyfriend, don't you?" he asked.

"No . . . I mean . . . yes," she said. Good grief, she had almost told him that she had a fiancé not a boyfriend. Cripes, she hadn't even told her mother yet.

Martinez gave her a slow smile, as if pleased with her indecisiveness.

"I'm still with Joe," she said. She was pleased that her voice sounded nice and firm.

"I'd be disappointed if you weren't," he said.

Okaaaaay, now she was confused.

"What do you mean?" she asked.

Martinez rose from the couch after giving Jack one last scratch beneath his chin, which elicited much purring.

"I mean I'd be disappointed in him if he

let you go," he said. "You're the kind of girl a guy spends his life looking for."

Mel blew out a surprised laugh as she rose to stand as well. Now she knew he was teasing her.

"Yeah, right," she said. "As if a guy like you would give me the time of day."

He crossed to the door and she noticed his silhouette, backlit by the window, was a solid mass of muscle. She did not think there was even an ounce of fat on Detective Martinez.

"Oh, I'd give you the time of day," he said. Then he winked at her and added, "And night."

TWELVE

Mel felt her face get scorching hot, which had to look spectacular with her black eye. She could not believe the man was flirting with her now. Then she realized that he was probably doing it on purpose to distract her from the horror of the morning. She gave him a small smile.

"You're trying to keep me from freaking out about Sam, aren't you?" she asked.

"Is it working?" he countered.

"A bit," she said.

"Good," he said. "But just so we're clear, I meant what I said."

"Oh."

He smiled again and, feeling completely flustered, she snatched up an afghan from the futon and began refolding it even though it had been perfectly neat already.

"I'm sure Stan will want to talk to you after we're done with the crime scene," he said. He reached into his shirt pocket and took out a small white card. "My contact info is on here. Call me or Stan if you think of anything else, even if it doesn't seem important."

Mel took the card and glanced down at the stiff white paper with the embossed Scottsdale city emblem on it. It read *Detective Martinez* and listed several phone numbers and an e-mail address. She frowned.

"What is your first name?" she asked. "I don't think you've ever told me."

He grinned at her. "You're a smart girl. Figure it out."

He left, closing the door softly behind him.

The rest of the day dragged, as one by one the boot campers were questioned by Stan and Martinez. Amy was petulant, resenting the fact that Brigit and Hannigan seemed to have put aside their differences in the wake of their friend's murder. Although they didn't speak, Brigit and Hannigan sat together, not touching but each seemingly taking comfort from the other's presence.

Bonnie baked cupcakes while she cried, and Mel let her use the kitchen to channel her grief into some semblance of productivity. Justin looked shaken, and Angie had to take his fourth cup of coffee away from him because his shaky fingers made him look like he was having a seizure. Sylvia was morose, occasionally wiping away a tear, but otherwise she seemed to have closed in on herself, hugging her grief to her chest like a life preserver.

Mel watched them all as if she were attending a play. She felt removed from them and what they were feeling. They had a history that she knew nothing about. She didn't know about their relationships, their friendships, their enmity or their rivalries — well, except for Amy, who seemed to be disliked by everyone except Hannigan.

As she watched them, she couldn't help but wonder if one of them had been responsible for Sam's death. It made the marrow in her bones chill to think that a murderer could be among them. Still, she couldn't help but wonder: Did someone in this group have a reason to kill Sam? And if so, who was it and why?

"This is ridiculous!" Amy said. She'd taken to pacing the length of the kitchen, clacking back and forth in her spiky heels. "We're being held prisoner here."

"We have to help with the investigation in any way that we can," Hannigan said. His voice was controlled, not letting any emotion spill into it.

Brigit nodded in agreement.

126

"But who . . . how?" Bonnie blubbered the question that was weighing on them all. "I mean Sam was . . ."

Whatever she'd been about to say was lost as sobs wracked her body. Justin stood up and pulled her close, letting her soak his shirtfront with tears as he patted her back.

"It had to have been a mugging gone wrong," Brigit said. "Sam always got everywhere early. He must have surprised a criminal trying to break in and was killed for it."

"There was no sign of any attempt to break in," Angie said. "And he had his watch and wallet on him."

Brigit looked about to protest, but Mel added, "Why would anyone break into a cupcake bakery when there are art galleries and jewelry shops all around us? It doesn't make sense."

"But then . . ." Bonnie lifted her head from Justin's shirt and sniffed. "Who would have killed Sam? I mean, do you think he had an enemy?"

The room went still. Mel hadn't known Sam personally, but she really didn't think his skull had been crushed by a stranger. She did not, however, know how to say it tactfully.

Luckily, Justin finessed the situation with

well-spoken truths.

"Sam was a polarizing personality," he said. "People generally either loved him or hated him."

Bonnie looked about to protest, but Justin just tilted his head and said, "Just because you're one of the ones who loved him don't discount the fact that not everyone did."

Bonnie nodded and sank into a seat at the table.

The back door opened and Detective Martinez and Uncle Stan strode in. As a veteran on the force, Uncle Stan always had a new partner. She noticed that he seemed more at ease with Martinez than he usually was with his trainees. She figured it was because Martinez had experience in another city. Either way, they seemed to have a good rapport and, since Uncle Stan was getting up there in years, it made Mel feel better that he had a partner who was more his equal.

"Excuse me, folks," Uncle Stan addressed the group. "I want to thank you for your co-operation. Please understand this will be an ongoing investigation, and my partner and I will be in touch with many of you when we have more questions, but for now, you're free to go."

"Well, it's about time!" Amy shouldered

her way past the rest of them towards the kitchen door.

"Amy, wait!" Hannigan ordered. "We need to make a decision about the gala this weekend. We still have a commitment to bake one thousand cupcakes."

"You can't be serious!" Amy huffed. "I don't ever want to come back to this crappy little bakery again."

Angie growled low in her throat, and Mel put her hand on her arm. "This isn't about us."

Angie blew out a breath and visibly shook off her ire.

"We have to do this," Ian said. "Sam would have wanted us to."

"That's bull!" Amy argued. "Sam hated this almost as much as I did — maybe more. He thought it was a complete waste of time. You heard him say so!"

The last was directed at Mel, who said nothing. This wasn't her decision or her argument.

"Things are different now," Brigit said. "We will all be here tomorrow, every one of us, and we will bake those damn cupcakes in Sam's honor, and he will be remembered at the gala for being the brilliant journalist that he was."

Brigit's voice broke on the word *brilliant*,

and Hannigan reached out to put his hand on her shoulder, but he never made contact, pulling his hand away at the last second.

"Anyone who doesn't show can consider their career at *SWS* over," Brigit said. "Understood?"

Amy glowered, but with a stiff nod she turned and stormed out of the room.

"Go," Brigit said to the others. "It's been a hell of day."

Justin, Sylvia, and Bonnie left the kitchen in Amy's wake.

"Do you think this is a good idea, Brigit?" Hannigan asked. "I'd be willing to hire someone to finish the cupcakes for the gala."

"No, it has to be this way," she said.

"Why?" Hannigan asked.

"Because we may have a murderer in our midst, and I for one want them caught," Brigit said.

With that, she draped the handles of her purse on her forearm and strode from the kitchen. After a moment's pause, Hannigan followed her.

Uncle Stan and Martinez exchanged a glance.

"Do you think she counts herself in that statement?" Angie asked.

"Doesn't matter," Uncle Stan said. "*We* do."

Angie went to lock the front door behind the boot campers while Mel walked Uncle Stan and Detective Martinez to the back door.

"I'd prefer it if you didn't stay here tonight," Uncle Stan said.

"Don't worry," Mel said. "I'll be fine."

"Melanie," he said in his stern detective voice, "I don't want to have to call your mother."

"Uncle Stan, are you threatening me?" she asked.

"*Threaten* is such a harsh word. I'd prefer *coerce*," he said.

"Oh, yeah, that term gives me the warm fuzzies," she retorted.

"Stay somewhere else," he said. "Just for tonight."

"Fine," she said. "I'll call you later and let you know where I land."

"Thank you," he said. He planted a smacking kiss on her forehead and headed down the stairs to the alley.

"Good call," Martinez said. "He'd worry about you otherwise."

"I know," she said.

He smiled at her.

"What?"

"Nothing," he said. Mel didn't believe him, but he gave her no chance to question him when he said, "So, I'll see you tomorrow."

"Yeah, see you tomorrow — Eddie?" she asked.

He gave a surprised laugh and then grinned at her.

"No, Eddie Martinez is my drunken cousin who has nose-hair issues. Nice try, though."

"I'm going to figure it out," she said through a laugh. "Just you wait."

"I've got nothing but time," he said. He looked like he was going to say more, but instead he turned and headed down the steps. "See ya."

"Bye," Mel said, and she watched him follow Uncle Stan around the side of the building.

"So, what is up with tall, dark, and surly?" Angie asked as she stepped outside to join Mel.

"I wouldn't call him surly exactly," she said.

"Really? Because when he brought you in for questioning a few months ago, charm did not seem to be his most memorable quality."

"He's different when he's not about to arrest your mother," Mel said.

"Good to know," Angie said. "Listen,

there has been no word from Tate in response to my texts or messages. Should we call his office?"

"Yes, his secretary always knows where he is," Mel said. "It's like she has GPS on him."

Angie pulled out her phone and hit Tate's name in her contacts file. She put the phone to her ear and waited while it rang.

"Hi, Mrs. Gurney, this is Angie, is Tate in by any chance?"

There was a pause, but Mel could distinctly hear Mrs. Gurney sounding very upset on the other end of the line.

"Wait, I'm sorry. I can't understand you," Angie said. She gave Mel an alarmed look. "No, I didn't know. He what? Are you sure?"

There were more sounds of hysteria on the line.

"It will be all right, Mrs. Gurney," Angie said. "Yes, Mel and I will talk to him. We'll find out what's happening. Don't worry."

"What's going on?" Mel asked as Angie ended the call.

Angie looked at Mel, her brown eyes wide and her jaw a bit slack. "Tate quit his job."

THIRTEEN

"What?" Mel gasped. "No, you must have misheard."

"Believe me, that is highly probable given the amount of blubbering Mrs. Gurney was doing, but she was very clear when she said that she came in the this morning to find he had packed up his stuff and was gone. The only thing he left behind was a present for her, diamond earrings, and a note thanking her for her years of service."

"Is she out of a job?" Mel asked.

"No, she said she'll be transferred to someone else, but that made her cry even harder, since she loved Tate like a son."

Mel looked at her, and Angie shrugged. "That's what she said."

"Did he mention quitting to you?" she asked.

"No, you?"

"Not a word," Mel said. "Should we call his house?"

"I don't know," Angie said. "I can't believe he didn't tell us."

"I need a cupcake," Mel said. She strode to the walk-in refrigerator and pulled the heavy door open. "You want one?"

"Two," Angie said. "A Chocolate Espresso and a Chocolate Mint Chip, please. I need a double chocolate shot to get over this day so far."

Mel grabbed Angie's choices and then two of the same for herself, giving herself permission to go back for a Blonde Bombshell if need be.

They were quiet while they ate. Angie got up to get them each a glass of milk, but neither of them spoke until they had scraped the last of the frosting off their plates.

"Okay, I'm restored," Angie said. "Shall we go to Tate's apartment and see if he's there?"

"We might as well," Mel said. "I can't face the thought of opening the bakery. It would just seem wrong."

"What did Joe say about the whole thing?" Angie asked.

"What do you mean?"

"When you called him," Angie said. "Wasn't he freaked out that a man was murdered right by his girlfriend's apartment?"

"I haven't called him yet," Mel said.

"What?" Angie asked. "Why not? Are you two having a tiff?"

"Not exactly," Mel said. Now was her chance. She could tell Angie that Joe had asked her to marry him but that they'd been keeping it quiet and now he was getting impatient. Angie would understand, right?

"Come on, spill it," Angie said. "Just because he's my brother doesn't mean you can't tell me if you're having issues."

And there it was. She couldn't tell Angie about the engagement or anything. Angie was Mel's best friend and Joe's sister, and she would be hurt that they hadn't told her they were engaged, and she'd be upset if they were having problems. Mel couldn't do that to her.

"I just don't want to worry him," Mel said.

"Yeah, on top of that black eye you've got going, he'll probably go all mother hen on you," Angie said with a laugh. Mel cringed. "Oh, jeez, you didn't tell him about the eye either?" Mel shook her head.

"He is going to be so unhappy with you," Angie said. "You know he lives for that 'ride in and save the day' stuff."

Mel nodded. She did know. In fact, sometimes she wondered if Joe was only with her because she seemed to need so much rescuing. She shook her head, feeling disloyal even thinking it. Joe loved her and she loved him. They were just approaching a new level in their relationship and it was making her cautious, which she was certain was perfectly normal.

"Come on," she said, leading the way through the front of the bakery. She still didn't want to go out the back way. "Let's go to Tate's. I'll even let you drive, since I'm still monocular."

"Can that word be used as an adjective?" Angie asked.

"It can now," Mel said.

They locked the bakery door behind them and headed for Angie's sedan. She cranked the radio to a rock station, and they hummed along as they went. Tate lived just up the street, but they had to get through several lights before they reached his swank building, where he lived in a corner penthouse overlooking the Arizona Canal.

As Angie navigated the parking garage, the radio announcer's voice filled the car. "And now here's a new song from one of our own native sons. This baby is burning its way up the charts, sung by none other than Roach, the drummer of the Sewers, here's 'Angie.' "

Angie stomped on her brakes so hard that

they squealed and Mel was sure they left a chunk of rubber on the asphalt.

"Oh, no, he didn't!" Angie said.

"Shh!" Mel hushed her. Her ears were straining as she listened to Angie's ex-boyfriend sing about their breakup and his heartache. Surprisingly, Roach had a deep voice that resonated with emotion, and Mel felt herself getting choked up.

"I didn't know he could sing. I thought he was just the drummer," Mel said. "Did you know he could sing?"

"I'm going to kill him," Angie said. "How could he do this to me?"

"He's an artist," Mel said. "That's what they do."

"Not with my life!" Angie protested.

A honk blared behind them, and Angie glanced into her rearview mirror to see a Cadillac Escalade perched on her bumper, looking like it wanted to give her a push.

"Keep your shirt on!" she yelled, as if the driver could hear her.

She parked in the first available spot and switched off the engine.

"Are you okay?" Mel asked.

"I'm fine," she said. "No, I'm not. Is he insane?"

"He's working through your breakup."

Mel said. "It sounds like he was deeply in love."

Angie glared at her.

"Well, it does," Mel said. She pulled a tissue out of her purse and blew her nose. "He made me water up and everything. Look at me, I'm a mess."

"Oh, my god, we broke up months ago." Angie rested her head on her steering wheel.

"Did he mention the song to you?" Mel said.

"No, because I would have told him not to even think about it," she said. She fished her phone out of her purse. "I need to call him. That boy has some explaining to do."

"Do you want to do that while I go see Tate?" Mel asked. "Or maybe you should wait until you calm down?"

Angie looked from her phone to Mel and back to her phone. She gave a quick nod.

"You're right," she said. "I don't think I've reached reasonable just yet. Let's go. I'll deal with Roach later."

It sounded like Angie was going to be doing some serious Roach stomping. Mel almost felt sorry for him, but really, he had to be expecting it after writing a song about her and their breakup.

Mel wondered if his purpose all along had been to win Angie back with his music. She didn't say as much to Angie — she didn't have a death wish, after all — but she was pretty impressed with Roach right now.

They made their way into the bottom of Tate's building. The lobby was done in Italian marble with several deep green velvet couches and a thick Persian carpet in one corner, and an enormous flower arrangement in the center. Mel could see Hal, the doorman, in the mailroom, assisting the mailman, so she and Angie went right to the bank of elevators.

Since they watched movies with Tate just about every weekend, they both had a key card to the elevator and knew the pass code to his apartment. Angie seemed preoccupied, so Mel fished out her card and used it to summon the elevator. They stepped in and hit the penthouse button.

The elevator made a soft *whoosh,* and in moments they were on the topmost floor. There were four penthouse apartments, and Tate had the one that faced southeast. Mel and Angie crossed the smaller lobby, which also had a huge flower arrangement in the middle of it, and stopped in front of Tate's door.

Mel rang the bell, and they waited. If Tate wasn't at work or at the bakery, he would most likely be home. No one answered, however, and Mel frowned.

She and Angie exchanged a look, and Angie rapped on the front door with her knuckles. Still, there was no answer.

"I'm using the code," Angie said, and she tapped in the code that would unlock the door on the keypad next to the door.

They heard a click as the door unlatched, and Angie grabbed the handle and turned it. She looked at Mel before she pushed it open, and Mel nodded. Angie entered the apartment, and Mel followed.

The sight that met their eyes stopped them both in their tracks.

"What happened?" Angie asked. Her voice echoed in the empty room. Gone were all of Tate's furnishings, including his enormous television and comfy couches.

"At a guess," Mel said as she took it all in, "I'd say he's moved out."

"Yesterday," said a voice from the door.

Mel let out a shriek and spun around while Angie stiffened as if ready to fight off an attacker. There was no need, as it was Hal, the doorman. He looked at them with a sad smile, and Mel realized that he didn't like being the bearer of bad news.

"I take it Mr. Tate didn't tell you he had moved out?" he asked.

"No," Angie said. "He neglected to mention it."

"What's going to happen to the apartment?" Mel asked.

"A realtor was in here this morning," Hal said. "He didn't say as much, but I assume Mr. Tate is going to sell it. Are either of you interested?"

Mel and Angie exchanged a look. In a dream world, they would be able to buy a place like this.

"Uh, no, I don't think so," Mel said.

Hal looked sad. "It's a real loss to lose Mr. Tate. He was a good tenant, always pleasant and never loud. No one ever complained about him."

Mel knew that there were a few pseudo celebrities living in the building who were not well liked. One was a movie actress whose star had waned who was known for going out and getting roaring drunk and bringing the party back to her penthouse. Darby Meeks was her name, and she lived catty-corner from Tate. On several occasions they'd seen her taken out by the paramedics when she'd overindulged. Mel had never understood it. Darby had wealth and fame, and she chose to squander it in a parade of drugs and alcohol, letting the world see her still beautiful face covered in her own snot and tears with vomit running down her front. It was pathetic.

"You don't think Darby's antics finally caused him to move, do you?" Mel asked Angie.

"No, Darby's been in rehab out in Wickenburg for a month," Angie said. "Besides she was afraid of coming near Tate after I clarified his situation for her."

"Ah," Mel said.

Darby had taken to showing up at Tate's front door buck naked with a rose in her teeth and holding a bottle of champagne. She had made the mistake of doing it on a night when Angie had opened the door.

"I can't believe we'll never watch movies here again," Angie said.

"I can't believe he didn't tell us he was selling," Mel said. "If he's moved out of here, where is he living?"

"Let's ask him," Angie said. She took out her phone and called Tate again. Still, there was no answer.

"Hal, I suppose we should leave our pass cards with you," Mel said. She handed him hers and Angie did the same.

Hal looked choked up, but he took the cards with a nod as if accepting the inevitable.

"Come by the bakery anytime," Mel said.

"I'll always have a Red Velvet waiting for you."

"Aw, thanks, Miss Mel," Hal said. He blew his nose into a handkerchief he'd pulled from his pocket. "I'm going to miss you girls."

He opened his arms wide, and Mel and Angie exchanged an uncertain look before stepping into his embrace. They shared an awkward hug and an even more awkward ride down in the elevator.

As they crossed the parking garage to Angie's car, she looked at Mel and said, "That was more emotional than I expected."

"I know," Mel agreed. "I knew Hal was fond of us, but I didn't expect tears."

"Some people are really bad with change," Angie said. "I thought Tate was one of them, but now I don't know what to think. He's quit his job and moved out of his apartment. It's like he's having a major midlife crisis."

"He has been acting odd," Mel said. "Where do you suppose he's living now?"

Angie was silent as they got into the car. Her face was grim, and she looked worried.

"What are you thinking?" Mel asked.

"I think he's met someone," Angie said. "And he's too chicken to tell us."

"No, he hasn't," Mel said. "You know how

he feels about you."

"I thought I did," Angie said. "And when I broke up with Roach, I thought Tate might finally *do* something."

"No, huh?"

"Nothing. Nada. Zip. Zilch. Zero. I think he changed his mind," Angie said. "I think he wanted me when he couldn't have me, but now that I'm available, he's panicking. He's probably on his way to Costa Rica right now to get away from me."

"You're nuts," Mel said. "He's crazy about you. I'm sure there is a logical explanation for everything that is happening."

"Really?" Angie asked. "Lay it on me, because I'd love to hear it."

"Well, I don't know what it is," Mel said. "But I'm sure it will make sense once we hear it."

"Uh-huh," Angie said.

She started the car and pulled out of the parking garage. Mel turned her head and stared out the window as they left the luxury apartments for the last time. She didn't want Angie to see the doubt on her face. What could be happening with Tate? She didn't want to say it out loud, but for the first time she wondered if he had met someone new.

FOURTEEN

Mel had some choices for where to spend the night. She could bunk with Angie, who had a small house in the neighborhood that surrounded Old Town. It would be nice to be with a friend, someone who had gone through the trauma of finding Sam with her.

But she had a feeling Angie was going to be busy talking to Roach about his new hit single. She was still pretty steamed, and Mel didn't want to intrude on her letting her ex-boyfriend have it.

Then of course there was her mother, Joyce, who would love to have Mel spend the night, but she would wonder why, and Mel would have to tell her about the body. As it was, Mel was hoping that the news reports of where the body had been found would be vague, so that her mother might not find out it was beside the bakery. It would only cause her to worry and insist that Mel move home, which was not going to happen.

Of course, crashing at Tate's would have been an option, but since he had up and moved and was not returning calls, she had no idea where Tate's was anymore.

Her brother Charlie lived in Flagstaff, so he was out, and she couldn't see staying with Uncle Stan, because he would want to know why she wasn't bunking with her boyfriend, which brought her full circle to why didn't she want to stay with Joe.

She loved Joe; she had loved him since she was twelve years old and he was the sixteen-year-old heartthrob of the local high school. Joe was the whole package: smart, kind, and funny, not to mention tall and handsome. He was a dedicated attorney and believed in the judicial system and its ability to regulate society. She knew it was her own poor self-esteem that made it hard for her to believe that Joe was in love with her, a cupcake baker, but there it was.

The man could have anyone he wanted, anyone, and he had chosen her. She could not wrap her brain around it and sometimes she couldn't help but wonder why. Why did Joe want to marry her?

Oh, she knew he had a mythic sweet tooth and he loved her cupcakes, but that certainly didn't seem like enough of a reason to marry someone.

Then again, she knew she wasn't the chubster she'd been when they were in school. She'd spent some time in Paris, studying to be a pâtissier and had learned to have a healthy relationship with food and not one where food became her go-to for sadness, happiness, loneliness, and boredom.

She knew she was a confident businesswoman and that Joe was proud to have her come to his lawyerly events because she cleaned up okay and she could carry on conversations with local business leaders with intelligence and charm. She knew this, but old insecurities never died, they just waited until she wasn't paying attention so they could rear up and bite her on the butt. Maybe she wasn't a chunky adolescent on the outside, but most of the time, she sure felt like one.

She knew her hesitation about staying with Joe was grounded in her desire not to talk about the marriage thing. Add to that the fact that if she stayed with Joe, he'd see her eye, and she'd have to tell him about Sam's murder and, yeah, she had a feeling that conversation wouldn't be much better than if she was having it with Joyce.

She didn't enjoy being in her apartment

that evening. She couldn't stop thinking about Sam, and when she glanced out her window, the yellow crime-scene tape with which they'd marked off the area where his body had been found flapped in the breeze as if daring her to come by so it could snatch her into its death grasp, too.

A shudder traveled down her spine, and she pulled her window shades closed. She knew she'd been on pain meds last night, but she still wondered how someone could have smashed Sam's skull in without her hearing.

It made her think it must have been someone Sam knew, since he hadn't shouted for help. Which then made her wonder if it was one of the cupcake boot campers, which frankly gave her the heebie-jeebies.

She packed up the necessaries for herself and Jack and headed over to Joe's house. She texted him before locking up her apartment, asking if she could come over and, naturally, being the perfect guy, he had texted back an affirmative. No hesitation. No questions asked.

Joe lived in a two-story townhouse right off Central Avenue in Phoenix. It took Mel about a half hour to get to Joe's, and she pulled into his two-car carport, parking beside his Prius. His front door opened before she had shut off her engine, and Joe met her as she stepped out of the car.

"How are you?" he asked.

Mel stepped out of the car and Joe's eyes opened wide.

"What happened to your eye?"

"Wrong place, wrong time," she said.

"Explain," he said with a frown.

"I stepped into a scuffle between two of my cupcake boot campers yesterday and didn't duck in time," she said.

"I just got off the phone with Uncle Stan," he said. "He told me about Sam Kelleher. Are you all right? Can I do anything?"

"Yes, take him," Mel said. She handed him Captain Jack, who was yelling at her and had yelled at her the entire ride over. He didn't like cars. "He's very cranky."

"Oh, come here, little buddy," Joe said, and he cradled Jack close to his chest. Jack gave a mollified purr and began to butt Joe's chin with his head.

Joe planted a quick kiss on Mel's bangs, took her overnight bag, and led the way into the house. Mel shouldered Jack's tote bag of food and toys and followed with his litter box.

Joe's townhouse was about as different from Mel's apartment as two places could get. His place was all sleek lines and curves made of steel and granite, featuring black leather furniture with apple green accents, while Mel's place was more a hodgepodge of antique pieces and was decorated in browns and blues with floral patterns mixed with stripes and matching snuggly chenille pillows and throws on the futon.

She put Jack's litter box in the laundry room off the kitchen, and Joe followed with Jack to show him where it was. He then put down Jack, who scampered off to go and investigate. Mel always brought him to Joe's when she spent the night, as he liked to go adventuring in the bigger house.

"Don't break anything!" she called after him.

"He's fine," Joe assured her. He held open his arms. "Need a hug?"

Mel heaved a soul-deep sigh and fell against him. Joe caught her close and held her tight. He was warm and strong, and she realized that for the first time all day she felt safe. Safe enough for the tears that had threatened repeatedly to spill out. She tried to gulp them back, but Joe had already seen what was coming.

"It's okay," he said. He ran his hand up and down her back. "Let it out."

"He was dead!" Mel said, as if this was news. "I saw his hand, and then when I went over there was a pool of blood and the back of his head was crushed."

A shudder rippled through her from her hair follicles to her toenails. Joe just kept holding her until the tremors passed.

"The magazine people were all freaking out, and Uncle Stan and his new partner and the crime-scene crew came. We haven't been able to find Tate, and then there was this song on the radio and Angie was so mad," she said.

Joe's hand stopped moving on her back. "Sorry, you lost me."

"Roach was singing a song about him and Angie on the radio," she said. "It's a hit that's burning up the charts."

"Uh-oh. How did she handle that?" he asked.

"Not well," Mel said with a shake of her head. "And Tate is missing."

"What? What do you mean missing?" he asked.

"We tried to call him about Sam, but he didn't answer, so then we thought we'd call his office, but his secretary said he'd quit."

"Quit?" Joe asked. "But I thought he was happy there. He's like a genius at making money, isn't he?"

Mel shrugged. "It gets worse."

Joe just looked at her.

"We stopped by his apartment, and he's moved out," she said.

"To where?"

"We don't know," she said. "He didn't even tell us he was moving."

Joe frowned. He obviously did not like what he was hearing.

"It's weird, isn't it?" she asked.

"And you haven't heard from him?"

"Not a peep," she said. "I'm worried about him. Angie thinks he's met someone."

"What do you think?" he asked.

Mel thought about it for a moment. "I don't know what to think."

A chime sounded in Mel's purse. It was "Tara's Theme" from *Gone with the Wind,* her ringtone.

"I have to get that," she said. "It might be Tate."

Joe nodded.

Mel checked the number. It was Angie. She shook her head at Joe before she answered.

"Hey, Ange. What's up?"

"I think we need to call Tate's parents," Angie said. "They have to know where he is."

"Agreed," Mel said. "So why don't you call them?"

"I was thinking we should stop by the

153

house," Angie said.

"Really?" Mel asked. "Why?"

"Because I think that's where Tate is, and I think if we show up, his parents won't give us the brush-off," she said. "But if we call, they might."

Mel thought about it for a minute. Angie was right. They needed to find Tate and let him know what was happening. He was a partner in their business, and their friend. She wouldn't rest easy until she knew where he was and what was happening with him.

"I'm at Joe's," Mel said. "Can you pick me up?"

The doorbell rang and Joe went to answer it. Angie stood in the doorway with her phone. She ended the call, and asked, "Hi, Bro. So, Mel, are you ready to go?"

Joe did not look happy when they left, but Mel promised to bring him a spinach calzone from Spinato's, one of their favorite Italian restaurants, on her return and he looked somewhat placated.

"Call me as soon as you know something," he said. He hugged Angie and planted a kiss on Mel and stood in the doorway waving good-bye with Captain Jack lying across his shoulder.

"They make a cute couple," Angie said.

"They sure do," Mel agreed as she got

into the passenger seat.

About 80 percent of her wanted desperately to be back in the townhouse with Joe and Captain Jack, but she knew the nagging 20 percent of her that would worry about Tate would never let her rest.

Tate's parents lived in the same neighborhood as Mel's mother and Angie's parents, except where the Cooper and DeLaura families had a nice view of Camelback Mountain, Tate's family actually lived on the mountain.

Angie and Mel had spent most of their weekends in high school in the Harpers' built-in theater watching old movies and giving their popcorn machine a workout. Driving up the winding road, Mel felt a sudden nostalgia for the simplicity of those days, when there were no dead bodies, police investigations, or complicated relationships.

Angie parked in the circular driveway in front of the house. The Harpers' mansion was one of the oldest on Camelback Mountain, built in the forties with a decided Frank Lloyd Wright influence. Like his famous Scottsdale residence Taliesin West, the Harpers' house was built from native stone nestled in concrete and had a squared-off look with cantilevered ceilings and redwood beams.

Where the other mansions sat on the mountain like blemishes with their ostentatious turrets and towers and ridiculous vaulted ceilings, the Harpers' mansion seemed to nestle right into the side of the mountain as if the intent of its organic design was to return the house to the earth once the residents were finished with it.

Angie and Mel got out of the car and climbed the three short steps which led them into a courtyard, built of the same concrete and boulders as the house. The front doors were set back between the two wings of the house that had square floor-to-ceiling glass walls framed by large beams of redwood.

Angie reached the door first and raised her fist to knock. The door swung open before her knuckles could connect, and she almost rapped Mr. Harper, Tate's father, on the chest. Luckily, her response time was quick enough and she didn't connect.

"Good evening, Melanie, Angela," he said. "I'm assuming you are here with news."

FIFTEEN

Mel and Angie exchanged a confused look.

"News about . . . ?" Mel asked, letting the question dangle.

"Darling, where are your manners?" Mrs. Harper appeared beside her husband. "Invite the girls in."

"Sorry." Mr. Harper huffed out an irritated sigh and stepped aside. "Please come in."

Mel sensed it wasn't an invitation as much as an order.

She and Angie followed the Harpers into the foyer, which had a highly polished mahogany floor that led down into a sitting room, where a fire was going and a view of the city of Phoenix could be seen from the floor-to-ceiling windows.

"It's good to see you both," Mrs. Harper said as she took in the sight of them.

The Harpers were not a huggie-kissie sort of people. Where Mel's mother would have hugged the stuffing out of them and the De-Laura family would have smothered them in cheek pinches and kisses, the Harpers stood stiffly, staring at them as if uncertain of what to do.

"Please, come in and have a seat," Mrs. Harper invited them.

Tate's mother was a sweater-and-pearls type of lady; her manicure was always perfect and matched the fastidiousness of her thick silver hair, which she wore in a chin-length bob.

Despite the workday being long over, Mr. Harper was still in a pale blue dress shirt and tie over crisply pleated navy slacks and brown loafers. In all the years she'd known him, Mel had never seen him don jeans or shorts; in fact, she couldn't even imagine it.

"May I bring refreshments?" a voice asked from the doorway that led to the kitchen.

An older woman dressed all in black appeared behind the Harpers. It had been a long time since Mel had seen Mrs. Ada, the Harpers' live-in housekeeper, and she noted that the gray-haired lady with the sturdy build didn't seem to have aged a day since the last time she'd seen her.

"Hi, Mrs. Ada," Mel and Angie said together.

"Would you girls like a nice root-beer

float?" Mrs. Ada asked.

"You remembered," Mel said.

"I'm not likely to forget," Mrs. Ada said with a grin. "I must have made hundreds of those over the years for you and Mr. Tate."

Her hazel eyes sparkled at them and, if the Harpers hadn't been standing there watching, Mel would have crossed the room to give her a big hug. As it was, she just smiled back, and Mrs. Ada gave her a small nod as if she understood.

"I think iced tea would be fine," Mr. Harper said.

Clearly he was anxious to get the discussion underway, and Mel wondered what he thought they had to report. She had a feeling they were doomed to disappoint the Harpers.

Mrs. Ada left the room, and the four of them sat down on the stiff brown leather couches that faced the fireplace. Despite the warmth coming from the fire, the room felt cold to Mel; she wondered if it was the stone or the people in the room that made her feel that way.

She didn't dislike the Harpers; in fact, they had been very kind in welcoming Angie and Mel into their home every weekend, and Mel had always gotten the feeling that they were somehow relieved to have them there, so that they wouldn't be obliged to spend too much time with their son.

"Now, please tell us what brings you here," Mrs. Harper said.

"We're looking for Tate," Angie said. "We have to tell . . . that is, there is some news we need to share with him."

Mr. and Mrs. Harper exchanged a look. They must have developed a code no one could crack, because Mel could read nothing in their expressions, but they each obviously knew exactly what the other was thinking.

"Why did you come here?" Mr. Harper asked.

"Because he's moved out of his apartment," Mel said, "and he's not answering his phone, so we thought he might be here."

"You know that he quit his job today," Mr. Harper said. He was watching them closely.

Angie nodded. "We talked to his secretary."

"Did you know he planned to quit?" Mr. Harper asked.

Mel could hear the expectation in his voice, as if he was hoping someone could clarify what his son had done. She hated to disappoint him, but there was no alternative.

"No," she said. "He never said a word. We

160

were stunned."

Mrs. Ada arrived back in the room carrying a tray with four glasses of iced tea. They thanked her for the tea but waited until everyone was served before they continued their conversation.

"So, I take it he isn't here?" Angie asked.

"No," Mrs. Harper said with a shake of her head. "We've heard nothing from him since his father discovered his letter of resignation this morning."

"I hate to pry," Angie said. "I know it's none of my business, but did he say why he was doing all of this?"

Mel knew Angie was trying to find out if there was a woman involved, and she prayed for Angie's sake that there wasn't, because she feared it would crush her best friend.

"No, he didn't," Mr. Harper said. He sounded angry, and Mel felt Angie stiffen beside her. "It was nothing more than a lousy form letter. It could have been from any of my employees."

"It's all very distressing," Mrs. Harper said.

Mel got the feeling Mrs. Harper had been listening to her husband rant and rave for the better part of the evening, and she cast the woman a sympathetic glance.

"You bet it's distressing," Angie said. She

took a long swallow of her iced tea. "I can't imagine what he's thinking. I mean, who up and quits his job and moves without telling anyone?"

Mel thought back to when she'd ditched her marketing career in Los Angeles and moved back to Scottsdale to attend culinary school. She hadn't said a word to anyone.

"Well, there could be a variety of reasons," she said. "I mean, maybe he —"

"No, there's only one reason," Angie interrupted. She *thunk*ed her glass down onto a cork coaster on the coffee table. "He is being a selfish brat, and he needs a good kick in the pants, since obviously that is where his brain is presently situated."

"Hear, hear!" Mr. Harper cheered. He put his glass on the table, too. "That's the first sense anyone has talked all day."

"Now, we don't know why Tate is making these decisions," Mrs. Harper said. "He could have very good reasons for what he is doing."

"For quitting the family business?" Angie asked doubtfully.

Mr. Harper shot her a look of approval, and added, "And not telling his friends where he is?"

Angie nodded at him. "And excluding his family from his decision-making?"

162

"As well as his business partners," Mr. Harper added.

Mel glanced between Angie and Mr. Harper, as did Mrs. Harper. It was clear Angie and Mr. Harper were allies in their annoyance with Tate, while Mrs. Harper and Mel were more inclined to wait and see what he had to say for himself. Mel wished Tate were here to see this. She never thought she'd see the day when Mr. Harper unbent enough to have a conversation, never mind be in perfect agreement, with Angie.

"He has a lot of explaining to do," Angie said.

"Indeed," Mr. Harper agreed.

"Be that as it may," Mrs. Harper said. "I'm really more concerned with where he is right now."

And there it was, a mother's love for her son, bringing the entire discussion full circle to the fact that someone that all four of them loved was missing.

Mel didn't sleep well at Joe's. He had a queen-size bed that was as soft as a cloud. She should have slept like a baby, even after the horror of the day and her worry about Tate, but no. Comfort wasn't exactly comfortable. Mel knew each individual lump in her futon mattress, and she missed angling her body around them just so. Captain Jack had no such problems, as he chose a nice, fluffy pillow to sleep on — hers — and spent the night snoring in synch with Joe.

Was this what married life would be like? Mel stared at the ceiling while she thought about moving in here with Joe. She tried to imagine how her florals and plaids would blend with his black leather. She couldn't picture it. She tried to picture him moving into her shoebox of an apartment above the bakery — no, that didn't work either.

She could feel a complete freak-out brewing just underneath her skin. She tried to breathe through it. No decisions had to be made today. She was fine. Life was fine.

Her phone chimed from its spot on the bedside table. She glanced at the clock. It was five in the morning. Who would be calling her at five in the morning? Joe grumbled and rolled over. Maybe it was Tate.

Mel sat up in bed and grabbed the phone. She checked the number and sighed. It was her mother.

She pressed the button to talk as she tiptoed from the room, grabbing a sweatshirt of Joe's on the way.

"Mom, is everything all right?" she asked. She pulled on the sweatshirt and went down the stairs to the kitchen. She might as well start the coffee.

"What do you mean is everything all right?" Joyce asked. "There was a murder right outside your bakery!"

"I know," Mel said.

"You know?" Joyce parroted her. "And you didn't call me? I turned on the morning news, and there is Gina Mendoza standing right outside your bakery, talking about a murder."

Mel could hear her mother's television in the background. Joyce was quiet, and Mel could tell she was watching the news again.

"Mom, hello? Mom!"

"That Gina is so cute," her mother said. "I love how she wears her hair. Could you run downstairs and get me her autograph?"

"I'd love to Mom," Mel said. "But I'm not home. Captain Jack and I are at Joe's."

"Dear Joe," Joyce sighed. "How is he?"

"Asleep like most normal people at five o'clock in the morning," Mel said.

She wrestled a coffee filter into the pot and measured out enough scoops for the two of them. She hit the button and was immediately comforted by the sound of the coffee machine beginning to drip hot java into its glass carafe.

"Well, I'm glad you had the sense not to stay at the bakery," Joyce said.

"Uncle Stan made me promise to stay elsewhere."

"Stan knows about the murder?" Joyce asked.

"He's the lead detective for the investigation," Mel said. "And since Sam Kelleher, the victim, was one of my cupcake boot-camp participants, Stan thought it best if I —"

"You knew him?" Joyce interrupted. She sounded stunned. "I thought it was just a robbery gone wrong that happened to be outside your bakery."

"No," Mel said. "I found Sam when I went to open the bakery yesterday."

"*You* found him? Oh, my lord, Melanie Cooper, what have you gotten yourself into this time?" Joyce asked.

"Nothing," Mel protested. "I'm just holding a cupcake boot camp for the staff of *SWS* magazine. I have nothing to do with anyone getting murdered."

"That's it. You're selling the bakery," Joyce said.

Sixteen

"What?" Mel asked. She *thumped* her head softly against the wooden front of Joe's kitchen cabinet. "Why would I do that?"

"Well, obviously cupcake baking is a much more dangerous profession than we first anticipated," Joyce said. "It's like the dead bodies are lured in by your buttercream."

"Not my fault," Mel said.

"I know, but, honestly, you're not getting any younger, honey, and you have a good guy now. Maybe you need to start looking at the next phase of your life."

"Like getting married and having babies?" Mel asked.

There was enough coffee for a cup now. She hurriedly poured herself one and put the carafe back.

"Your *younger* brother, Charlie, is married and has two gorgeous boys," Joyce said.

"Are we competing?" Mel asked. "I was unaware."

167

"Obviously, because if you were competing, I'd have grandbabies from you by now," Joyce said.

"Mom," Mel said. It came out as a ten-syllable whine, but she was powerless to stop it.

"Don't you want marriage and babies?" Joyce asked.

"I don't know," Mel said. And there it was. She really didn't know.

Joe staggered into the kitchen. He had bed head, and his eyes were puffy with sleep. His T-shirt and long flannel pants were wrinkled, and he cradled Captain Jack in one arm. He let out a yawn and Mel felt her heart trip over itself at the sight of him. She loved him, of that there was no question, but was she ready for "until death do us part"? She didn't know.

"Listen, Mom, I have to go," she said.

Joe's eyebrows shot up, and Mel gave him a pained nod.

"All right," Joyce said. "Well, call me later and tell me what's happening; otherwise my friend Ginny and I will be over to see you."

Mel smiled. Her mom didn't even candy-coat the threat.

"I promise," Mel said. "Love you."

"I love you, too," Joyce said. "And give my love to dear Joe."

Mel ended the call and dropped her phone on the counter. Usually she used milk and sugar in her coffee, but today she felt like she needed to mainline the caffeine, so she drank it unforgivingly black.

"Mom, huh?"

"Ugh."

"Does she still call me 'dear Joe'?" he asked. He was grinning.

"Yes," Mel said. "Every time she mentions your name, in fact."

"I like your mom," he said.

He had fed Captain Jack and poured his own coffee. Now he looped an arm around Mel's waist and pulled her close so that they leaned side-by-side against the counter while they sipped their coffee.

Mel knew it was a moment of peace in what was otherwise going to be a very long, very difficult day. She tried to memorize the feeling of calm, knowing that she was going to miss it later.

By ten o'clock that morning, that feeling of calm was no more than a poignant memory. The bakery had reopened. Unexpectedly, a crowd of gawkers awaited the unlocking of the doors, and Mel wondered what they were hoping to see. A chalk outline on the floor?

Marty made it pretty clear that they were in the cupcake business not the corpse business. The more ghoulish of the gawkers left, but the rest consoled themselves with cupcakes.

The *SWS* crew met up in the kitchen. They had the sunken eyed, weary look of zombies, and Mel had a feeling that not one of them had slept the night before.

"Are you sure you're all up to this?" Mel asked as they gathered around the steel table.

Ian Hannigan stood by the door with his arms crossed over his chest.

"We're fine," he said. "What do we need to do to have the cupcakes ready by the gala on Saturday?"

"Get baking," Mel said.

The lack of enthusiasm was not unexpected. Her own desire to bake had been curbed by finding Sam in the alley yesterday; still, she had a business to run.

"Listen, I'm happy to do the baking for you," she said. "I don't think anyone would fault you for canceling the boot camp."

"No, we can do this. We will do this. For Sam," Brigit said. She was wearing jeans and a form-fitting, long-sleeve jersey shirt in ruby red. Even casually dressed, Brigit exuded a stylishness that was impeccable.

"I really don't see Sam giving two hoots about whether we make cupcakes or not," Justin said.

"That's not the point!" Brigit snapped. She looked as if she was going to say more, but she didn't. Instead, she took her purse outside. Mel had a feeling she was going for a cigarette break.

"Go ahead and start, Mel," Hannigan said. "I'll talk to her."

Mel and Angie had planned to treat the cupcake boot camp just like one of the baking classes they held periodically. With Ian and Brigit outside, that left Justin, Sylvia, Bonnie, and Amy in the kitchen.

In no time, the room was filled with the sounds of ingredients being poured and spatulas scraping the sides of bowls, and the whir of mixers.

"Baking always makes me feel better," Bonnie said to Mel as she paused beside her.

"Me, too," Mel said. "I was in culinary school when my dad died. I think it helped me to work out my grief."

Bonnie stared at her for a moment, and Mel wondered if she had just shared too much.

"My mother passed when I was sixteen," Bonnie said. "I have four younger brothers and sisters. I became the family cook. It helped. I always felt as if my mom was in the kitchen cooking with me."

Mel nodded. She could see that. Joyce drove her crazy, no question, but she could imagine that she might feel her mother's presence in her kitchen, primarily because the kitchen had been her mother's base of operations when she and Charlie were kids. It was where she had interrogated them over homemade plates of Rice Krispies Treats and chocolate milk.

"Excuse me, is the batter supposed to be winding its way up the beater?" Sylvia asked. She was using a hand mixer, and it looked as if her cupcake batter was doing a "creature from the bottom of the bowl" sort of thing as it rose up and tried to strangle the beaters.

"Yikes!" Justin said. " 'Well it's kind of a — kind of a mass. It keeps getting bigger and bigger.' "

"*The Blob*," Mel said, identifying the movie quote.

"Nice," Justin said.

"I think it needs more milk," Angie said from across the table. "Otherwise you're going to have a pet."

"Would it be housebroken?" Sylvia asked as she looked into her bowl. "That would

172

be a step above my last two husbands."

Everyone was silent, and then Angie started to laugh, which set off the rest of the room. It was a good sound. The only one not laughing was Amy.

The back door opened, and Hannigan and Brigit walked in. Her eyes were red, and Mel didn't think it was cigarette smoke that had made them that way.

"How many husbands have you had, anyway?" Amy asked. She looked sourly at Hannigan and Brigit. It was easy to see she was feeling jealous and angry and looking for a target. Lucky Sylvia.

"Oh, let me count," Sylvia said while Angie worked on her batter. "The first one I married because he was gorgeous. Never marry a man for his looks. Beauty fades."

Justin snorted. "I'll remember that."

"The second one I married for his money. Never do that, either. If you spend like I do, the poor bastard will be broke in a year."

Amy let out a huff of disgust as she dumped her dry ingredients into a large bowl and sifted with more vigor than was required.

Bonnie, on the other hand, had lowered her head and was hiding her smile.

"The third one I married because his children were so cute, and I thought I might like to be a mama." Sylvia shook her head. "Come to find out, I don't like children."

Brigit and Hannigan took the remaining seats at the table. Together they began mixing the ingredients that had been measured out, and Mel noticed that they moved together as if in a dance, where each partner knows the other so well they flow together seamlessly.

"The fourth one —"

"Fourth? You have got to be kidding me!" Amy said.

"I married him because he was younger, and I thought it would be exciting," Sylvia said. "It was like being married to a toddler. He did not understand the things an older and wiser man would."

"Four? How did you find four husbands? You have had more than your fair share of husbands," Amy said. She was glaring at Brigit and Hannigan, but her attack was at Sylvia. "You are a husband hog!"

Sylvie shrugged. "So, I married yours and mine. I think you owe me a thank-you for marrying the clunkers."

"I refuse to work like this!" Amy said. "All of this chatter and nonsense. It's just stupid."

Justin and Bonnie exchanged a surprised look.

"I think it's fun," Bonnie said. "I never knew those things about you, Sylvia. It's fascinating."

"You would think so, you cow," Amy snapped. "You married your high school sweetheart and have no life. I'm sure anyone's sordid existence is more interesting than yours."

Mel felt a hot burst of anger spark inside of her. She had no doubt that Amy felt free to insult Bonnie because Amy was a size zero while Bonnie was more in the double digits. Amy undoubtedly believed that a woman's worth was equivalent to the number on her scale, and the smaller the better.

"Shut up, Amy," Justin said. "You have no right to be nasty to Bonnie just because you're a miserable twig. Have a cupcake and stop being such a b—"

"Justin!" Hannigan cut him off. "That's enough."

Justin looked unrepentant.

"Everyone hates me," Amy wailed. "They have since the first day I showed up at the office."

"With that enormous chip on your shoulder, is it any wonder?" Brigit asked. "Really, I can't imagine why Sam hired you. You have no respect for anyone's work. You act as if you're the magazine's savior simply because you're young."

"I do not," Amy protested. "Sam was mean to me. He belittled my writing and edited it so much that it wasn't even recognizable."

Brigit rose from her seat and stared Amy down.

"That's because it was terrible. Frankly, your journalism chops are weak. I told Sam that, and he agreed. He wouldn't let you get away with the crap writing you were doing, he forced you to be better, and you hated him for that."

"I did hate him," Amy said. "But only because he forced me to sleep with him to get this job, which, as it turned out, is a joke."

Seventeen

Everyone in the room stared at Amy in wide-eyed disbelief.

"What?" she asked. "Wasn't it my turn to share?"

"I don't believe you," Brigit said.

"Well, you'd better," Amy said. "Because I have the smutty text messages from him to prove it."

"You'd better not do anything that discredits Sam's standing in the journalism community," Brigit said.

"Or what?" Amy asked.

"I'll ruin you," Brigit said.

She said it with such cold, calculating precision that Mel had no doubt that she could do it and that she would do it if provoked.

"What's the matter?" Amy taunted her. "Are you jealous that your boy preferred my" — she paused to cast a nasty look at Bonnie — "size zero?"

With that she shoved her mixing bowl away from her and strode out the kitchen door.

"I'd better go and talk to her," Hannigan said.

"Don't you dare give in to her," Brigit said. "She is slandering Sam. We can't let her get away with that."

"Precisely why I'm going after her," Hannigan said.

"What are you going to do?" Brigit asked. "Give her a promotion?"

Hannigan looked as if she'd slapped him. "What exactly are you accusing me of?"

"You're going to cave in to her hysterics and keep her on, aren't you?"

"What would firing her do for us?" he asked.

"It would improve the art department," Justin said. Both Brigit and Hannigan glared at him. "Oh, that wasn't an open question? Sorry."

"I'm going after her," Hannigan said. "If what she says is true, that Sam had her sleep with him for her job, then she could come after us with a lawsuit that would kill the magazine."

"Since when do you care about the magazine?" Brigit asked.

"I've always cared," he said.

178

"Oh, save it," Brigit snapped. She made shooing motions with her hands. "Go after the little girl. I hope you're very happy together."

"Brigit!"

Hannigan looked like he would have yelled at her if there wasn't an audience, an audience that was riveted watching them.

"Go! Just go!" Brigit yelled. She stalked across the kitchen, opened the door to Mel's office, and slammed it so hard behind her that it rattled on its hinges.

Hannigan let loose a string of colorful curses and then followed Amy out the kitchen door.

"I think that was a bad call," Sylvia said.

"What do you mean?" Angie asked.

The kitchen door banged open and Marty glared at the group.

"Will there be any more forthcoming drama from here?" he asked. "Because in case you people haven't noticed, we've got a business to run, and I can't keep coming up with excuses for why there is so much noise coming from the kitchen."

"Sorry, Marty," Mel said. "I'll try to keep it quieter."

"What have you been telling people?" Angie asked.

"That our chief baker likes to watch soap

179

operas while she cooks, which was working until those two idiots came running through the bakery, making me look like a big, fat liar."

"Which you are," Justin said as he scooped batter into a cupcake pan.

"I prefer embellisher of facts, if you don't mind," Marty said.

"My mistake," Justin said. He looked like he was trying not to laugh.

Mel and Angie took the first batch of cupcakes and put them in the convection oven.

"Just so we're clear," Marty said.

The door swung shut behind him.

"I think the drama is only just beginning," Bonnie said. "We are going to have to work a lot faster if we're going to get these cupcakes done by the gala, and we can't have people just leaving in a snit."

"Sounds like we're not done with the drama," Angie said. "The investigation into Sam's death is ongoing and, with what Amy said, I have a feeling it's going to get messy. Not to mention, there is obviously some serious tension between Hannigan and Brigit."

She said Brigit's name in a whisper, and they all glanced cautiously at the door to Mel's office. It didn't fly off of its hinges in an explosion of upset, so Mel figured she couldn't hear them.

"What is the deal between Hannigan and Brigit anyway?" she asked. "There is a hostility there that you usually only see between —"

"Lovers?" Sylvia supplied.

"Well, yeah," Mel said.

"Back in the day, when they were all doing hard news," Justin said. "Hannigan and Brigit were lovers, which was complicated."

"Why?" Angie asked.

"Hannigan was married," Bonnie said. Her tone made it clear that she didn't approve, and Mel saw the flash of the other woman's wedding ring in the kitchen light.

"It happens," Sylvia said. "Especially when you are in a foreign country and think you may not get home."

"It never happens to me," Justin said, looking put out.

"That's because you don't do hard news," Bonnie said. Justin just looked at her and she turned bright red. "Oh, I'm sorry. I didn't mean it *that* way."

Justin grinned at her. "You're forgiven."

"The way I heard it, Brigit wanted Hannigan to leave his wife so that they could be together, but Hannigan turned her down," Bonnie said. "That's when she left newspapers and started working for magazines on the brink of extinction. She has a real gift for turning them around."

"Thank you," Brigit said from the open doorway to Mel's office.

Everyone in the kitchen jumped and Bonnie let out a little shriek, which she quickly turned into a cough.

"Just so you know," Brigit said. "Your office walls apparently carry sound instead of shutting it out."

Sylvia, Bonnie, and Justin all hung their heads in the perfect posture of shame. Mel nudged Angie, who was beside her, and they quickly hung their heads, too.

"It's all right," Brigit said. "After all, any of that is easy enough to find on the Internet gossip sites."

Mel looked up at her and saw that she looked older than she'd seen her till now. The fine lines around her eyes and mouth seemed deeper, and they didn't appear to be laugh lines but rather looked like they'd been caused by stress.

Mel had seen the beginnings of lines forming around her own eyes, but she had been okay with them because they looked like they were caused by joy. She had the overwhelming urge to fetch Brigit a cupcake.

"Sam's death is going to drag it all up again, I suppose," Brigit said with a sigh. "Detective Martinez said as much. I suppose I should get prepared for when they dig into my relationship with Hannigan."

"Maybe they won't go there," Bonnie said.

Angie rolled her eyes at Mel. Angie had been dragged into the limelight during her relationship with Roach. She knew what it was like to open the curtains in the morning and have a photographer hanging upside down from a rope tied to the eaves while trying to get compromising pictures of her.

"Oh, they'll go there," Brigit said. "Especially, since I'm responsible for his wife's death."

No one moved. Mel thought it looked as if they were playing a game of freeze tag and everyone had been nailed except Brigit.

"When you say you're responsible . . ." Justin trailed off.

"Oh, not like that," she said. "I didn't stab her or shoot her, as tempting as that was. No, I used my gift for investigative journalism and I wrote an exposé on her family."

Mel noticed that both Bonnie and Justin made O's with their mouths and that Sylvia's eyes went wide. She didn't know if it was because they all were surprised by Brigit's candor or because her reporter's skill was something fearsome to behold.

"I think she might have preferred that you shot or stabbed her," Bonnie said.

So that answered that. Clearly Brigit's reporting skills were legendary.

"It was a loathsome thing to do," Brigit admitted. "Of course, if her family hadn't been connected to the mob, it might not have been such a big deal."

"You took on the mob?" Bonnie asked. The timer on the oven rang, and Mel went to get the cupcakes. This batch would stay in the chiller until the day of the gala, when they would frost them.

Angie hurried over to help her, and they listened while they set the tins on the back counter to cool.

"It's not so much that I took on the mob, as that I exposed the connections they had to several very wealthy Long Island families, one of which just happened to be Hannigan's wife's family."

"What happened?" Sylvia asked.

"Death threats mostly," Brigit said. "The documentation that I uncovered and published showed a long trail of political corruption. They were in disgrace and became social pariahs."

"So, how did this cause his wife's death?" Justin asked.

"Image was everything to Casey," Brigit said. "She was one of the most fashion forward of New York society, and she lived for her balls and parties and charity galas."

They waited for Brigit to continue, and she glanced around the kitchen at them and gave a rueful smile.

"No, the irony that Hannigan and I are working together on a charity event is not lost on me," she said.

"I wanted to humiliate Casey. She wouldn't divorce Ian, because she was petrified that she'd be disgraced amongst her little clique. Well, I decided to give her what she was so afraid of by outing her family as a bunch of thugs and thieves. A week after the story broke, she killed herself. Hannigan has never forgiven me. In fact, I've never forgiven myself."

"You couldn't have known that she would —" Justin protested.

"No, but if I hadn't been motivated by revenge, the story never would have been written. Her family was scum, no question, but there are much worse villains out there. I didn't need to put the glaring spotlight on them. I did it out of spite. That's not being a professional journalist. I should have been better than that, but I wasn't."

"And that's why there is so much hostility

between you and Hannigan?" Mel asked.

"Pretty much," Brigit said. "I think we both feel a lot of guilt, and neither of us has ever been able to let it go."

"Did Sam work on that story with you?" Angie asked.

"Why do you ask?" Brigit asked. She looked cautious.

"Well, the other day, I remember Hannigan saying to Sam that he had chosen whose side he was on. Was he mad at Sam, too?"

"Yes, he was," she said slowly. "Because when I left Hannigan, Sam stayed with me and helped me investigate Casey's family."

"You don't think — ?" Bonnie stopped herself in mid-sentence as if she wasn't sure she should utter what she was thinking.

"That Hannigan killed Sam in revenge?" Brigit asked. "Given that the man has more money than a small oil-rich nation, it seems unlikely. He could have crushed Sam in so many other ways. Besides, if he did go after Sam, then he'd surely come after —"

"You," Mel and Angie said together.

Brigit looked alarmed. "Yeah, me."

Eighteen

They spent the rest of the morning in a baking frenzy. It seemed the crew was collectively trying to forget the morning's conversation, partly because it seemed farfetched and partly because there was enough truth to it to make it terrifying.

The magazine staff headed out to lunch at the nearby Los Olivos Mexican restaurant, leaving Mel and Angie to confer with Marty about how business was going. He seemed to have everything under control out front, and Oz was coming in after school to provide backup.

Mel had to talk to him once about not grilling the customers about where they bought their other baked goods. Marty had gotten it into his head that Olivia's spy could be a chatty customer who shopped at Olivia's Confections as well as at Fairy Tale Cupcakes and had inadvertently blabbed to Olivia about what was happening in their bakery.

"Have you heard from Tate yet?" Angie asked Mel as they wiped down the kitchen to prep for the afternoon's baking session.

Mel had checked her office phone and her cell phone three times; so far there was nothing. Angie had checked her phone as well, but the only messages were text messages from Roach — they were still arguing about his song — and her brothers.

"Has he been missing for twenty-four hours yet?" Angie asked. "Can we file a missing-persons report?"

"I already talked to Uncle Stan about it," Mel said. "He said we should really leave that up to his parents."

"Will they do it?" Angie asked. She paused to scrape some spilled ingredients into the trash can.

"I would think so," Mel said. "But what if he wants to remain missing?"

"Who wants to remain missing?" a voice asked from the kitchen door. It was Detective Martinez.

"Uh . . ." Mel hesitated.

Martinez filled the doorway with his broad, well-muscled frame, and she felt as if his sharp, dark eyes saw every single detail of the kitchen at a glance. She felt her face grow hot, as if she and Angie had been caught doing something wrong, which was ridiculous.

"Tate Harper, our business partner, is missing," Angie said. Obviously, she did not feel as cautious about giving out information to the homicide detective as Mel did.

"Since when?" he asked.

"Since yesterday when he quit his job and moved out of his apartment," Angie said.

Martinez looked at Mel as if to verify the story. She nodded.

"He went missing after the murder?" he asked.

"Yes, but —" Angie began, but Mel interrupted.

"He had absolutely no connection to Sam Kelleher or anyone at the magazine," Mel said.

"Are you sure of that?" Martinez asked.

Mel knew it was critical that she maintain eye contact as she answered. "Yes."

Martinez was the first to look away, and she found that oddly satisfying.

"Is he a drinker, a drug user, a gambler?" he asked.

"No, no, no," Angie said. "In fact, up until he disappeared, I would have thought he was perfectly content with his life."

"Was he in a relationship?" Martinez came in and sat down at the table. Both Angie and Mel sat with him.

"No," Mel said.

"Even an online one?" Martinez asked. "You know, a lonely middle-aged man sometimes picks up with the women they meet on these match sites on the Internet, and the next thing you know he walks away from his entire life for a woman across the country."

"He would have told us," Angie said. She sounded overly firm, and Mel could tell there was a part of her wondering if it was true.

"Well, for his sake, I hope not," Martinez said. "I've seen people arrive at their 'soul mate's' house only to find that the picture of the young hottie they thought they were talking to is actually a flaccid geriatric."

"You think Tate might have been snookered by an old man pretending to be a hot young woman on the Internet?" Mel asked.

"It happens." Martinez shrugged.

"Ish," Mel and Angie said together.

"We have to find him," Angie said.

"Where have you looked so far?" Martinez asked.

"His workplace, his apartment, and his parents' house," Mel said.

"Is there any place that he goes that might be special to him?" Martinez asked. "A coffee shop, a park, a church?"

"Here," Mel said. "He liked to be here with us."

Martinez looked around the room. "I can see why. It's got a nice vibe, this place."

"Yeah, except that someone was murdered right outside of it," Mel said.

"Speaking of which," Martinez said, "where are your cupcake people? I have a few questions for them."

"Well, the ones who are left went out for lunch," Mel said. "They should be back within the hour."

"What do you mean the ones who are left?" he asked.

"Well, I'll tell you, Viggo." Mel looked at him, and he quirked one eyebrow up.

"Viggo? Really?"

"You could be a Viggo," she said.

"Viggo is a dog's name," he said.

"Or a hot actor's name," Angie said. "What exactly are you two talking about? I thought you were going to tell him about Amy."

"Amy Pierson?" he asked.

"Yes," they said together.

"What do you know?" Immediately, he had his detective face on, and Mel knew that any fishing for his first name was over. It was just as well. She hadn't thought of any other good ones.

She and Angie told him all of the morning's events, about Amy hating Sam and sleeping with him, and about Brigit and Hannigan.

"I knew about Hannigan and Brigit," he said. "That was big news when he bought the magazine. Did not know about Kelleher and Amy, which brings up a host of possibilities.

"Do you mind if I wait for them out front?" he asked. "I want to go over their statements when they get back, but I can catch up on some paperwork while I wait."

"Not at all, make yourself at home," Mel said.

He smiled at her and Mel felt her breath catch. The man's smile was a stunner, and she was pretty sure he could use it in his arsenal to apprehend suspects, especially any of the female persuasion.

"I've got it!" Angie shouted and jumped out of her seat. "Come on, Mel."

"Got what? What are you talking about?" Mel asked as she stood. Martinez did the same.

"A place that's special to Tate," she said. "I think I know where he went."

Angie opened the door to the bakery and leaned around the doorjamb.

"Marty, Detective Martinez is staying in the bakery to work for bit," she said. "Hook him up with a four-pack on me. The man is a genius."

"Thanks," Martinez said. "I think."

Angie gave him a solid thump on the shoulder with her fist. This sort of affection from Angie had knocked Mel to her knees upon occasion, but Martinez didn't even flinch. Mel had to admit it: She was impressed.

"Come on," Angie said as she hustled to the back door.

"Let me know how it goes," Martinez called after them.

"Will do, . . . Gregor?"

He shook his head. "Gregor Martinez? That's your best guess?"

Mel shrugged. "Am I right?"

"Not even close," he said.

Mel saw him leave through the kitchen door as Angie pulled her out the back door, slammed it shut, and locked it.

"What was *that*?" Angie asked.

"What was what?" Mel asked, hoping she sounded innocent as opposed to, well, defensive.

"You're flirting with Martinez," Angie said. She stomped down the stairs, and Mel sincerely hoped the steps weren't a substitute for her head.

"I am not," she scoffed as she followed.

"Oh, puhleeze," Angie said. She led the way down the alley in the opposite direction from where Sam's body had been found, which was still marked off with yellow tape.

"I know flirting when I see flirting. So, what gives?"

"Nothing gives," Mel said. "And I'm merely trying to figure out his first name."

That caused Angie to stop in her tracks. "We don't know his first name?"

"No, and when I asked him, he refused to tell me, so it became a sort of joke to try and guess it," she said.

"You could just ask Uncle Stan," Angie said as she resumed walking.

"Where's the fun in that?" Mel countered.

"And that's what makes it flirting," Angie said. "You're actively engaged in joking around with the man."

Mel felt her face flame hot with guilt at Angie's use of the word *engaged.* Oh, man, if she knew that Mel and Joe were engaged, this would be so much worse. Then again, maybe now would be a good time to tell her. Yeah, Mel didn't have to feel her back to verify that chicken wings had abruptly sprouted.

"I am not flirting," she protested. "Anyway, I thought we were looking for Tate. What's your grand idea?"

Now it was Angie's turn to blush. She blew out a breath as if trying to cool herself off from the inside.

"Okay, so you know how Martinez — wow, we really don't know his first name, do we?" she asked.

"Already established," Mel said, and she rolled her hands, signaling Angie to continue.

"Anyway, he asked if there was any place special that Tate likes to go," Angie said.

"The bakery."

"Beyond the bakery," Angie said.

They walked from the alley to the street, and Angie went to the right. They passed several shops and the tattoo parlor where Mick, the tattoo artist, nodded to them while working on the ankle of a young woman who did not appear to be enjoying herself.

"Did I mention that Roach wanted us to get matching tattoos?" Angie asked.

"Was that part of the breakup?" Mel asked.

"No, I kind of liked the idea." She paused. "Just not with him."

"Ah." Mel tried to picture Angie and Tate with matching tattoos. Since they couldn't even manage to pull together a first date, it was hard for her to see them in matching ink.

"So, back to Tate. Beyond the bakery would be where?" Mel asked.

"He's taken to hanging out on the green in the Civic Center Mall," Angie said. They crossed the street, and strolled past several fountains and sculptures.

"Since when does he hang out here?" Mel asked.

"Remember the cooking competition we were in last spring?" Angie asked.

"You almost died," Mel said. "It's embedded in my brain for life."

"Yeah, well, remember when I was still pretty weak and Tate had to carry me out of there?"

"Yeah." Mel got misty at the memory. "You asked him for help, and he said, 'As you wish.' "

"At the time, I wasn't sure he meant what I thought he meant," Angie said. She paused to scan the park. There was no sign of Tate, lounging in one of his power suits at any of the picnic tables.

"Angie, we live movie quotes," Mel said. "There is no way you didn't know that he was quoting Westley from *The Princess Bride.*"

"Hey, I was in a weakened state from my near-death experience," Angie said. "Plus, I was still dating Roach, so it was awkward."

"Whatever," Mel said. "What's your point?"

Angie bit her lip and looked distinctly uncomfortable. "I think that's why he hangs out here, because that's the closest we've ever come to telling each other how we feel."

Mel nodded. It made sense. Besides, she didn't have the heart to embarrass Angie any more than she already was.

"Well, it's about the only lead we've got," she said. "Let's do a sweep. I want to get back before the boot campers."

Together they worked the park with Angie looking to the right and Mel looking to the left. They had covered most of the park when they came upon Robert Indiana's LOVE sculpture with the *L O* perched atop the *V E,* done in red and blue.

It stood happily on its slope of grass, but there was something wrong. Mel could see a person's foot peeking out from just behind its cement base.

"Oh, no," she said. She felt all of the blood drain out of her face, and she got the spins.

"What is it?" Angie whipped around. "Do you see him?"

"No, but I think we may have found another body," Mel said.

Nineteen

Angie looked in the direction that Mel was pointing, and she gasped.

"What is it with you?" she asked as they hurried across the grass towards the foot. "You attract bodies like bees to pollen. It's not right."

"Hey, it's not just me," Mel said as she pulled out her phone, getting ready to call the police. "You've been with me for most of the bodies. And it's your fault we're here now looking for Tate, so this one is on you."

"Hey!" Angie protested.

They rounded the sculpture to see a scruffy-looking man in khaki shorts and a grungy T-shirt lying down with his head on a backpack. His eyes were open and his chest was moving up and down. He was not dead.

"Do you two think you could keep down?" he asked. "I'm trying to nap."

Mel squinted at the man. Beneath his day-old beard growth was a familiar square jaw and laughing eyes.

"Tate?" Angie asked. She rushed forward, and he sat up, opening his arms to hug her, but she shoved his arms away and got right in his face and shouted, "Have you lost your mind?"

He looked surprised and then shrugged and reclined back on his backpack. "No."

"No?" Angie yelled. "That's all you have to say for yourself — no?"

"You asked me a question," Tate said. "And I answered it."

Mel could see that Angie was about to pop her cork, so she kneeled down beside her, and said, "Tate, what's going on?"

"Presently, I'm being accosted in the park by two ladies while I try to read," he said. He lifted a book from the grass beside him. "And you?"

Now Mel could feel her temper heat up. If Tate was going through something, that was fine, but his attitude was really becoming annoying, as if he were the only one who had something going on.

"Well, let's see," she said. "We've been frantically searching for you only to find out that you've moved out of you apartment —"

"— quit your job —" Angie added.

"— and not told anyone, us or your

parents, what is going on," Mel finished.

"You spoke to my parents?" he asked. He lowered the book.

"Uh, yeah," Angie said with a nice dollop of sarcasm that was the verbal equivalent of a slap upside the head.

"Are they mad?" he asked.

"And worried," Mel said.

"You need to let them know you're okay," Angie said.

"I sent them an e-mail this morning," he said.

Angie shook her head in disgust.

"What?" he asked. "We're not like your family. We don't shout everything out."

"Well, maybe you should," she snapped.

Tate looked mutinous and to Mel's surprise, instead of yelling, Angie crossed her legs and put her hands on her knees palms up. She took several deep breaths as if trying to channel an inner calm.

"Why didn't you tell us what you were doing?" Angie asked, her voice low and soft, letting him know without words how worried she'd been. "We're your best friends."

Tate gave her a sad look, as if he knew he'd hurt her but he hadn't seen any other option.

"I didn't want you to talk me out of it," he said.

"Out of what?" Mel asked. She was not yet as calm as Angie. She moved from kneeling to sitting, mostly to keep herself from standing and kicking Tate. "I'm not even sure what it is exactly that you're doing."

"I want to be like Ian Hannigan," he said. "I want to be a self-made man."

Mel and Angie exchanged a confused glance.

"What exactly does that mean?" Angie asked.

"It means" — Tate paused to close his book and sit up, before he continued — "that I have to prove to myself and to you that I am worthy of you."

He reached out with one hand and cupped Angie's cheek. Mel suddenly felt like an intruder, and she wondered if it would ruin their moment if she abruptly crab-walked away from them.

"But you are worthy," Angie protested.

"No, I'm not," Tate said. "You made me see that, Mel."

"What? Huh?" Mel asked.

"When we were up at Juniper Pass a few months ago, you told me that I was too chicken to tell Angie how I felt because I've never had to work for anything because everything has always been handed to me."

"Whoa, kind of harsh," Angie said with a wide-eyed look at Mel.

"I didn't like hearing it," Tate said. "But it was true."

"No, it's not," Angie protested.

"Yes, it is," he said. "I was a legacy at Princeton because of my dad, I was hired right into the family business after school, and I've shot up the ladder there through sheer nepotism."

"Tate, you're a financial wizard," Mel said. "It's not all been handed to you."

"Well, I don't know that, do I?" Tate asked. "And neither do you. I need to prove myself, Angie. Before you and I see what's between us, I need to know that I'm worthy of you."

"Tate, it doesn't matter," Angie protested. "I know you're worthy. I lo—"

"No!" Tate cut her off. "Don't say anything yet. Let me prove that I can make it on my own so that you know you've picked the right guy."

"I already know that," she grumbled. Then she turned to Mel and snapped, "You just had to go and open your big, fat mouth, didn't you?"

Mel sucked in a breath. Even though her exterior was now on the slender side, the chubby adolescent inside of her was devastated that her best friend would use the words *big* and *fat,* even if only in regard to her mouth.

"I did it for you," Mel argued. She rose to her feet and began brushing stray bits of grass off her legs. "I was trying to get him to —"

"Well, a whole heck of a lot of good it's doing me, isn't it?" Angie interrupted, also standing.

"How was I supposed to know he was going to take it to heart like this?" Mel asked.

"Maybe you should think before you speak," Angie snarled.

"Mel, Angie, come on. We're all friends here," Tate said as he stood and subtly moved between them.

"And maybe you should rein in your temper," Mel said. "You know we wouldn't even be in this mess if it wasn't for you. Did you ever think of that? Huh?"

"Me?" Angie gasped as if she'd been struck. "How do you figure this is my fault?"

"Because we would not be having a cupcake boot camp with one camper murdered, if you could have just controlled your temper during the photo shoot!" Mel yelled.

"Excuse me," Tate said. "Did you say someone was murdered?"

Enraged, Mel turned on him. "Yes, Mr.

Self-Absorbed. If you hadn't been so busy with your personal crisis, you might have answered one of our messages and heard the news that Sam Kelleher was murdered right outside the bakery."

"When did this — ?"

"Yesterday!" Mel yelled. "Now, if you two will excuse me, I'm taking my big, fat mouth back to work."

"Mel!" Tate called after her, but Mel waved him off.

She was halfway across the park before she dared glance over her shoulder. Tate and Angie sat on the base of the sculpture with their heads together, paying no attention to her departing figure. *Fine, be that way.*

She knew it was childish of her, but she had really expected Angie to run after her and apologize, and when she hadn't, Mel felt hurt and miffed.

Mel left the park behind and stepped back into Old Town Scottsdale. She figured her boot-camp people would be back, and she hoped the afternoon would prove more productive than the morning.

She decided to enter through the back way, as she didn't want to field any questions from Marty about where Angie was. As she came around the corner of the building, a flash of pink hair moving at high

205

speed made her jump back with a yelp.

Her first thought was that it was the killer, and her insides spasmed accordingly; her second thought was that she was going to wring Oz's neck.

The pink tornado that had passed her was going full speed down the alley to shoot up a hastily erected skateboard ramp, off of which the rider did a complicated twirl thing and then came back down, zipping past Mel once again.

"Nice!" Oz yelled from where he was sitting on the back steps.

Mel watched as the skateboarder stopped right beside Oz, and they exchanged a backhanded high five and a knuckle bump.

" 'The pool is for swimming!' " Mel called over to them as she approached.

Oz looked up and grinned, bobbing his head in approval and making the fringe that covered his face all the way down to his nose bob, too.

"*Lords of Dogtown,*" he identified the movie quote. "Excellent."

"Tate made me watch it after we hired you," she said. "He said it would give me insight into the whole skater universe."

"Did it?" Oz's friend asked.

"Only in a 'where it all began' sort of context," Mel said.

"Beginnings are critical," Oz said. "Mel, you remember my friend Lupe."

Mel glanced at the slender youth standing beside Oz. She had thought it was a boy, but now she could see the definite curves beneath the girl's outfit of unrelieved black. Her hair was styled much like Oz's in that it hung over her face down to her nose, but her fringe was an electric pink color.

"Hi, Lupe. Wasn't your hair green last time I saw you?"

"I like to change it up," Lupe said.

"The pink is a bold choice," Mel said. Then she turned to Oz, and said, "You two can't skateboard in the alley. If you break a bone, I'll be liable."

"We won't," he protested. "We're pros."

"Take it to the Wedge over in the park," Mel said. She used her "this is not negotiable" voice.

"Oh, man," Oz began, but Lupe interrupted. "It's cool. I'll break down the ramp. You're supposed to start work in five minutes anyway."

They shrugged at each other in some silent teenspeak that Mel didn't understand.

Lupe propped her board, which boasted a pretty spectacular red skull on its underside, against the wall and jogged over to their hastily constructed ramp.

"So, you're spending a lot of time with Lupe, huh?" Mel asked as she passed Oz on the steps.

"Just friends," Oz said, clearly anticipating the direction her question was going.

"Well, tell your friend she can have a cupcake on the house for that sweet alley that she did in the air."

"It's called an ollie," Oz corrected.

"Really?" Mel asked. "I could have sworn —"

"Yes, I'm quite sure," Oz said.

Mel looked at him closely. His lip rings were trembling, and she could tell he was trying not to laugh.

"Ollie, then," she said.

As she closed the door behind her, she saw Oz burst out with a laugh as he hurried to help his friend break down their ramp.

She couldn't help but smile. They reminded her of, well, of her and Tate when they had first become friends. She hoped Lupe proved to be as worthy of Oz's friendship as Tate had been of hers. Then she remembered that she was mad at him and turned back to the kitchen, scowling.

"How did it go?" Detective Martinez asked.

Mel jumped and spun away from the door. The kitchen door was swinging shut behind him, and she realized he must have come in just after she did.

"Good," she said. "We found him."

"Is he all right?" Martinez asked.

He had his detective face on, and Mel met his inquisitive glance directly, so he had no doubt about what she said.

"Tate was shocked to hear about Sam Kelleher," she said. "Completely, utterly shocked."

Martinez gave her a slow smile. "I like that."

"What?" she asked.

"That you are so absolutely sure of your friend's noninvolvement in the murder and that you want me to be sure of it as well."

"Why does that amuse you?" she asked.

"Because it's very loyal of you," he said. "And I don't see a lot of that when I'm questioning people. Like this magazine crew —"

His voice trailed off, as if he thought better of what he had been about to say, but Mel was curious. Who at the magazine was willing to throw over the others?

"Are they all pointing fingers at one another?" she asked. She went for a sympathetic tone to draw him out, but he grinned, as if he knew exactly what she was doing.

"You are so your uncle's niece," he said.

"That is the exact same tone he would have taken to get more information."

"So, you're not falling for it?" she asked.

"Not even a little," he said.

They studied each other across the kitchen. Mel liked him. He had a real sense of right and wrong, good and bad, up and down.

"So, given that my kitchen is empty, I have to ask: Did you haul all of my boot-camp cupcake bakers off to jail?" she asked.

"No, but only because I don't have enough evidence to stick on any of them yet," he said. "I have them sitting out front, writing statements about exactly what they knew about Sam Kelleher. Somewhere in there I've got to get a lead."

"And while you do that, Uncle Stan is doing what exactly?" she asked.

"Trying to track down the murder weapon," he said. "The medical examiner had a few ideas of what might have been used to cause the blunt trauma to the back of the skull, and Stan is out canvassing the neighborhood with some uniforms. If they recover the weapon, it could turn the case around for us."

"Is it not going well?" Mel asked.

"Well, we're past the first twenty-four-hour mark, which is crucial," he said. "The more time that passes, the harder it will be to trace the killer."

"What about Amy Pierson?" Mel asked.

Martinez lifted his eyebrows, and asked, "Care to share something?"

"Other than personal dislike, sadly, I don't know anything more than what I've already told you. But I just can't help thinking that she has the most motive given her twisted relationship with Sam," she said. "And no one likes her."

"I got the feeling of general dislike for her in the interviews and as far as her relationship with Kelleher, it's under investigation," he said. "Unfortunately, the DA, as you probably know, likes us to have something a bit more solid than animosity."

"Pity," Mel said.

"Speaking of the DA, how are things with you and Joe DeLaura?" he asked.

Mel knew there was absolutely no reason why she should feel uncomfortable talking to Martinez about Joe, and yet that was exactly how she felt. If she was completely honest with herself, it was because she didn't want Martinez to think of her as being in a relationship, which was so completely wrong. Right?

So she met his gaze and forced a smile and did the right thing. "Things are good, great, things are great."

"You know what I can't believe?" Martinez asked.

"What?"

"That Joe hasn't gotten a ring on that finger of yours," he said. "I'd have thought he'd have a lock on you by now."

Mel felt her face flash as hot as an oven fire.

"Oh, no way! You're engaged?" Martinez asked.

TWENTY

Mel couldn't answer. She hadn't even told her mother; she certainly wasn't going to tell Martinez. She heard the door to the bakery open and assumed it was Oz. She didn't want him overhearing this, either.

"So, have you set a date?" Martinez asked. "And where's the rock? If you're engaged, DeLaura better pony up a serious sparkler for that left hand."

Mel started to shake her head, but a shout of fury interrupted her.

"What?"

Mel spun around to see Angie standing in the open door with her hands planted on her hips, looking outraged.

"When? And why didn't you tell me?" Angie hollered.

Oz came in behind Angie, took one look at her gladiator posture, and turned back around.

"I'll just go around the side," he called to Mel.

"Angie, Detective Martinez was just teasing me," Mel said. "Really."

She whipped around and narrowed her eyes at him in a look that promised impending pain if he didn't go along with her, "Right, detective?"

"Yep," he said immediately. "Just joshing."

Angie glanced suspiciously between them.

"Because that would be a *huge* thing to keep from your best friend," Angie said. "Unforgivably *huge.*"

Mel felt the sweat bead up on her forehead. Then she got mad. She still hadn't forgiven Angie for earlier.

"Well, maybe if I do get engaged I'll just keep my big, fat mouth shut about it," she said. "So there."

" 'So there'?" Angie mocked. "Really? So lame."

"Go away," Mel said.

"Fine, I'll go help Marty and Oz out front," Angie huffed. She strode past Martinez and hit the swinging kitchen door harder than necessary.

"Still mad?" a voice asked from the back door.

Mel turned to see Tate standing there.

"Yes," she said. "But not so much at you."

214

"Good, because I have something to ask you," he said.

He glanced over her shoulder, and said, "Oh, hi, detective."

Martinez nodded at him, and Mel could tell his detective brain was still wondering why Tate had disappeared right after Sam's murder.

"Come on," she said. "We can talk in my office."

She didn't look to see what Martinez thought of this; she just led the way. Tate followed her inside, and she shut the door. Brigit's stuff covered most of her desk, and her own things were in a pile on the floor. Mel felt her mood dip even lower. If this week did not end soon, she was pretty sure she was going to punch some poor sap right in the nose for no other reason than he'd be crowding her personal space bubble and she would have had it.

"What is it?" she asked.

"Can I have a job?" he asked.

Mel starred at him. He looked terrible: wrinkled and unshaven, and he had a faint unemployed odor about him that was not pleasant.

"You're serious?" she asked.

"Yes," he said. "Just until I figure out what I'm going to do."

"Fine," she said. "Report to Angie. She'll work you into the schedule."

"Thanks, Mel," he said. "You're the best."

He turned to leave, but she stopped him with a hand on his arm. "Where are you living now?"

"Oh, I've got a line on a place," he said.

"You know you could stay with me or Angie," she said.

"I know," he said. "But then I wouldn't really be doing all this on my own, now, would I?"

"Tate, when I said all of those things, it was just to get you to build up the courage to tell Angie how you feel, not to walk away from your whole life," she said.

"Yeah, I know, but you made me realize that my whole life is a sham," he said. "I was born with a silver spoon in my mouth. I've never earned anything on my own."

"Yes, you have," Mel said.

Tate tilted his head and gave her a doubtful look. "Name one thing."

"My friendship," she said. "You were my first real friend."

He gave her a small smile and then opened his arms. Mel hugged him and then quickly stepped back, holding her nose.

"As your boss, I insist you go up to my apartment and shower," she said. "To put it

216

kindly, you stink."

"Still, harsh," Tate said.

"Git," Mel said, and she tossed him the key to her apartment.

The door shut behind him, and she sighed. What a mess. Tate's life was a complete disaster, and she couldn't help but feel that it was a little bit her fault. Angie was mad at her, and she probably had a small right to be, although Mel wasn't completely sure about that. And now she had lied to Angie about being engaged, and if the truth got out, it was going to be ugly.

There was a soft knock on the door, and she imagined it was Brigit coming to lay claim to her office again.

"Come in," she said.

To her surprise it was Detective Martinez. He closed the door behind him, and Mel felt as if her already small office had shrunk to the size of an old-fashioned phone booth.

"I think I owe you an apology," he said. "I didn't mean to cause trouble between you and your friend."

He looked genuinely regretful, and she was grateful.

"It's not your fault," she said. "Things are just — complicated."

"How complicated?" he asked, taking a step towards her.

Mel stopped breathing. She had to look up to meet his gaze, and she felt dizzy, with him standing within inches of her. This was bad. This was very bad.

"Very complicated," she whispered, afraid to move or even stir the air around them and invite more trouble than she could handle.

Martinez reached out and cupped her chin. His black eyes searched her face as if trying to read her beneath the surface. Mel felt her heart rate kick up into a zone where she was pretty sure people stroked out from sensory overload.

"If you are not engaged, go out with me," he said. "If you are engaged, reconsider."

His mouth was just inches from hers, and Mel could tell he was about to kiss her. She knew she should step away. She knew it, and yet she didn't move.

"Hey, Martinez, your interviewees are done with their written statements!"

The office door slammed open and Marty stood there. He took them in at a glance, crossed his arms over his chest, and didn't budge.

Even though nothing had happened, Mel wanted to whither like an autumn leaf and blow away on the wind. Martinez, however, was not even fazed.

"Think about what I said." He let go of her face and stepped around Marty and out of the office.

Marty watched him go and then whipped around to look at Mel. She held up her hand, and said, "It's not what you think."

"Oh, yes, it is," he said. "The detective quite obviously has a thing for the cupcake baker."

"Ugh." Mel put her hands over her face. "What am I going to do?"

"What do you want to do?" Marty asked.

"Nothing!" Mel protested. "I don't want to do anything!"

"If you didn't want to do anything," he said in a reasonable tone, "then you wouldn't have been in here alone with him to begin with."

"Don't you have some place to be?" Mel asked.

She was afraid her legs were going to give out, so she circled her desk and sat in her chair. She put her head down on the one spot of her desk that wasn't buried in stuff.

"Mel, listen to me." Marty's voice lost its usual gruff edge. "It's okay."

"No, it isn't," she said. "It is definitely not okay."

"Look at me," Marty ordered.

Mel raised her head but only because she

knew he wouldn't go away if she didn't. Marty ran a hand over his bald dome. He seemed to be picking his words very carefully, which caught her attention. Marty grumbled more than he talked, so if he was making an effort, she owed it to him to pay attention.

"I had one." He held up his right index finger as he spoke. "One great love, and I married her."

Mel gave him a small smile. Despite Marty's lothario way with the ladies, she knew that he had loved his late wife totally and completely.

"I know," she said. "You got lucky."

"No," he said. "I listened to this." He tapped his heart with the same finger he'd been holding up. "You should, too. It won't lie to you."

"But I'm so confused," Mel said. "I've loved Joe since I was twelve years old."

Marty gave her a small smile, and said, "But you're not twelve anymore."

"No," she agreed.

"Mel, whatever you're feeling, it's right," he said.

She blew out a breath. "I don't know what I'm feeling. Should it be this complicated?"

"It isn't," he said, "if you're brave enough to look down deep."

"Ugh," Mel groaned.

"You don't want to be them," Marty said, and he jerked a thumb at the open door. "I mean, look at Hannigan. He stayed with a woman he didn't love and lost the love of his life. And Kelleher, he stayed by the woman he loved, but she never loved him. You don't want that."

"What do you mean about Kelleher?" Mel asked.

"It's obvious, isn't it?" Marty asked. "He was a grade-A journalist working on a glorified tabloid. Why?"

"Because newspapers are dying?" Mel asked.

"No, because he was in love with Brigit, and he wanted to be near her any way he could," he said.

"How do you know this?" she asked. "Did he say that?"

"He didn't have to," Marty said. "It was obvious every time he looked at her."

"Do you think Hannigan knew?" she asked.

"Yes, and I think it drove him crazy. Otherwise why would he have bought the magazine?" Marty asked.

"What about Brigit?" Mel asked. "Do you think she knew?"

"That both men were in love with her?"

Marty asked. "Hard to say. She's not as easy to read."

"You know what this means?" Mel asked.

Marty shook his head.

"It means Hannigan could be the murderer," she said.

"I did not say that!" Marty protested.

"Yes, you did."

"Nuh-uh," he said. "We were talking about relationships, and I merely pointed out that some people make the wrong choice and have to live with it and it sucks."

"But think about it: We thought that Hannigan might have killed Sam because he helped Brigit exposé his wife's family, but what if it's more than that?" Mel asked. "What if it was a crime of passion?"

"Do you really think that, after all of these years, he decided now was the time to kill his rival?" Marty asked.

"Maybe it was an accident," she said. "Maybe he thought he could handle working in close proximity to them, but then he couldn't and he just snapped."

"Who snapped?" a voice asked from the open door.

Marty and Mel both jumped and turned to find Brigit in the doorway. She was looking at them with one eyebrow raised in question.

"A customer," Marty said quickly. He turned back to Mel, and said, "Don't go looking for trouble to keep yourself distracted from what you need to be thinking about — if you get my meaning."

"Yeah, I get it," she said.

"Excellent," he said. "Well, I'm off for the day. Call me if you need to, you know, talk."

He was so charmingly awkward when he offered that, Mel rose from her seat and crossed the small room to kiss his cheek.

He turned such a vibrant shade of flustered old-man pink that Mel had to laugh. He let out a grumble and stepped around Brigit to leave.

"Bonnie said if we're going to stay on task, we need to get baking," Brigit said.

"She's right," Mel said. She went to leave the little room, too, but Brigit held her back with a hand.

"What were you really talking about?" she asked.

Mel knew they hadn't fooled her. She wasn't surprised. She could see the others gathering in the kitchen, and she gave Brigit a level look.

"We were trying to decide if Hannigan still loved you enough to murder for you."

TWENTY-ONE

Brigit stared at her for a second and then tipped her head back and laughed. Surprisingly, she did not laugh without humor but rather as if Mel had just said the funniest thing she'd ever heard.

"Sorry," Brigit panted after a moment. She wiped at her eyes, and then said, "But I haven't laughed like that in a long time."

"I take it you think we're off base," Mel said.

"Off base, honey? You're not even playing in the right ball game," Brigit said. "Hannigan loathes me."

"Loathing is a pretty intense emotion," Mel said. "Kind of the flip side of love, isn't it?"

"Mel!" Bonnie called from the kitchen. "We've got to kick this into high gear if we're going to be ready by the gala."

"We're on our way," Mel said. "Brigit, I have to ask: Were you and Sam lovers?"

"That's none of your business," Brigit said, not meeting her eyes, which Mel took to mean yes.

She followed Brigit out to the kitchen, where Angie and Bonnie were directing Justin and Sylvia in their cupcake-baking factory line. About halfway through the first batch, Hannigan and Amy arrived.

His face was set in stern lines, and she looked subdued, as if she'd been forced at gunpoint to come back, which Mel suspected wasn't far off the mark.

Amy didn't apologize for her behavior; she merely set to work, keeping her head down. Mel would have felt sorry for her if she weren't such a nasty person.

It was not a pleasant afternoon, with Amy actively avoiding everyone, Hannigan and Brigit studiously ignoring each other, and Mel and Angie not yet back on friendly terms, either.

Mel could tell that Angie was still mad at her over the Tate situation, which she thought was unfair, but her own guilt at not telling Angie about her engagement kept her from pursuing the matter. Instead, she chose to focus on Hannigan.

He was a self-made gazillionaire. He did not have to be here, and yet he was. Why? Mel could think of no other reason than the unresolved feelings he had for Brigit, whether it was rage that she had caused his wife's death, or the desire to have her back, she didn't know. The man gave nothing away.

They worked through the dinner hour until Bonnie and Mel did a quick count of the cupcakes and gave everyone the all-clear to go home.

Mel was just swabbing down the kitchen when Uncle Stan and Detective Martinez appeared at the back door.

"We're breaking down the crime scene, Mel," Uncle Stan said. "This should clear out the gawkers."

"Thanks," she said.

Uncle Stan made his way to the coffeepot and poured both himself and Martinez a cup. Mel shook her head when he asked if she wanted one. She was so tired from sleeping poorly at Joe's that she just wanted to climb upstairs to her apartment and sleep for a solid twelve.

She glanced at the clock on the wall. Given that it was already after eight and she had to be up at six, it didn't seem likely.

"Any luck finding the murder weapon?" she asked.

Uncle Stan and Martinez took seats at the steel table, shifting when Mel moved around them to clean. She noticed that Martinez barely moved when she scoured the tabletop, bringing them into dangerously close proximity. She had tried not to think about him all day, but having him here made it virtually impossible.

"No luck yet," Uncle Stan said. "How did boot camp go?"

"If by that you mean, did someone spill their guts and confess to Sam's murder?" Mel asked. "No."

For a nanosecond both Martinez and Stan had looked hopeful.

"Did you find out anything about the staff that is suspicious?" Mel asked them.

Martinez exchanged a look with Uncle Stan, and Mel knew they were silently trying to decide what to tell her.

"Oh, come on," she said. "I'm with them every day. I see stuff."

Uncle Stan gave a small nod. "Fair enough. The most interesting fact so far is that Amy Pierson's the only one without an alibi for the night Sam was murdered. Bonnie was shopping with her husband, Justin was at an art opening with his partner, Sylvia was at a dinner at Bruno Casio's."

"Is that a restaurant?" Mel asked.

"No, he's a pompous windbag, who throws extravagant dinner parties every week for the fashionista set," he said. Mel could tell by the curl of his lip that he hadn't taken to Bruno.

"Brigit and Hannigan were wining and dining some resort big wigs to get them to advertise in the magazine," Martinez concluded

Mel sat down with a thump. The back door opened, and in strode Joe, carrying Captain Jack in one arm.

"Well, look what the cat dragged in," Uncle Stan said as he stood and shook hands with Joe.

"More accurate than you know," Joe said.

He went to hand the cat to Mel, but Martinez rose from his seat and intercepted the cat.

"Hey, how ya doin', big fella?" he crooned and Jack purred his approval. "Remember me?"

"You've met Captain Jack?" Joe asked, frowning.

"Yeah, when I was up in Mel's apartment," he said.

Uncle Stan's head whipped between the two men, and Mel knew it wasn't just her who felt the rise in the testosterone level in the room. She scooped her cat out of Martinez's arms and glared at him. He was baiting Joe on purpose, and she did not approve.

"They met when he was questioning me about finding Sam's body," Mel said.

"Oh, and how is that investigation going?" Joe asked. He sounded perfectly polite, but Mel suspected that it was a dig at their lack of a lead. She noticed that both Uncle Stan and Martinez looked grumpy at the question.

"It's going," Uncle Stan said. "If you hear anything of note, let us know, Mel."

He stood and drained his coffee cup in a couple of swallows. Martinez did the same. Uncle Stan kissed Mel's cheek on the way out, and Martinez stopped in front of her to scratch Jack under the chin.

"See you tomorrow," he said.

Mel closed the door after them, feeling as if there was more to what Martinez was saying than what he'd actually said and wondering if anyone else had heard it.

She turned to face Joe and found him studying her as if trying to figure something out. Yep, he'd heard it, too.

"I don't like this," he said.

"Like what?" Mel asked.

"You working so closely with —" He paused as Mel moved around him, checking to make sure that everything in the

229

kitchen, including the coffeepot, was shut off for the night.

"With?" she asked as she crossed to the back door and opened it.

Joe shut off the last light, and Mel watched him step past her onto the landing. His face was backlit by the streetlights in the parking lot across the alley, and she couldn't read his expression.

"With all of these murder suspects," he said.

Mel felt relief sweep through her that he hadn't said *Martinez.*

"Since the magazine people decided to go through with the boot camp, I don't have much choice."

"I'm really surprised that Stan is okay with it."

"I think he's feeling a bit desperate," she said as she led the way up the stairs.

Jack purred, and Mel could tell he was happy to be coming home. She opened the door, and he leapt from her arms and scampered across the room.

Mel switched on the light and went to see what she had to offer for dinner, when Joe grabbed her hand and stopped her.

"Mel, what's going on?" he asked. "There's something more bothering you than the murder, isn't there?"

She opened her mouth to deny it, but she knew it would be a lie. She didn't want to lie to Joe ever, but she wasn't exactly clear on what she was feeling either.

"We found Tate," she said.

He held her gaze for a moment, and Mel was pretty sure he saw the swirling vortex of doubt inside of her, and then he nodded as if he was telling her he knew there was something else and that he knew she wasn't ready to talk about it yet.

"How is he?" he asked, letting her go.

"He quit his job, he's moved out of his apartment, we found him hanging out in the park, and now he's working for me," she said. She opened the freezer and found a frozen pizza. She held it up, and Joe nodded.

"Wow, that's a pretty big life downshift," he said as he took a seat at the breakfast bar. "Did he say why he's doing all of this?"

Mel took a bottle of wine out of her wine rack and handed it to Joe, who reached for the corkscrew while she got two glasses out of the cupboard.

"He says it's because I said he had everything handed to him and that he didn't know how to earn anything on his own," she said.

"Harsh."

"Well, I said it when we were at the rodeo, and I only meant that he wasn't going after Angie because she was a challenge and he was chicken. How was I supposed to know he was going to scrap his entire life?"

"No argument here," he said.

"Now Angie is mad at me, and we're not exactly on speaking terms," she said. She unboxed the pizza and slid it into the oven as Joe poured the wine.

She knew she sounded as if she was feeling sorry for herself, and she knew she was, which only made her feel even more lousy. Because Sam Kelleher had been murdered, and she was pretty sure if someone had given him a choice, he'd have chosen to have his best friend not speaking to him instead of being dead.

"Angie will get over it," Joe said. "It's probably misdirected anger, and she's really mad at Tate."

"I don't know," Mel said. "We didn't speak all day except for one time, and that didn't go well."

Joe pushed a glass towards Mel. "Is there anything else you need to tell me?"

Mel felt a hot flush warm her face. She took a sip of wine and studied him over the rim of the glass. She had a moment of panic that he knew that Martinez had pretty much asked her out and told her to rethink her engagement. Should she bring it up or let him do it?

"Are you all right, Cupcake?" He reached out and took her glass away. Mel felt a fuzzy warm glow bloom inside of her and looked down to see that she'd drained the glass.

"Oh. Oops," she said.

She looked back up and saw his chocolate brown eyes looking at her with such concern that she wished she could just kiss him and make all of the doubts and nonsense she was feeling go away.

"What is it?" he asked. "Just tell me."

"I don't want to get married," she said.

Whatever he had been expecting, that was definitely not it. He blew out a breath, opened his mouth to speak, and then closed it. He glanced down at the counter, picked up his glass and took a long sip and then put it back down.

"I see," he said.

"No, you don't," she said.

"It sounded pretty clear," he said. He backed up from the counter. He put one hand on the back of his neck as if he wasn't sure what to do with himself. "So, are we calling it then?"

"What do you mean?" she asked.

"Well, if you don't want to get married to

233

me, then I'm really not sure where that leaves us," he said.

"Joe, it's not that I don't want to get married to you," she said. "It's that I don't want to get married period."

"Why not?" he asked. "You know, the first day I walked into the bakery and saw you in the kitchen, I knew I wanted to spend the rest of my life with you."

"You did?" she asked. He had never told her that before.

"Yep," he said. "One look at you, and it was as if I'd been hit by lightning. I still feel that way when I look at you."

"Oh, Joe," she said. She made to come around the counter, but he held up a hand, indicating she should stay.

"It sounds like you have some thinking to do," he said. "I'm going to go home, and when you know what you want, call me."

"But can't we talk about it?" she asked.

"We could," he agreed. "But here's the thing: I know I want to wake up next to you every day for the rest of my life. I want you to feel the same way, and I don't want to feel like I've talked you into it."

He crossed the room and opened the door. Mel would have called him back, but what could she say? That she'd changed her mind? That she suddenly wanted to get married? She didn't.

"Call me when you know what you want," he said. "Even if it isn't me."

Mel felt her throat get tight. She would have called him back just to tell him she loved him, but she couldn't get the words out. She just nodded and watched mutely as he closed the door between them.

TWENTY-TWO

Captain Jack sashayed around the corner, looked Mel in the eye, and yowled as if he knew she'd just thrown his kitty daddy to the curb.

"That's nothing," Mel said through the lump in her throat. "Wait until my mother hears about this. She's going to make Tarzan's call sound like a whimper."

Captain Jack began to lick his chest as if he would not dignify that remark with an answer.

The timer on the oven went off, and Mel grabbed a pot holder and pulled out the piping-hot pizza. The thought of food right now made her stomach turn.

She reached for her cell phone. It was instinct to call Angie to talk, but she couldn't. Joe was Angie's brother. There was no way she could be impartial about what was happening between them; besides, Mel would have to confess about their engagement, and she couldn't imagine that going well. Understatement of the decade.

That left Tate. She doubted he'd answer his phone, but it was worth a try. She called. He didn't answer. She hit redial. Still he didn't answer. She sent a text. He did not respond.

Mel thought about giving up; obviously, the man did not want to be disturbed. But really, she had no one else, and she had some stuff going on. He was her oldest friend, even older than Angie, and even though he had his own crap right now, he really needed to be there for her. Besides, what better way to get out of his own head than to listen to her whine?

She called again. On the fourth ring, a very testy voice asked, "What?"

" 'He'll keep calling me, he'll keep calling me until I come over. He'll make me feel guilty. This is uh . . . This is ridiculous, okay I'll go, I'll go, I'll go, I'll go, I'll go,' " Mel replied with one of her favorite movie quotes.

"*Ferris Bueller's Day Off,* very nice. Now, what is so critical?" Tate asked.

"Joe and I just broke up," she said. Mel thought it quite amazing that her voice only cracked at the end and that she didn't burst into tears.

Tate swore. "Come outside."

"What?" she asked. "Where are you?"

"Just come out," he said.

"Oh, man. You've moved into a box in the alley," she said. She made sure the oven was off, patted Captain Jack on the head, took her keys, and stepped outside. She did a quick visual off the alley but didn't see him.

"I'm not living in a box," he said. "Well, not exactly."

"Tate, don't you think you're taking this too far?" she asked.

She quickly locked her door and scanned the area again. An arm waving at her from the parking lot caught her attention. Tate was hanging out the window of their cupcake van.

"You're kidding me, right?" she asked.

"Nope, not kidding," he said. "Come on over."

Mel switched off her phone and ran down the stairs. The big white van with the Fairy Tale Cupcakes logo on the side was parked in its usual spot in the lot adjacent to the bakery. The van technically belonged to Oz, but Tate had put a small fortune into it to turn it into the sweet ride that it was. Marty and Oz took it to events to pimp their cupcakes, and occasionally people hired them to use it for parties and such.

As Mel approached, Tate rolled up the back door and held out his hand to help her up. Mel stepped carefully into the back of the van.

"You've made quite a little nest for yourself here," she said.

Tate pulled the door down and turned on his camping lantern.

"Oz said I could crash in it until I get a place," he said. "Have a seat."

Mel sat on the sleeping bag he'd rolled out between the banks of freezers that ran along each side of the van. Tate closed his open laptop and sat beside her.

It was quiet in the van, and the soft glow coming from the lantern made it quite cozy.

"Cookie?" Tate offered. He held out an open pack of Double Stuf Oreos, and Mel took three. "We'll have to share the milk."

He put an open carton between them. It reminded Mel of junior high school, and she smiled. It seemed like just yesterday Tate had been an overly tall, skinny boy with a cowlick that wouldn't be tamed and a love of junk food and old movies that rivaled her own.

"So, what happened with you and Joe?" he asked.

Mel nibbled her cookie. Now that she had someone to talk to, she didn't know what to

239

say. Maybe she should have kept it between her and Captain Jack.

"Come on," Tate elbowed her. "You don't drop a bomb on someone and then refuse to give details about what happened. Did he cheat on you? I'll pound him."

Mel looked at him, and he bit his cookie and nodded.

"Yeah, you're right, this is Joe we're talking about," he said. "He'd never cheat. It's not in his DNA."

"He asked me to marry him," Mel said.

Tate choked on his cookie, and Mel handed him the carton of milk. When he finished slugging back enough milk to dislodge the Oreo in his throat, he wiped his mouth with the back of his hand and stared at her with wide eyes.

"What did you say?" he asked.

"I said yes," Mel said.

Tate beamed at her. "That's . . . wow . . . I'm really happy for you."

Mel looked at him again and waited.

"Wait a minute," he said. "Proposal. Yes. Breakup. Something here is not adding up."

Mel sighed.

"Explain," he said.

"Joe asked me to marry him at the end of the rodeo," she said. "I said yes, but I wanted to keep it quiet for a while. You know how my mom is."

"True that," Tate agreed. "She'd have you decked out in a poofy meringue and marched down the aisle before the sun set on the day he proposed."

"Exactly," she said.

"So, how long were you going to keep it quiet?"

"At first, I figured just a few months," she said. "But now . . ."

"Mel, you have been in love with Joe De-Laura since you were twelve," Tate said.

She looked at him in surprise.

"Yes, I knew. Heck, everyone knew," he said. "That boy would walk into the room and you'd get that moony look on your face. And heaven forbid he spoke to you, because then you'd turn bright red and go hide. Truly, even as your best friend, it was so embarrassing."

"And now I've lost him," she said. She twisted an Oreo apart and scraped the filling off with her teeth.

"That's disgusting," he said.

"I'm heartbroken, it's allowed," she countered.

They were silent for a few minutes while they polished off some more cookies.

"Mel, I have to ask. Is it the detective?"

"What do you mean?" she asked. She

knew her face was heating up, and she was grateful for the dim lighting in the van.

"Oh, please. Marty told me he walked in on you and Martinez," he said.

"Nothing happened," Mel protested.

"But it could have," he said. "Couldn't it?"

"Yeah," Mel said.

She felt on the verge of tears, and Tate must have heard it, because he moved the milk carton out from between them, threw an arm around her shoulders, and hugged her close.

She glanced up and found his face just inches from hers. Why couldn't she have fallen for him when they were twelve? He glanced at her and grinned as they exchanged a look of perfect understanding.

Mel knew she didn't have to say it. They both felt it. As much as they loved each other, they had never ever felt that way, and they never would.

"Tate, why is this happening?"

"At a guess?" he asked. "I'd say you're scared."

"Scared of what?"

"Death."

Mel would have questioned him further, but the back door to the van rolled up, startling them both. Tate clutched her closer as if preparing to throw her behind him in case it was Sam's murderer coming to kill again.

Instead, it was Angie. She took in the scene in a glance and, with a stricken look, she started to back away.

TWENTY-THREE

"Oh, hell no!" Tate snapped and he climbed over Mel and hopped to the ground, catching Angie about the waist and spinning her about.

"I'm sorry — I didn't realize — Oz told me — I was worried —" Angie's stammer was cut off in the middle when Tate pulled her close and planted a kiss on her that was the single most romantic thing Mel had ever witnessed.

She knew she should look away, but when Angie twined her arms around Tate's neck and the kiss deepened, Mel found herself sighing with joy. It was just so right seeing them together.

Tate broke the kiss and leaned his forehead against Angie's. "It's you I want. No one else. Do you get it, you ninny?"

Obviously incapable of speech, Angie nodded.

"But I have to prove to myself that I'm

good enough for you."

Angie looked as if she would protest, but he shook his head at her.

"You're just going to have to be patient. Clear?" he asked.

Again, Angie nodded. Tate released her with a grin.

"I think I kissed her speechless," he said to Mel. "Who'd a thunk?"

Mel looked at Angie. She did seem to be in a bit of a stupor, and Tate was walking with a self-confident swagger she'd never seen on him before.

He climbed back into the van and gently pushed Mel out. Looking quite pleased with himself, he said, "Now go away, both of you."

He rolled the door down. Mel turned to look at Angie and wondered if they were on speaking terms yet.

"He called me a ninny," Angie said. Then she broke out in a smile that was blinding in its brilliance. "That should not be as charming as it is."

"Come on," Mel said as she threw an arm around her shoulders. "I'll buy you a cup-cake."

They crossed the alley to the back door of the bakery. Mel didn't look at the corner where she'd found Sam's body. It still freaked her out that it could have happened while she was sleeping in her apartment, completely unaware.

Angie went right to the walk-in and came back with two of Mel's Moonlight Madness Cupcakes. They were her insomnia special: chocolate cupcakes with vanilla buttercream, rolled in coconut and each topped with a Hershey's Kiss. Mel poured them each a glass of milk, and they sat at the steel table in the center of the kitchen.

They'd each taken a restorative bite and washed it down with a sip of cold milk when Angie finally spoke, addressing the situation between them.

"I'm sorry I said you had a big, fat mouth," Angie said. "It was mean and stupid and you didn't deserve that."

Mel blew out a breath. "It's okay."

"No, it isn't." Angie shook her head. "You're my best friend, and I treated you like garbage. Let me make it up to you."

Guilt stabbed Mel as sharp as a pinprick.

"You really don't have to do that," she said.

"No, I do," Angie said. "Tell you what: I'll take over cleaning the bakery every day."

Mel shook her head and took another bite of her cupcake.

"I'll give you a foot rub," Angie offered.

"Tempting but really not necessary."

"I'll do lunch with your mother in your place," Angie said. "I'll let her grill me about you and Joe, and I won't let anything slip."

Mel dropped her cupcake back onto the plate and wiped the extra frosting off of her fingers.

"What's wrong?" Angie asked.

"I owe you an apology, too," Mel said.

Angie paled and pushed her cupcake away. She clenched her fingers together and took a fortifying breath.

"It's you and Tate, isn't it?" she asked.

"Oh, by all that is holy, no!" Mel yelled and slammed her hand on the steel tabletop, making it ring like a gong.

Angie blinked at her in surprise. Mel seldom lost her temper and she very rarely yelled.

"Let me be perfectly clear," she said. "Tate is my F-R-I-E-N-D! Friend! That's all that has ever been between us — EVER!"

"You don't have to shout," Angie said. "I'm not hard of hearing."

"Really?" Mel asked. "Because I have been saying this for years, and yet you keep suspecting that Tate and I have a thing for each other when we don't."

"But —" Angie began, but Mel interrupted.

"Joe and I broke up."

"What?" Angie looked stricken, and Mel wished that she had cushioned the news a bit more. "Does your mother know?"

"Not yet," Mel said.

"But why?"

Mel sighed. "You know how you just apologized for being mean today?"

"Yes."

"You said you wanted to make it up to me," Mel said. "Do you think you could not freak out about what I'm going to tell you?"

"Maybe," Angie said.

Mel glanced up. Angie's dark brown gaze was boring holes into hers, so she quickly looked at the tabletop to avoid being blinded by the intensity of her friend's stare.

"And I'm going to need you to forgive me in advance," Mel added.

"What?" Angie asked. "How can I when I don't even know what you've done?"

Mel shrugged. She knew she should take the hit of Angie's ire like a woman and just tell her what was going on, but having Angie not speaking to her today had been pretty lousy and she really didn't want to go through it again.

"Scale of one to ten, how bad is it?" Angie asked.

Mel considered if the situation had been reversed and Angie hadn't told her that she and Tate had been engaged for months and not told her. Yeah, it was pretty bad. What had Angie said earlier when Martinez had been teasing her? That it would be a *huge* thing to keep from her. Mel knew it was a major oops in best friend protocol.

"Nine point five," Mel said.

"Oh, my god. You killed Sam Kelleher, didn't you?"

"What? No!" Mel said. "How could you even think that?"

"Well, a ten on the friend scale means you need help hiding the body," Angie said. "Since you don't need that, I figured the next level down would be a confession of murder."

"Yeah, if you're an ax-wielding psychopath," Mel said. "Sheesh."

"So, what is it then?" Angie asked. "Spill it already! The suspense is killing me."

"I lied to you earlier," Mel said. She glanced up, looking at her friend with regret. "Joe and I were engaged."

The hurt in Angie's eyes was worse than Mel had anticipated. She reached out across the table and grabbed her friend's hand.

"I'm really sorry," she said. "I should have told you, but I just wanted to keep it to myself for a while."

"It's cool, I understand," Angie said. But it was clear from the strained quality of her voice that she didn't. "So, why did you break up?"

"He wants to get married, and I don't," Mel said.

"Why not?" Angie asked.

"I don't know," Mel said. "I've been trying to figure it out, but I don't know what's holding me back."

"Fear," Angie said.

"Of what?" Mel asked. "I've loved Joe for as long as I can remember. What could I possibly be afraid of?"

"Marriage is a big step, even if you're crazy in love with someone," Angie said.

"If Tate proposed to you right now and wanted to run away with you, what would you do?" Mel asked.

"Grab his hand and never let go," Angie said.

Mel let out a heavy sigh. "What if Joe gives up on me?"

"He won't," Angie said.

"How do you know?"

"Because he's my brother, and I've never seen him this crazy about anyone before."

"Yeah, until he dumped me," Mel said.

"What did he say exactly?" Angie asked.

"That he thought I needed time to think and that he didn't want to feel as if he'd talked me into marrying him," she said.

"And what about Martinez?" Angie asked.

"What about him?"

"Mel, I'd have to be six feet under not to notice that he's interested in you," Angie said. "Are you interested in him, too?"

Mel did not want to answer. Angie kept her gaze unwavering, and Mel put her head down on the steel table.

"My whole life I was the fat chick," she said. "I never had one guy like me, never mind two."

"So, this is an ego thing?" Angie asked.

"I'm shallow and pathetic, aren't I?"

Angie laughed. "No, you're human. Look, I love my brother, and I love the two of you together. But if he's not the right one for you, then I won't be mad at you for finding someone else."

"Honest?" Mel asked as she raised her head.

"I just want you both to be happy," Angie said. "You know, you've been together for a year. The initial magic usually wears off between six to nine months. I mean, look at Roach and me. We barely made it to six months."

"And now he's writing *Billboard* chart-toppers for you," Mel said.

"Don't remind me," Angie cringed.

"If you weren't already in love with Tate, would you have stayed with Roach?" Mel asked.

Angie frowned. "I don't know."

"Why are relationships so complicated?" Mel asked.

"Because men are stupid," Angie said.

"That's gender bashing," Mel argued. "Not all men are stupid."

"Mine is unemployed and sleeping in a cupcake truck," Angie said. "Stupid."

Mel had to give her that one. She thought about the dynamics of the relationships they'd been watching for the past few days: Hannigan and Brigit. Sam and Amy. Sam and Brigit. Hannigan and Amy. It was all so messy.

"Do you think it was stupidity that got Sam Kelleher killed?"

"I don't know," Angie said. "If you had to pick any of the magazine people as the murderer, who do you think did it?"

"Amy," they said together.

"She has no alibi," Mel said.

"She admitted that she hated him and had slept with him for the job," Angie said. "If Sam and Brigit were a couple, don't you think Brigit would be angry that he was sleeping with a woman who was younger than her and obviously gunning for her job?"

"So you think Brigit killed Sam?" Mel asked. "I don't know. Her grief seemed pretty genuine when we found the body."

"What about Hannigan?" Angie asked. "He obviously still has feelings for Brigit."

"But he ran out after Amy today," Mel said. "She's obviously chasing him. Do you think there's anything there?"

"Hard to say," Angie said. "And what of the others, Bonnie, Justin, and Sylvia? Do any of them have a history with Sam?"

"They are all in the industry," Mel said. "And they all seemed pretty choked up over his murder."

"Couldn't you squeeze out a few tears if you were a murderer, to cover you tracks?"

"Probably. I know Uncle Stan and Martinez are stressed, trying to find the murder weapon and narrow the suspects down," Mel said.

She was pleased that she could say Martinez's name without blushing. Really, there was no need. Nothing had happened between them. So he had expressed an interest in her and she was flattered. As Angie said, she was only human.

"Maybe there will be a break in the case

soon," Angie said. "It'd be nice if it was cleared up before the gala. Speaking of which, how are we doing with that?"

"We'll be fine," Mel said. "Bonnie seems to run a tight ship, and the others have stepped up."

"I have to admit, I'll be glad when it's over and our kitchen is ours again," Angie said.

She threw out the remains of their cupcakes and stood. "Are you sure you want to stay here tonight?"

"I'll be fine," Mel said. "I've got Captain Jack the watch-cat, and Tate is just in the truck below."

"All right, I'm going home then," Angie said. "But call me if you need me."

"I will," Mel said.

They hugged at the door, and Mel locked up behind them. She watched while Angie went to her car, which was parked a few spaces from the cupcake truck, before she went into her apartment, locking the door behind her.

She took out her cell phone, wanting to call Joe to see if he was as miserable as she felt, but she put it on the counter instead. It wasn't fair to him. He had told her to call him when she knew what she wanted, and she was still unsure.

Was Angie right and they had just hit that

254

time in the relationship where the magic had worn off? She thought about the way he smiled at her, and she felt herself get warm from the inside out. No, the magic wasn't gone. She just wasn't ready to make the next leap, and he was.

A chiming version of "Tara's Theme" from *Gone with the Wind* sounded from her phone, and Mel snatched it back up, hoping it was Joe.

As she read the number, she groaned. It was her mother.

TWENTY-FOUR

"Hi, Mom," Mel answered.

"Melanie, I just called dear Joe's house, and he said you were home. What's going on? I thought you were staying with him," she said.

"No, just for last night," Mel said. She tried to keep her voice light to keep Joyce off track.

But Joyce wasn't her mother for nothing. "What's wrong?"

"Nothing," Mel protested.

"Melanie, do not fib to me."

Mel sat down on her futon. So much for keeping Joyce off track.

"Really, other than a body being found outside my bakery, everything is just peachy-keen," she said.

"Do not try to sidetrack me with sarcasm and a murder," Joyce said.

"Mom." Mel knew her voice came out in an exasperated huff, but she was powerless to stop it. Despite being well into her thirties and a successful small business owner, when Joyce mothered her, Mel morphed right back into a twelve-year-old again.

"What does dear Joe have to say about you staying there?" her mother asked.

"Stop calling him dear Joe," Mel said, irritated. "He's Joe, just Joe."

"Okay," Joyce said, sounding equally irritated. "What does 'Joe just Joe' have to say about you staying there."

"He thinks it's fine," Mel said. "In fact —"

She almost said they were no more, but she snapped her mouth shut just in time to stop the words that would break her mother's heart.

"In fact what?" Joyce asked, her voice was suspicious, as if she had an inkling of what was to come.

"In fact, it was his idea," Mel said. Not a total lie, Mel reasoned, since he was the one who had left. "He didn't want me to build up a phobia about being here by myself."

"Dear Joe is so sensible," Joyce said with a burst of obvious relief.

Mel's phone beeped, signaling another call was coming in. She didn't bother to check it. No matter who it was, they were saving her bacon. She'd be happy to talk to a car insurance salesman if it would keep her from blabbing the bad news to her mother and opening a can of drama she had no wish to deal with at this moment.

"I've got a call coming in that is probably him," Mel said. "I'd better go."

"Give him my best, honey," Joyce said. "I love you."

"I love you, too, Mom," Mel said.

She ended the call and took the other before it vanished.

"Hello?" she answered.

"So, my partner just got a phone call from a certain assistant DA," the voice said. "He wanted Stan to check on you, but he didn't say why."

"Martinez?" Mel asked.

"Hi, Mel. What's going on?" he asked.

She took a moment to note that his voice was deep and very pleasant on the phone.

"Nothing," she said. She knew that the single word weighed as much as an elephant and was about as inconspicuous.

"Aw, come on. Talk to me," he said. "Stan was about to call and check on you, but I told him I'd do it since he's stuck on another line, running down a lead. You can't give me 'nothing' as a report. What kind of detective would that make me?"

"Are you trying to charm me?" she asked.

"Is it working?" he countered.

"Maybe just the tiniest bit," she said.

"Then tell me what's happening?" he asked. "Are you okay?"

"I'm fine, Richard," Mel said.

A snort sounded on the line, and she knew she'd gotten him.

"Richard Martinez," he said. "Yeah, it has a certain ring to it. But, uh, no, that's not it. Back to you. Is there anything you care to share?"

She wasn't going to talk to him about her personal life. She hadn't said no to marrying Joe so that she could date Martinez. Yes, he was attractive, but her personal life was shreddle right now, and she didn't see herself dating anyone until she figured out what was going to happen with her and Joe.

"Nope, nothing to share," she said. "So, about Sam's murder."

"What about it?" Martinez asked. His voice was wary, and she was glad she'd caught him off guard.

"I was just wondering how the investigation was progressing," she said.

"Not as easily as we'd like," he said. "Still no murder weapon, plenty of motives, and a list of suspects as long as my arm."

"Is that why you're both working late?" she asked.

"Yeah," he said. "Hannigan has connections in city hall, and he's applying pressure to solve this thing, which is trickling down with all of the finesse of a sledgehammer."

"Is Uncle Stan on his usual diet of antacid tablets and jumbo-sized coffees?"

Martinez chuckled. "Yep."

They were both quiet for a while, and then Martinez's voice dropped to a low tone, and Mel suspected there was someone standing nearby and he didn't want to be overheard.

"So, are you going to tell me what's going on with you and Joe or not?"

"Not," Mel said.

"Why not?" he asked.

"You're a detective," she said. "Anything you need to know, I'm sure you can figure out on your own."

"I do enjoy a challenge," he said.

He sounded more than eager, and Mel wondered if maybe she should have given him the "I'm not ready yet" speech.

A voice that sounded alarmingly like her Uncle Stan grumbled on Martinez's end of the call.

"Duty calls," he said. "Talk to you tomorrow?"

"Sure," she said.

"Over dinner?" he asked.

"Doubt it," she said. "I expect to have no

life until after Saturday's gala."

"I'll look forward to next weekend then," he said. He ended the call, and Mel stared at the phone in her hand as if it were a live snake and she wasn't sure how it had gotten there.

She had not said she would see him next weekend. How had he gotten that idea? Did he think they had a date? She could feel herself start to panic, and then Captain Jack came roaring around the end of the futon, slapping the cap of a milk bottle across the floor while he chased it, and her panic vanished.

Martinez was just being funny. There was no date on the books. She just wasn't used to having anyone actually pursue her. When she and Joe had gotten together, they had been thrust together because Mel was the suspect in a murder case. Because she'd had a crush on him forever, all he'd had to do was ask her out and she was his.

With Martinez, it was different. She hadn't liked him when they'd first met, and she was pretty sure he'd felt the same way about her. Oh, the attraction was there, but she'd gotten in the way of his investigation and he'd let her know how irritating he found that. Now, ironically, they were on the same team.

Mel believed that everything in life happened for a reason. She frequently had no idea what the reason was at the time it was happening, but later she always managed to look back and see an aha moment where everything that had happened made sense.

Right now, she couldn't imagine that she would ever feel that way, but she had to believe that, whatever growing pains she and Joe were going through, they were going through them for a purpose. And the same was true of Martinez's appearance in her life. He was here for a reason; she just didn't know what it was . . . yet.

Mel slept hard that night. She had thought she'd toss and turn and fret, but the day had worn her out. Captain Jack snuggled the top of her head like a furry hat while she slept and they both snored.

When she woke up and staggered to the bathroom, she was pleased to see that Amy's love tap had faded to mottled green-and-purple bruising, but the lumpkin was clearly no more. She was not sorry to see it go.

Sadly, she didn't own any makeup other than eyeliner, mascara, and lip gloss, so she couldn't use anything to cover up the knuckle print under her eye.

She ate breakfast, played with Captain

Jack, and hurried downstairs to the bakery. Tate was already there, eating a yogurt while reading the paper at the kitchen table. The coffeepot was full and hot. Yay.

She took one look at the bed head he had going, and said, "Feel free to use my shower."

"Thanks," he grumbled, and folded up the sports page and headed upstairs, doing a fair impression of a cranky old man. Obviously, the time he was spending with Marty was rubbing off on him.

Mel scanned the headlines. There was a follow-up article about Sam's murder, and the reporter made it clear that she felt the investigative skills of Uncle Stan and Martinez were lacking. Ouch. That had to hurt. She did note that the reporter referred to Martinez without using his first name, which made her even more curious about what he was hiding. It had to be bad, really bad.

The entire magazine crew was in and baking by ten o'clock. Hannigan had banned the cameras after Sam's murder, feeling that it was too intrusive on the grief the staff might be feeling, but Chad the photographer arrived with the rest of them to take some still pictures of them at work to include in a piece Brigit was writing about the gala, which had been adjusted to include a memorial to Sam.

Mel was pleased with their progress on the cupcakes but knew that tomorrow was going to be an all-out whisk-to-the-wall day to finish frosting and decorating the cupcakes in time for the evening's gala.

Mel was in the walk-in chiller when the back door opened to the kitchen. She could hear the murmur of voices and assumed that Angie was dealing with whoever had dropped in.

As she slid the rack of cupcakes onto the shelf, she heard a shout. There was the sound of voices raised in anger, and she hurried out of the freezer to see what was happening in her kitchen.

Uncle Stan was standing nose to nose with Ian Hannigan while the rest of the group looked on with matching looks of surprise on their faces. The only one who didn't look shocked was Brigit.

"This is ridiculous," Hannigan was saying. "She and Sam were — friends."

Mel knew he had been about to say something else but had obviously thought better of it.

"If you don't get out of the way," Uncle Stan said, "I'll be taking you in for obstruction of justice as well as bringing her in for questioning. Now stand aside."

Twenty-Five

Uncle Stan and Hannigan stared at each other for a moment. Finally, Hannigan moved so that Uncle Stan could approach Brigit.

"Ms. MacLeod, if you'll come with me," he said.

"Certainly," she said.

She didn't look surprised, and Mel wondered why. Hannigan put out an arm to stop her when she went to get her handbag out of the office.

In a low voice, he said, "I'll call an attorney and meet you at the station. Do not answer any questions without an attorney present."

Brigit gave him a small nod. Mel sidled up next to Uncle Stan.

"What's going on?" she asked.

He gave her a fond look. "I'm not at liberty to say."

"Aw, come on," she said. "You're killing me."

He gave her a look that reminded her so much of her dad when he had been exasperated with her that she sucked in a sharp breath. No matter how much time passed, there wasn't a day that she didn't miss her dad, who had crossed over to the "wrap it in bacon and fry it" diner in the great beyond over ten years ago.

"I'm a homicide detective," Stan said. "Your word choice is unfortunate."

"Sorry. What I mean is that I'm in an all-hands-on-deck situation here, and you're taking one pair of my hands and the other is sure to follow," she said.

"Can't be helped," Stan said. "We've got a lead, and questioning Brigit is key."

"*We* meaning you and Martinez?" Mel asked.

"He is my partner," Stan said.

Stan was watching Brigit and Hannigan, whose conversation had gone down to a whisper. Mel followed the line of his gaze and saw that Amy was watching them as well, and Mel noted that she seemed to have quite the self-satisfied smirk on her face. The others seemed to be busy pretending to work under Angie's direction while furtively watching the goings-on around them.

Uncle Stan was in full-on detective mode, and Mel figured, since he was distracted, this might be a good time to do some investigating of her own.

"So, when you and Martinez are hanging out back at the station," Mel said, "what do you call him?"

"What do you mean?" Stan asked. He gave her a sideways glance, keeping his focus on Brigit.

"Well, Martinez, is a bit formal," she said. "So, I figured you'd call him by his first name — which would be . . . ?"

Stan gave her his full attention and broke into a grin.

"You don't know his first name," he said.

"Too obvious?" she asked.

"Way," he said.

"So, do *you* know it?" she asked.

"Of course. He's my partner," he said.

Brigit and Hannigan were making their way across the room towards them.

"Well?" Mel prodded him.

"Oh, no, I'm not telling," Stan said. "If Martinez wants you to know, he'll tell you."

"But you're my uncle," she protested.

"And he's my partner," he said. "By the way, I noticed he's taken a particular interest in your bakery. Is there anything you want to tell me?"

Again, he looked so much like her dad that Mel felt a sudden need to confess all. Thankfully, Brigit and Hannigan joined them at that moment, preventing her from an awkward bout of full disclosure.

"Nope," she said. "Not a thing."

Uncle Stan gave her a level look, and said, "He's a good guy, Martinez, you know, if you need to know that."

Mel thought it spoke pretty well of Uncle Stan to give her a thumbs-up on Martinez when she knew very well that he and Joe were pretty tight.

"Duly noted," she said, and he nodded.

"I'm ready now," Brigit said.

"Excellent," Uncle Stan said.

Stan looked at Brigit with what Mel assumed was supposed to be a bolstering smile, but it came out more like he was battling indigestion.

Mel marveled at the way every man who came into Brigit's orbit seemed to feel the need to take care of her. Even Uncle Stan wasn't immune, as he attempted to make taking her in for questioning seem like a routine errand and not the big deal that it was.

Brigit was one of the toughest women Mel

had ever met. She certainly didn't need to be coddled, but there was something about her, a refined ladylike grace, that brought out some latent sense of chivalry from the men in her life.

Mel wondered if that was why Sam had been unable to let her go. He had given up his career as a hard journalist to be with her. Did he regret it? Especially when he realized she would never love him like she loved Hannigan?

What could have happened between them that had the police interested?

The door shut behind Uncle Stan and Brigit, and the pretense the others had been maintaining of working evaporated like hot steam.

"Why do you think they want to talk to her?" Justin was the first to ask the question on all of their minds.

"I don't know," Mel said as they all looked at her. "My uncle didn't say."

"Well, I'm going to the station," Hannigan said. "I'll make sure she has the best representation money can buy."

"What?" Amy asked. "You're going to help her?"

"Of course," Hannigan said. He turned to look at the young art diretor. "I'd do the same for any of you."

"But she caused your wife's death!" Amy shouted. "How can you run to her side like a whipped dog?"

Hannigan's face flushed scarlet, but Amy's eyes glittered with jealous rage. She was well past caring if she offended him or not.

"Mind your manners," Hannigan snapped. "I'm your boss, and you'd better not forget it."

Amy opened her mouth to argue, but Justin nudged her hard in the side, jarring some sense into her, and she shut her mouth.

"And for the record, let me be perfectly clear: Brigit did not cause my wife's death," Hannigan said.

They all watched him. Sylvia and Bonnie looked as if they were frozen in place. A small frown creased Angie's forehead and Mel knew that Angie was as surprised by what Hannigan said as she was . . .

"Yes, Brigit wrote an exposé that brought ruin to my wife's family, but frankly, it was long overdue. They were a miserable, corrupt bunch, and justice needed to be served. And yes, my wife took her life shortly after the article came out, but the truth is, she had a history of mental instability, and she probably would have done it anyway."

Hannigan paled as he spoke, and at the

end of his disclosure, he looked like a dishcloth that had been wrung out and left to dry. He turned to Mel and gave her a nod.

"I trust you'll get it done," he said.

He gestured to the kitchen, and Mel assumed he meant the baking of the cupcakes for the gala. It wasn't stated in the form of a question, and the door banged shut behind him when he left.

"Well, you heard him," she said, since no one resumed motion after the door shut.

Everyone pitched in immediately — everyone except Amy, who took off her apron and dropped it onto the table with no regard for the baking materials in front of her. Flour went one way, sugar went another, and when a bottle of vanilla extract looked about to pitch over, Angie grabbed it.

"Going someplace?" Angie asked her with a scowl.

"Home," Amy said. "I'm done."

"Oh, what's the matter?" Bonnie asked. "Are you sore because the boss chose his longtime love over you?"

"Shut it, Tons-o-Fun," Amy said. "I can't help it if I suddenly have a sick headache."

"You could lose your job over this," Justin said. He didn't sound as though he thought this was a bad thing.

"Oh, please. Brigit is going down for Sam's murder," Amy said. Then she clapped a hand over her mouth as if she'd blurted the words out unintentionally. Mel suspected otherwise.

"What are you saying?" Sylvia asked.

"Nothing," Amy said with a shrug. "But I'll be surprised if any of us have jobs when it's over. In fact, I think my time would be better spent looking for a new job than decorating cupcakes."

"What did you do?" Justin asked. His eyes were narrowed in suspicion.

"I don't know what you mean," Amy said as she strode to the door.

"Amy, if you set Brigit up —" Justin's voice was a low growl.

"A murderer doesn't need to be set up," Amy snapped. "She just needs to be caught."

She pushed through the swinging door into the bakery, leaving them all staring after her.

"She's evil!" Bonnie hissed.

"She's a woman scorned," Sylvia said. "Which makes her very dangerous."

"Doesn't that seem a little old school?" Mel asked. "I mean, I would like to think women have evolved beyond that, emotion-ally."

"Does she look like the poster child for emotional maturity to you?" Angie asked.

"Good point," Mel conceded.

"I'm going to make sure she left," Angie said. "Be right back."

"All right," Bonnie said. "Let's try to get as much done as we can. I don't want to at-tempt to decorate one thousand cupcakes tomorrow right before the gala."

Sylvia, Justin, and Bonnie began to buzz around the kitchen. Mel and Bonnie coordi-nated the use of the oven so that the flow of the kitchen took on the atmosphere of an assembly line.

When a half hour had passed and Angie hadn't reappeared, Mel poked her head into the front of the shop to see what was hap-pening.

Marty was behind the counter assisting a customer while Angie and Tate were clean-ing up the tables and booths. Well, Tate was cleaning while Angie tagged along after him, joking and laughing.

Tate paused in his cleaning to lean close to Angie and whisper something low in her ear that made her blush a pretty shade of pink. Mel was hit low and hard with a burst of jealousy that stunned her.

"About time, huh?" Marty asked.

Mel forced her gaze away from her friends and looked at Marty. He took one look at her face and made a clucking sound with his tongue.

"Now, don't be like that," he said. "They're still your friends. They'll always be your friends. They're just finally discovering each other."

"But I'm going to be shut out of it," Mel said.

She knew she sounded pathetic, but there it was. She was afraid that when Tate and Angie became a couple, they'd forget all about her. They might prefer to be alone instead of getting together for their weekly old-movie night. And what if they turned into one of those groping couples, who every time they were within a few feet were pawing at each other, oblivious to everyone around them? She'd hate that.

"Well, I should hope so," Marty said, sounding alarmed. "I'm not a prude, but there's a reason couples are generally twos and not threes. Besides, you won't lose them. Your friendship runs too deep for that."

"How do you know?" Mel asked.

"Look at all that you've been through," Marty said. "No one has bailed yet."

"Good point," Mel said. "You know, I just want my kitchen back. I want my bakery back. I want Sam's murder solved, and I want things to be normal again."

Marty looked at her. Angie giggled at something Tate said, and Marty looked at them and then back at Mel, and asked, "When exactly has anything ever been normal around here?"

TWENTY-SIX

The front door opened and in strolled Oz and his friend Lupe. They wore all black, from their fingerless gloves to their Vans, and they carried their skateboards tucked under their arms.

"Afternoon, my peeps," Oz said. "Lu, will you take my board for me?"

"Sure," she said. "I'll bring it back after your shift."

"Cool," he said.

They exchanged a complicated hand-shake, and then Lupe took his board, tossed the pink fringe that hung over her face out of her eyes and zipped out the door.

"I rest my case," Marty said. "There is nothing normal about this place."

"Okay, you've got me there," Mel said. "Still, I'll breathe easier once Sam's killer is caught."

"I bet it's someone he wrote about," Oz said as he joined them behind the counter.

"Rich people don't think the rules apply to them. I bet someone put a hit on him."

Mel looked at Oz through narrowed eyes. "Don't tell me, let me guess: you recently had a Godfather movies marathon?"

" 'You think that would fool a Corleone'?" Oz asked with a grin.

Mel shook her head and then smiled at Marty. "Nope, not normal. Angie, quit flirting. We have work to do."

Angie jumped and spun around. When she saw all three of them watching her and Tate, she turned an even deeper shade of pink.

"I was not flirting," she grumbled as she began to walk towards them.

Tate grabbed her by the apron strings and pulled her back. Then he whispered something in her ear that made Angie squeal.

"Oh, ugh, she just made a girly-girl squee noise," Oz said.

"Yep, it's sickening," Mel agreed.

"I think it's cute," Marty said, and both Mel and Oz looked at him as if they thought he'd been body snatched, and he groused, "What?"

"Whew, for a second there, I thought we'd lost him, too," Oz said.

"There's nothing wrong with being a little sentimental," Marty said. "It wouldn't hurt you, you know."

"Nope, not me," Oz said. "Girls are nothing but drama. I have no room for drama in my life."

"Lupe doesn't seem full of drama," Mel said.

"That's different," he said. "She's just a friend."

Mel looked over Oz's shoulder at Angie, who joined them. Angie gave her a small smile, and Mel marveled at how much softer Angie seemed now that she and Tate were coming together as a couple. She had a sweet serenity to her that Mel had never seen before.

Angie looked like she could be wearing haute couture while she spent her days planning charity events. Mel could almost see Angie fitting in with the Harpers' country-club lifestyle. Next thing she knew, Angie and Tate would be the subject of an article for *SWS*.

Mel's eyes went wide at the thought. Not just because it was alarming to think of her friends in that light, but because of the story they would make.

She couldn't help but wonder how someone like Sam would twist the fact that Angie came from a loud Italian family with many brothers and Tate was an only child and heir of old money. Add in the facts that they had been friends since childhood, that Tate's fiancé had been murdered while Angie was the former arm candy of a notorious rock star, and you had some juicy reading. And a story like that could do some serious damage to a relationship just getting its footing.

What would Tate or Angie do if their relationship were dissected for the public at large? Mel knew her friends well enough that they would stand together. They were like that.

But what if they weren't? Could a poison-filled story be the final straw and cause one of them to commit murder? A shudder ran up Mel's back from the base of her spine to the nape of her neck.

Ever since they'd found Sam's body, she had thought the murderer had to be someone he knew. And the dynamic at the magazine was such that she really thought it was one of his coworkers — okay, she was convinced it was Amy. She still was for that matter, but now she had to wonder. Had Sam's murderer been seeking revenge because of one of his stories?

Mel's social set did not really run in that circle — well, with the exception of Tate, who only attended the command performances his mother insisted upon. If there was anyone in the know about *SWS* and the people they had written about, it was Tate's mother, Mrs. Harper.

"Angie, we have to finish these cupcakes today," Mel said. "Would you mind overseeing what's happening in the kitchen for a bit?"

"Not at all," Angie said, and she disappeared through the swinging doors with a wide smile.

"She's got it bad," Oz said with a shake of his head. "I'm going to wash up, and I'll be right back."

"I await your return with bated breath," Marty said.

Mel ignored them and approached Tate while he was wiping down the last booth. The bells jangled on the door, and Mel glanced over to see that Marty greeted the customer. She needn't have worried. It was an attractive woman in her mid- to late fifties, Marty's specialty.

"Tate," Mel said. "I need some help with an errand after work tonight. Are you available?"

He glanced at her. "My calendar is clear, boss."

"Cool, I'll see you then," she said.

Mel went back to the kitchen. It was time to do a serious survey of what was left to do for tomorrow. They had finished most of the cupcakes and were baking the final ones now. Decorating the last of the cupcakes was going to be priority one for the evening and morning.

"Bonnie, I'm thinking we can decorate everything except the ganache on the gluten-free chocolate cupcake and the whipped cream on the pumpkin cupcake," Mel said.

"Agreed," Bonnie said. "The buttercream lattice on the apple pie cupcake and the cream cheese on the pistachio-fig can be done today. Also, what about the brown-butter honey frosting on the corn cupcake?"

Mel thought about it for a moment. "I really would like to make it fresh tomorrow. But we'll need to brown the butter and then put it in the fridge to solidify. That's a bit of an extra step."

"I'll brown the butter today and refrigerate it overnight," Bonnie said. "It can soften tomorrow while we prep the ganache. The whipped cream on the pumpkin we can put on right before we leave for the gala."

Mel gave her a tired smile. "I think we may just pull this out."

They spent the rest of the day baking the final cupcakes and frosting the cupcakes that were ready. Justin surprised everyone with his heretofore unknown piping abilities, and he took over the apple pie cupcakes, making them look like adorable mini–apple pies. Mel had Sylvia and Angie roll the edge of the cream cheese–frosted pistachio cupcakes in crushed pistachios and then place slices of fresh fig vertically into the icing. The pinkish hue of the fig with its sliver of dark peel was very festive.

They had cooked into the early evening when Mel declared they were done. The magazine people left, looking exhausted. Amy had never returned to the kitchen, and Hannigan had called only to tell them that Brigit had been released and he was taking her home.

No one had said as much, but Mel thought the relief amongst the others was palpable. She didn't think it was just concern for their jobs or the desire not to be employed by a murderer, but rather, she suspected, they had a great deal of respect for Brigit and didn't want her to go to jail.

Mel and Angie cleaned the kitchen while Tate closed up the bakery. When the doors were finally locked and the day was done, Tate popped back into the kitchen.

"All right, Mel, I'm all yours. What needs doing?" he asked.

Angie looked between Mel and Tate, and

Mel included her when she said, "Just a quick errand. Do you want to come with us, Ange?"

"Where are we going?" she asked. Her voice sounded suspicious, and Mel knew it was because she was not as gullible as Tate.

"You'll see," Mel said.

"Does it have to do with the gala?" Angie asked.

"Yep," Mel said.

Sure, it was a stretch, but she didn't want to give too much detail or Tate might balk, and she had a feeling she needed him to get the Harpers to talk to her.

Mel ran upstairs to feed Captain Jack and get her purse while Tate and Angie locked up. They all met beside Mel's car, which was parked in the lot near the cupcake van.

She was tempted to ask Tate how he'd slept last night. She didn't imagine the transition from a king-size bed with sand-washed, 1200–thread count silk sheets to a flannel-lined sleeping bag was an easy one. She resisted. He was going to be sore enough at her when he figured out where they were going.

TWENTY-SEVEN

Tate didn't go into a full-on hissy fit until Mel turned onto the winding road that led to his parents' house.

"Oh, no," he said. "Mel, I can't be here."

"You have to," she said. "I need to talk to your mother, and you're my entrance pass."

"But I haven't seen my parents since I quit the business," Tate protested. "I wanted to wait until I got my feet under me a little bit more. You know how my father is."

"Yes, which is exactly why I need you with me," she said. "You distract him, and I'll question your mom."

"Question my mom?" he asked. "About what? Mel, have you lost your mind?"

"I need to ask her about the people and events covered in *SWS*," she said.

She pulled into the circular drive.

"Why would my mother know or care about anything in that magazine?" Tate asked.

"Your mom knows anyone who is anyone," Angie said from the backseat. "I have to agree with Mel on this one."

"And why are we doing this?" Tate asked.

"Other than to facilitate a reconciliation with your parents?" Mel asked. "We are doing this because I want to know who murdered Sam Kelleher."

"What I mean is, shouldn't you leave this up to Uncle Stan and Martinez?" Tate asked.

"Oh, I am," Mel said. "I just think if we can get some names to help out, we should. None of the cupcake boot campers have been arrested. That means they all have alibis, and even Amy, who doesn't, hasn't been arrested."

"Mel, I really don't think —" Tate began, but Mel interrupted.

"Listen. Most of the people at the gala tomorrow have been written about in the magazine. Now, who is going to have better luck than the police at getting these people to talk?"

"Us," Tate replied. His voice was low and unhappy.

Mel switched off the engine and opened her door.

Tate didn't follow, however, instead sitting with his arms crossed over his chest.

Mel looked over the roof of her car at Angie. "Work your magic."

Angie blew out a breath. "I'd have better luck if I used dynamite."

Mel didn't wait to see what weapon of choice Angie unleashed. She had complete confidence that Angie would get it done. To that end, she decided to up the ante by approaching the Harpers' front door and announcing their arrival, leaving Tate with no alternative but to face his parents.

As she knocked on the door, she heard grumbling coming from behind her and knew that Angie had managed to coerce Tate into getting out of the car.

"Very mature of you," Mel said as Tate stood beside her.

He said something under his breath that Mel did not think was a compliment, but she decided to let it go.

The door opened, and Mrs. Ada was standing there, scowling at them.

"Mr. Tate, where have you been?" she asked. Then she pulled him into a bear hug that looked as if it might have squished his innards.

"Hi, Mrs. Ada," Tate choked out as he hugged her back. "It's good to see you, too."

"Girls, you brought him home," Mrs. Ada said as she released Tate and reached around him to embrace both Mel and Angie. They were bone-crusher hugs, and Mel surreptitiously felt her side to make sure she hadn't punctured a lung.

"Who is it?" Mrs. Harper called as she came around the corner. "Oh."

She froze in the doorway, staring at her son as if he were a ghost.

"Hi, Mom," Tate said. He stepped forward and kissed her cheek, his lips barely brushing her perfectly made-up skin.

Mrs. Harper blinked rapidly and then, before he could step away, she put her arms around his middle and squeezed him in the most awkward and yet heartfelt hug Mel had ever witnessed.

"Oh, Tate," she sighed. "I've been so worried. We all have."

Mrs. Ada nodded in agreement.

"Come on in," Mrs. Harper said. "Ada, would you go get Mr. Harper?"

"Right away," Mrs. Ada said. She crossed the foyer and went down a hallway that Mel knew led to Mr. Harper's home office.

They took seats in the living room as before. Mrs. Harper kept her eyes on her son as if afraid he would disappear again.

"Where have you been?" she asked him.

"I've been striking out on my own," Tate said. "I decided it was time I proved to myself that I could be successful on my own and not because I was born with all of this." He gestured to the obvious wealth surrounding them.

"But —" Mrs. Harper began to speak, but then stopped as if she couldn't fathom why Tate would feel the need to prove himself.

Mel felt a twinge of guilt that all this upheaval was her fault. She cast a sidelong glance at Angie to see if she was thinking the same thing, but she wasn't looking at Mel but at Tate, and the glowing expression on her face was one of pride.

"Tate," Mrs. Ada came into the room. "Your father would like a word with you in his study."

Tate did not look surprised.

"This should be fun," he said.

Mrs. Harper gave him a worried look, and he smiled at her.

"Do you want backup?" Angie asked.

Tate grinned at her. "That would be epic, but no, I can handle it."

He rose from his seat and disappeared down the hall.

"Would you girls like a refreshment?" Mrs. Harper asked. "Coffee? Mrs. Ada just baked a chocolate cake that is divine."

Mel was tempted. She did love chocolate cake, but she shook her head, determined to stay on task.

"If you change your mind, just let me know," Mrs. Ada said, and she left the room.

Mel noticed she was headed down the hall towards the study, and she wondered if Mrs. Ada was planning to do some dipping in on the men's conversation.

"Mrs. Harper, have you heard of *SWS* magazine?" Mel asked.

"*Southwest Style*?" she asked. "Yes, I've had a subscription for years. I have all of the issues. They did a piece on my garden a few years back."

"I thought I remembered Tate telling me about that," Mel said.

She glanced at Angie, who was staring at the study door with a worried expression on her face. Mel knew she would have liked to have gone with Tate to face his father.

"May I look at a few of those issues?" Mel asked.

"Certainly, but why?" Mrs. Harper asked.

"I'm just curious," Mel said. "You know that we've been hosting a cupcake boot camp for the magazine's staff at the bakery?"

Mrs. Harper nodded.

"And one of their writers was found dead outside the bakery a few days ago," she said.

"I thought it was a mugging," Mrs. Harper said. She looked from both Mel to Angie. "It wasn't?"

"Afraid not," Mel said. "I think it may have to do with something he wrote about someone."

"He did write exposé types of articles, and some people were not happy to be the source of his material," Mrs. Harper said. She rose from her chair. "In fact I can think of one banker, a client of my husband's, who was particularly enraged. I keep the issues in my sitting room. Come, let's go look."

Mel and Angie rose and followed Mrs. Harper down the hall in the opposite direction of Mr. Harper's study. Mel noticed that Angie was lagging behind, as if her ears had the auditory power of a bat and could pick up the men's conversation. Mel was just happy that they hadn't heard any yelling.

Then again, this was the Harpers. They were not a yelling family like the DeLaura family. As they made their way into Mrs. Harper's study, Mel tried to picture the Harpers and the DeLauras united by a relationship between Angie and Tate. It boggled.

The sitting room was cozy, done in cobalt blue and white with stripes and a floral pattern jumbled together to give a feminine feel but not overly so. Mrs. Harper had a large bookcase that was stuffed floor to ceiling, and beside one of the chairs was a wicker basket full of yarn.

"My latest knitting project," she said. "A Fair Isle sweater for Tate."

"The colors are lovely," Angie said.

"Well, thank you, dear," Mrs. Harper said. As she turned towards the bookcase, Mel gave Angie a look as if to say, *Suck up.*

Angie winked and tapped her temple with her forefinger, letting Mel know that was exactly what she'd been doing, and she was feeling pretty smart about it.

"Here we are," Mrs. Harper said. She knelt down beside the bookcase. "Twelve years of the magazine."

She pulled out the earliest box and took out the first issue. It was the premier issue of the magazine and the cover featured Carla Stone, a Hollywood actress who made her home in Scottsdale.

Mrs. Harper handed it to Mel, who flipped it open to the masthead. Sure enough, Brigit was listed, as was Sam Kelleher. She didn't see Bonnie, Justin, Sylvia, or Amy listed, so she assumed they had all come later. She wondered about the former employees at the magazine.

Had any of them left the magazine and

harbored a grudge? She figured Uncle Stan had probably covered that, but it certainly didn't hurt to ask.

"I know this is a lot to ask —" Mel began, but Mrs. Harper interrupted her.

"Yes, you may borrow them all. I trust you to take good care of them."

"Thank you so much," Mel said. She put the issue back in its box and knelt down on the floor. Each year had a box, so there were twelve boxes total.

"Mel! Angie!" A shout came from the hallway. "Where are you? We're leaving now."

"Oh, dear." Mrs. Harper put her hand to her throat, as if she were unaccustomed to hearing such a loud voice in her home.

Angie bounded across the room to the open door.

"We're in here," she called.

"Fabulous. Let's go," Tate said. His brown hair looked disheveled, as if he'd been attempting to rip it out in tufts. His mouth was compressed into a straight line. Mel knew him well enough to know, he did this when he was trying to keep any angry words from getting out.

"Tate, what is it?" his mother asked.

"Dad and I are having a little disagreement," Tate said. "It's nothing for you to worry about."

He crossed the room and placed a gentle kiss on his mother's temple that did nothing to ease the worried lines that creased her forehead.

"If you leave this house without agreeing to come back to the firm, I will disown you," Mr. Harper announced as he strode into the small room. "You will lose everything."

TWENTY-EIGHT

"Ah!" Mrs. Harper gasped. "Dear, you shouldn't say things you don't mean."

"Oh, he means it," Tate said. His cheeks had bright red patches on them, and his eyes snapped with barely banked anger. "But you can't bully me into staying at Harper Investments, Dad. Disown me, go ahead. I don't care."

When Tate moved to storm out of the room, Mr. Harper stepped in front of him.

"Think about what you're doing, son," Mr. Harper said. "You're throwing away everything you've worked for —"

"You mean everything you've worked for," Tate said.

Mr. Harper made a slashing motion with his hand to indicate that Tate should shut up. Mel was in agreement here. There was nothing Tate could say that was going to make this any better.

"You are throwing away four years at

Princeton and ten years in the business and for what? To prove yourself to a girl?"

Mel felt her eyes go wide. What exactly had Tate said to his father?

"Yes, I am," Tate said. "I need to know that I can be the man she deserves."

"She's not even your social equal," Mr. Harper raged. He waved a dismissive hand at Angie and Mel felt a flash of rage light up inside of her that was so hot and fierce she was afraid she might torch the place if she opened her mouth.

"You're right," Tate said.

Angie hung her head, looking ashamed, and Mel gasped. How could Tate be such a snob? Now she wanted to punch him in the nose. She wrapped an arm around Angie and pulled her close. She started to lead her towards the door away from this horrible scene.

"She's not my social equal," Tate said. "She is far superior to me in every way and much more than I deserve."

Angie stopped in her tracks and turned to look at Tate. He reached out and grabbed her hand. He gently tugged Angie away from Mel and brought her close to his side. Then he gazed at her with a look of such tenderness and devotion that Mel felt her anger evaporate. Her throat got tight, and she glanced at Mrs. Harper to see that her eyes had gotten misty as well.

"Well," Mrs. Harper sniffed. "I think you've done enough damage for one evening, husband. You may now go back to your study and brood about it."

"But —" Mr. Harper protested.

Mrs. Harper held up her hand. "No, don't bother. I am not speaking to you. Go away."

Mr. Harper glanced at everyone in the room, let out a frustrated growl, and stormed out of the room.

Mrs. Harper stepped forward and put her right hand on Tate's cheek and her left on Angie's. "It's a perfect match, if you ask me, and I couldn't be happier."

Angie blushed and Tate grinned.

"Thank you," Angie said. "But I don't want to cause trouble within your family."

Mrs. Harper took Angie's hands in hers. "Mr. Harper has obviously forgotten that he is not my social equal. I come from old money, and he comes from no money. Ironic that he is now the bigger snob, isn't it?"

"I didn't know that," Tate said. "I always thought the Harpers were wealthy back to the *Mayflower.*"

"Oh, please. Dirt farmers at best," Mrs. Harper said. "Early on, your father hired a company to have his image overhauled, and I think he has quite forgotten his roots."

"I had no idea. I'm stunned," Tate said.

"As most people would be, which is why your father is so private about his background," Mrs. Harper said. "Your father tells everyone that we met at the country club. What he doesn't say is that I was there taking tennis lessons and he was there on the landscaping crew."

Tate's jaw did a slow slide open.

"When we fell in love, my parents forbid me from seeing him. He had to bust his butt to win my father's approval. I wouldn't have it any other way for my son."

She let go of Angie's hands, and said, "Make sure he's worthy of you."

With that, she left the room, leaving the three of them to stare at one another in amazement.

"The entire foundation of my life has just crumbled," Tate said. "This is —"

"Incredible?" Angie said. "Yeah." He nodded.

"Well, I'd love to stay here and distill this new information, but we've got to go. Come on," Mel said, realizing Tate was too stunned to move. "Help me with these boxes."

"Boxes?" he asked.

"Yes, your mom is letting me borrow her

magazines," Mel said. "I want to read up on Sam's articles in *SWS*."

"Mel, don't you think the police have already done that?" Tate asked.

"Of course they have," she said. "But they're not baking cupcakes all day long with the staff and getting to know them, are they?"

"No," Tate agreed. "Still, I get the feeling that Uncle Stan will be so unhappy about this."

"I disagree," Mel said as she handed him four of the boxes and then turned to do the same to Angie. "If he really didn't want my input, he never would have allowed us to continue the cupcake boot camp."

"You have to give her that one," Angie said.

"Very reluctantly," Tate agreed.

Mel scooped up the last of the boxes, and Tate led the way out of his mom's sitting room and through the house. Mrs. Ada met them at the door.

"I am so proud of you, Mr. Tate," she said.

Tate looked pleased and leaned down to kiss her cheek.

"Thanks, Mrs. Ada," he said.

She then put a brown paper sack on top of his armful of boxes.

"I packed you each a piece of my chocolate cake," she said. "You earned it."

She patted both Angie and Mel on the arm as they trooped out the door and shut it behind them.

"Good old Mrs. Ada," Angie said. "I knew she wouldn't let us leave without cake."

Mel and Captain Jack sprawled out on her futon. Captain Jack was attacking his catnip mouse while Mel read through the back copies of *SWS.*

She didn't know what she was looking for exactly, but after several issues she was beginning to understand Sam Kelleher the journalist very well, with just glimpses of Sam Kelleher the man mixed in.

His writing chops were exemplary. He pulled the reader into his stories with short, smart bursts of description that engaged her as a reader and made her want to know more. His profiles were carefully constructed deconstructions of the person of whom he was writing. Occasionally, he wrote pleasant pieces about genuinely nice people doing nice things. But mostly, his work was about not-nice people doing very bad things, and Mel could tell he delighted in being the one to bring them down.

What amazed Mel was that, although Sam had done the occasional nice interview, it was very apparent that he liked to expose people's dirty dark secrets, like the banker who was having an affair with his wife's sister and was so obvious about it that everyone interviewed already knew, including the wife.

Other stunners included the world famous environmentalist, who traveled by private jet and lived in a McMansion on the side of Camelback Mountain, where he'd installed forty thousand dollars worth of rare teakwood flooring. Sam had eviscerated him in the interview and then had included a picture of the man posing in his opulent home.

As Mel read the articles, she couldn't help but be stymied that the people agreed to have Sam write about them. Had they not read the magazine, or was their vanity such that having an article written about them overrode their common sense?

She was a third of the way through the magazines when her cell phone chimed Tara's Theme. She wondered if it was time to change it. She needed a different classic movie theme, maybe *Rocky* or *The Pink Panther.*

She looked at the display and saw Joe's name. Her breath hitched, and she hurriedly answered.

"Hello," she said.

"Hi, Cupcake," he said. "How goes boot camp?"

"Good," she said. "I think we're going to slide in sideways on our buttercream, but we'll make it to the gala."

He chuckled and Mel felt the warm gravelly sound all the way down to her toes. She missed him. She hadn't really taken the time to think about it since their tiff, but she missed him a lot.

"I'm sure you and your cupcakes will be as amazing as usual," he said.

"Thanks," she said.

There was a beat of awkward silence, as if neither of them were willing to break their tenuous connection by bringing up the unresolved issue between them.

"I miss you," Mel said.

Joe sighed. "I miss you, too."

Again, there was silence and Joe finally cleared his throat. "Promise me you'll be careful until the killer is caught."

"I promise," she said. "Besides, I have Captain Jack with me, and Tate is now living in Oz's truck in the parking lot, so I feel pretty well covered."

"I heard about Tate," he said. "The brothers have heard about him, too."

"Uh-oh," Mel said. "Do tell."

She relaxed back into the cushions. Talking about the brothers with Joe was familiar ground, and she smiled as she pictured Joe sprawled on his couch, debating what to do with his pack of crazy siblings. Joe was the middle of Angie's seven older brothers, and for all intents and purposes he was the voice of reason amongst them.

"Well, Dom and Sal think he's certifiable," Joe said. "Tony and Ray don't say it out loud, but I think they admire him for walking away from his fortune to prove himself."

"What about Al and Paulie?" she asked.

"Haven't heard from them yet," Joe said. "But I expect there will be a split decision."

"And what about you?" she asked. "What do you think of what Tate's doing?"

"I think he's doing it right," Joe said. "I think he's smart to do what he needs to do to make sure he's ready to be with Angie."

There was a pause, and then he asked, "Is that why you want to wait on getting married? You want to be sure?"

Mel stifled a groan. They had been doing so well. Why did he have to go and mention the marriage thing?

"Joe —" she began.

"No," he interrupted her. "Forget I said anything. I'm just trying to understand."

"I know," she said. "And I know my not

wanting to get married makes no sense to you, but I can't explain it any other way. I really and truly do not want to get married."

It came out a little harsher than Mel had intended, and she knew from the weighted silence pulsing between them that she had offended him. Again.

"It's late," she said. "I'd better let you go."

"Yeah, okay," Joe agreed. "Call me if you need me."

"I will," she said. "And the same goes for you."

Their good nights were stilted, and Mel had a feeling that they were never going to get past this. It made her feel miserable, but she didn't know what else to do. She didn't want to lose Joe, but she didn't want to marry him, either. What a mess.

To distract herself, she pulled another pile of magazines out of the box and began to read. She had a piece of scratch paper and a pen beside her, and every time she came across an article where Sam filleted someone, she wrote the name down.

She knew that both Martinez and Uncle Stan had probably already been down this list, but still, she was working with the staff of the magazine. Maybe she could learn more from them than the police could.

At the very least, it kept her from brooding about the disaster that was now her personal life. Captain Jack stretched his full length and let out a big yawn. She reached over and rubbed his belly, letting his silky-soft white fur twine with her fingers.

"Life is just easier when you're a cat, huh, fella?" she asked.

He blinked at her, licked a paw, and went back to sleep.

"I'll take that as a yes," Mel said, and went back to her pile of magazines.

"All right, everyone, we have to have these finished by three o'clock so they can be brought over to the gala," Mel said. "Other than Bonnie and Justin, who showed us his mad skills at frosting the apple pie cupcakes yesterday, have any of you used a pastry bag before?"

The entire boot camp — minus Amy, who had yet to show — was assembled in the kitchen. Angie and Mel had arrived early and had begun mixing up the last of the frostings.

Brigit and Hannigan were on one side of the table with the last of the pistachio cupcakes in front of them, while Justin and Sylvia were working on the corn cupcakes, and Bonnie had the gluten-free chocolate cupcakes with the ganache icing.

"All right, let me demonstrate the pastry bag," Mel said. She picked up the one in front of Brigit that was loaded with cream cheese icing. She twisted the bag until icing was packed down at the open tip.

The others watched as she squeezed the bag, keeping the pressure consistent. Starting at the outer edge of the cupcake, she made a perfect swirl of cream cheese frosting, and then placed a slice of fresh fig onto the top of it.

Hannigan was frowning, looking at the pastry bag with the intensity of a bomb technician trying to figure out how to defuse it before it exploded. Brigit looked intrigued.

"My turn," she declared. She took the bag from Mel and began to squeeze. A great lopsided dollop landed on the top of the cupcake.

"Consistent pressure," Bonnie said from across the table as she dipped a chocolate cupcake upside down into a bowl of thick, rich chocolate ganache.

"I was consistent," Brigit argued. "The bag is defective."

"Let me try," Hannigan said. He took the bag from Brigit and started at the outer edge as Mel had showed them. He swirled his way in, but the frosting veered off in a different direction, and he frowned.

Brigit laughed, and he glanced up at her. "What?"

"I think your frosting needs GPS tracking to find its cupcake," she said.

Hannigan lifted the bag and squirted a glob right onto Brigit's nose. Mel exchanged alarmed looks with Angie, waiting for Brigit to dunk his head into the frosting bowl, but she just laughed and wiped the frosting off with a gloved finger.

"See?" Brigit asked. "You can't even find your cupcake."

"It's not my fault that you're as cute as a cupcake," Hannigan said with a laugh.

Brigit turned a bright red, and Justin made a gagging sound across the table. Mel and Angie exchanged a look. Obviously, Hannigan and Brigit had kissed and made up.

"Okay, then," Bonnie said. "Let's get to it. Justin and Sylvia, you're on the brown-butter honey, let's see what you've got."

Both Justin and Sylvia mastered their frosting techniques pretty quickly, and soon the kitchen was humming with activity.

Mel waited until everyone was engrossed in their work before she broached the subject that had kept her awake for most of the night. She was hoping to catch them off guard, so that they would talk freely, as if it were just a conversation and not a fact-finding mission by her, which of course it was.

"So, I was wondering," she said, pausing to see if she had their attention. "Have any of you ever received death threats at the magazine?"

TWENTY-NINE

Justin let out a groan. "You sound just like the police."

"Oh, they already asked that?"

"About ten times in ten different ways," Sylvia said.

"Well, did you?" Angie asked, looking curious.

"I have gotten a few," Brigit said. "I always keep a record of them, and I turned them over to the police when they came into the offices and took Sam's computer."

"Do you know if he'd gotten any threats?" Mel asked.

"Oh, yes," Bonnie said. "Sam took those as compliments to his journalistic prowess."

"Stupid," Sylvia said with a shake of her head. "If he wasn't so vicious, he'd probably be alive now."

"That's harsh," Hannigan said. "Sam was a journalist. He was doing his job."

Everyone turned to look at Sylvia, and she

shrugged.

"Do you think it was someone he wrote about who murdered him?" Mel asked. "Maybe someone who wanted revenge?"

"It seems like suing the magazine for libel would be more effective," Justin said.

"Unless what he wrote was true," Brigit said. "Sam didn't slander anyone — ever. He was a journalist to the core. He only printed verifiable facts."

"Maybe he should have been more careful about what facts he printed," Angie said.

Mel fished a piece of paper out of her apron pocket. "I have a list of names," she said. "Can you tell me if you think the people on this list were capable of murder?"

Everyone stopped what they were doing to stare at her.

"Where did you get that list?" Justin asked.

"I stayed up late reading twelve years of *SWS* and noting the name of anyone who might have had a grudge with Sam," Mel said. "So, how about Blaise Stevens?"

"Oh, the environmentalist," Brigit said with a small nod. "The nonprofit booted him, but he became a pitchman for the Shopping Network; apparently, he has consumption issues. He was mad, but I think he actually landed in a better spot after the article."

Mel scratched his name off the list.

"Okay, then, how about Patrick Cleary?" she asked.

"The banker?" Justin asked. "Oh, yeah, he lost everything, including his bank, in the divorce."

"He did leave a few tasty voice mails and e-mails for Sam," Bonnie said. "But then he moved to Costa Rica and became an expat. I heard he has a thriving investment business down there now."

Mel scratched that name off her list as well.

"All right —" she began, but Sylvia cut her off.

"Are we really going to discuss every person who might have had an issue with Sam? I mean, don't we have a bigger issue to deal with right now?"

"A bigger issue than murder?" Mel asked.

Everyone was silent, and Mel got the feeling that her lack of sleep was causing her to fixate on finding Sam's killer with an intensity that the others found off-putting. She glanced at Angie, who was looking at her in concern.

"I have to agree with Sylvia," Brigit said.

"But —" Mel protested.

"No, we need to focus on the gala and the memorial to Sam we're including," Brigit said. She gave Mel a kindly look. "I know you want to help, but solving his murder is really up to the police, and today I want to focus on celebrating his life."

"She's right," Hannigan agreed. "They've got his computer. I'm sure they have a much better record of the stories he wrote, the impact they had, and who wanted him dead because of them."

"And they have the man power to find those people and arrest them," Justin said. "I know it must be creepy for you to have had a killer right outside your bakery, but the police will find them."

Mel wanted to argue that together they could whittle down the list of names to give to the police, but she could see that no one wanted to have this conversation.

Angie moved to stand beside her. "Let it go. We've stumbled upon enough dead bodies to last us a lifetime."

"I know, but he died on our property —" Mel began, but Angie interrupted with a shake of her head.

Mel blew the blond bangs off her forehead. The others had gone back to work on the cupcakes, and she knew it would do no good to badger them. She tucked her list of names into her apron. At the very least, she could give the names to Uncle Stan. Maybe there was a name on there that he had missed.

They took a short break for lunch — very short — while Mel and Angie prepped the last of the frosting to be used. Despite the inexperience of the group, the cupcakes looked amazing, and Mel was certain that their cornucopia was going to look fantastic at that night's festivities.

"So what are you two planning to wear to the gala?" Brigit asked Mel and Angie as the group resumed their places at the steel worktable.

"A clean apron," Mel said, glancing down at her frosting coated bib.

"Oh, no, this is a little more formal than that," Brigit said. "You'll be at our table, of course, so evening attire would do."

Angie looked at Mel with wide eyes.

"Oh, no," Mel said. "You don't have to invite us. We'll be just as happy hanging out in the kitchen, keeping an eye on the cupcakes."

Angie nodded vigorously.

"Don't be silly," Sylvia said. "Without you two there would be no gala. Of course you need to be there. Right?"

"Absolutely," Justin said. "You have to come."

"Agreed," Bonnie said. "Besides, don't

you want to see what everyone thinks of our creation?"

Bonnie extended her arms, and Mel looked at the rolling rack of cupcakes. They were a thing of beauty.

"All right," she said. "I'm sure I must have something to wear."

"Don't worry about it," Sylvia said. "I can hook you up. The fashion department has a storage room full of clothes."

"Not like the poofy skirt and big hair they put us in the last time?" Angie asked, looking worried.

Sylvia laughed and the others chuckled. "No, I promise."

Mel and Angie stood patiently while Sylvia quickly took their measurements with the tape measure she always carried in her purse. Then she shut herself in Mel's office while she talked to her assistant on the phone, instructing her on which dresses to bring by the bakery for Mel and Angie.

Oz and Tate pulled the cupcake truck around to the alley and loaded up the cupcakes to be delivered to the hotel that was hosting the gala.

Tate and Oz were going to make the delivery and set up the cupcakes while Marty worked in the bakery, giving Mel and Angie a chance to clean up from the day's work and get dressed.

Sylvia's assistant brought over three different dresses for each of them, and much to Mel's chagrin, the staff of the magazine stayed to help in the selection process.

"Oh, throw that one back," Justin said when Sylvia held up a green one in front of Mel. "It's going to bring out the green in the shiner Amy gave her, never a good look."

"We can cover the bruise with makeup," Sylvia said.

Brigit tipped her head to the side, studying the dress and Mel. "I agree with Justin. That dress is too loud for her."

"How about this one?" Sylvia moved to hold up a sapphire blue number in front of Angie.

"I like that one," Hannigan said.

"That's because blue is your favorite color," Brigit said.

Hannigan looked at her in surprise. "You remembered."

Brigit shook her head. "No, I didn't. Blue is everyone's favorite color."

"Not mine," Bonnie chimed in. "I like yellow."

"Yellow?" Justin asked. "No one likes yellow."

"I do," Bonnie insisted.

Mel noticed that Hannigan was looking at

Brigit with a small smile, and she wondered if this was exactly what he'd planned. The cupcake boot camp, forcing everyone together like this, had he done it on purpose to win Brigit back? If so, did getting rid of Sam Kelleher, his rival, factor into that? By all accounts, Hannigan was a ruthless businessman, but was he a killer, too?

"Mel, hello, over here." Angie was holding up a chocolate brown dress. "What do you think?"

Mel glanced at her friend and noticed that the entire room was watching her, even Hannigan, who must have noticed that she was staring at him.

"I think the rest of you are going to be late," she said. "Angie and I will pick out our own gowns and surprise you."

Brigit glanced at the clock. "Is that the time? We have to go!"

Sylvia's assistant shoved the gowns at Mel and Angie. They caught them in their arms, and Sylvia handed Mel a small makeup case.

"The cover up in here should match your coloring, just be sure to blend, blend, blend," she admonished. "You do not want foundation splotches or lines."

"Blend," Mel repeated. "Got it."

The boot campers scurried out the door

without a backward glance, and Mel and Angie hurried up the stairs to Mel's apartment to try on the gowns.

Mel knew immediately which one of the dresses she wanted to wear. Of the pink, green, and slate blue gowns, the slate won hands-down. It was a floor-length chemise with a sheer chiffon overlay of the same color. It made her hazel eyes darken to reflect its color, its lines accentuated her height, hid her extra weight and gave her that Greek-goddess feel that was missing from her everyday life.

Angie had a tougher time picking out her dress. Of the brown, ruby red, and sapphire gowns sent over, she was partial to the cut of the chocolate brown satin with the retro fifties-style collar and A-line skirt, but the ruby red complemented her coloring and hugged her curves suggestively, giving her the sensuous allure of a movie star.

"I like the brown," she said to Mel as she came out of her bathroom for the fourth time. "But this red one will knock Tate to his knees."

"Indeed," Mel said with a wolf whistle. "The poor boy won't know what hit him."

"Joe would feel the same about you," Angie said. "Why don't you call him and invite him?"

"Oh, I don't know," Mel said. "We're in a place called *awkward* right now."

"Did you break up?" Angie asked, sounding sad.

"Not as much as we're taking a break," Mel said. At least she thought they were taking a break. She felt the sadness bubble up inside of her, and her throat got tight.

"It'll be okay," Angie said. She put her arm around Mel and gave her a hug. "I'll make sure a picture of you in that dress just happens to show up on my brother's phone, and the man will beg you to be his with a ring or without one."

Mel hugged her back. She knew it wasn't that simple, but she really appreciated Angie's attempt to lift her spirits.

"Okay, now this is when you tell me that Tate will take one look at me in this dress and start panting, howl at the moon, and get over his need to prove himself," Angie said.

"Sorry, I missed my cue, didn't I?" Mel asked.

"Little bit," Angie agreed.

Mel stepped back and studied her friend. The ruby red gown draped her curves perfectly. Her makeup was light except for the eyes and lips, where she was all long lashes and glossy red. Yep, Tate was going to

318

have a well-deserved heart attack.

"He's going to maul you like a bear on a trash can full of apple cores," Mel said.

Angie blinked at her and then busted up with a belly laugh. "I love you."

"I love you, too," Mel said. "Now, let's go get it done."

On the way down the stairs, Mel stopped in the bakery's kitchen to retrieve the list of names she'd created from the magazine. She'd left it in her apron, which rested on its hook by the door, but when she felt around in the front pocket, it was empty. *Huh.*

Angie stood impatiently waiting for her as Mel scanned the floor.

"What are you looking for?" Angie asked.

"My list of names," Mel said. "I wanted to bring it tonight in case the opportunity presented itself to ask people questions."

"Oh, good grief. Let it go," Angie said.

"I can't," Mel returned. "Marty!"

Marty popped his head through the kitchen door. His eyes went wide at the sight of them.

"Well, look at you two. Hearts are going to be breaking all over town tonight," he said.

Angie and Mel both gave him dazzling smiles.

"Thank you, Marty," Mel said. "Hey, you didn't happen to see a piece of paper with a list of names on it, did you?"

Marty frowned. "Nope, I can't say that I did. Is it important?"

"No," Angie said. "It's not. Can we go now?"

She hooked her arm in Mel's and, with a wave to Marty, she hauled Mel out the door.

"It could be valuable," Mel said as they made their way down the steps.

"Yes, but we can't lose any more time looking for it," Angie said. "I don't know about you, but I'm dying to see how the cornucopia turned out."

Mel nodded. She supposed she had to let go of her list. And Angie was right, Bonnie had hired a carpenter to build a huge cornucopia to display the cupcakes, and she was excited and nervous to see it.

They took Mel's car to Del Sol, a five-star resort nestled at the base of Camelback Mountain just minutes from Old Town Scottsdale, where the gala was being held. She handed her keys to the parking valet and paused at the base of the stairs to hitch up the skirt of her gown so she could navigate the steep steps that led to the terrace and the ballroom.

A uniformed doorman held the door open

for them, and Mel took a quick glance at her reflection in the glass door to check that her short blond hair was keeping the frothy shape into which Angie had whipped it, and to make sure the purple-green remnants of the shiner Amy had give her were completely covered by the makeup Sylvia had pushed on her.

The entryway was gorgeous, with a highly glossed brown stone floor and silver starbursts hanging above between rectangular shaped lamps, giving the modern space a retro twist.

Mel and Angie followed the horde of tuxedos and glittery gowns into the ballroom. A large black-and-white framed photo of Sam Kelleher met them at the door. It was Sam in his prime, when he sported a thick head of hair and the wiry build of a man whose meals were grabbed in between chasing down leads, back when he'd been writing for the *Los Angeles Times.*

The tables in the ballroom had been set with black cloths, and the centerpieces were tall, clear glass cylinders filled with water, with green apples and burgundy pomegranates bobbing below a wide white candle floating on the top.

Mel scanned the room, looking for the cupcake cornucopia. She saw several large bars that already had lines forming, as well as a huge ice sculpture carved into the shape of the *SWS* magazine logo.

"Over there," Angie said. She grabbed Mel's hand, and they wound their way through the tables towards the dessert display.

The horn of plenty was a huge golden structure. The opening was at least five feet high and five feet wide, and the cupcakes were displayed coming out of it on tiers, as if they were pouring out of the opening. The back of the cornucopia curled up into the air, and bouquets of different-colored mums had been tucked all around its base.

"Wow," Mel said. "It's even better than I imagined. The carpenter they hired outdid himself."

Tate appeared from behind the display, and said, "Breathtaking."

"It really is," Angie agreed as she turned to face him.

"No, I meant you," he said.

THIRTY

Angie flushed the same color as her dress, and Tate, who was still in a T-shirt and jeans with his bakery apron over them, held out his arm to her.

"Walk with me," he said.

Without a word to Mel, Angie took his arm, and they walked off with their heads pressed together.

A sharp pang of envy stabbed Mel, not because she didn't want Angie and Tate together, but because she wished things were as simple between her and Joe right now. She wished he were here, but she had run him off by not wanting to get married, and now she had to live with it.

"Mel!" A voice called her name, and she turned to see Uncle Stan making his way across the room towards her.

He gave her a once-over and grinned. "Wow, who knew that, behind the frosting and sprinkle-covered T-shirts, there was a raving beauty looking to get out?"

"I knew," a voice said, and Mel turned to see Martinez approaching from the other direction.

The look he gave her scorched, and Mel held her silver clutch purse to her middle as if it could help her catch her breath.

Uncle Stan glanced between them with an interested look, and Mel forced a smile, and said, "Thank you both, but I think the real attraction is the cornucopia. I can't believe we pulled it off."

Chad, the photographer, was snapping pictures of the display, and Mel hoped that *SWS* planned to use them in the magazine. It would be great publicity for the bakery.

"I didn't know you two were going to be here," she said to her uncle with a swift glance at Martinez that included him in the conversation but didn't give out even a smidgeon of a flirtatious vibe.

"A gala that now includes honoring our murder vic," Uncle Stan said. "Couldn't miss it."

"You look good in a dark suit," Mel said.

"Really? Because I feel like a pallbearer," Uncle Stan said.

He hooked a finger in the collar of his dress shirt. Like his older brother, Mel's father, Uncle Stan was a portly fellow, and his starched collar and snappy tie looked to be strangling him.

"I'm going to work the room," Uncle Stan said. "The police chief and the mayor are over there, and I want to do some damage control, since they're pretty unhappy with our lack of a lead at the moment."

"Need backup?" Martinez asked.

Stan glanced at him and then at Mel. She knew his sharp gaze wasn't missing the fact that Martinez was standing closer to her than a mere acquaintance would.

"No, I got it," Uncle Stan said. "Why don't you keep an eye out for any of our persons of interest?"

"Will do," Martinez said.

They watched him leave, and then Martinez turned to Mel, and asked, "Walk with me?"

She couldn't help but note it was the same thing Tate had said to Angie. She scanned the room, not sure of what or who she was looking for, but when the gorgeous gowns and sharp suits started to blur in front of her, she nodded.

Like Uncle Stan, Martinez was wearing a suit, and it hung off of his broad shoulders as if it were made for him. It was black, as were the shirt and tie he wore underneath. It gave him a dangerous edge that Mel had to acknowledge was just the teensiest bit thrilling.

"Come on," he said. "I don't bite . . . very often."

Mel let out a nervous laugh and walked beside him as he led her out the door to the patio outside. The sun was setting, and the south side of Camelback Mountain was absorbing the red and pink hues of the sunset into its pores and returning the glow.

"So, where's your date?" he asked.

"She's off with her soon-to-be boyfriend," Mel said, and she nodded towards the corner of the patio where Tate and Angie stood apart from the rest of the crowd, getting lost in one another's eyes.

"Ah," Martinez said. "Can I get you a drink?"

"No, thanks," Mel said as they passed a small bar. "I'm too nervous. I haven't seen any of the boot-camp people arrive, and I am hoping that they are as impressed with the display as I am."

"They will be," he said. "It's extraordinary."

His voice was so certain that Mel couldn't help but beam at him. His breath caught, and his black eyes crackled with heat.

"If I wasn't on duty, I'd kiss you," he said.

Mel felt the air rush out of her lungs in a

whoosh.

"I'm still figuring things out," she said.

"I know," he said. He ducked his head and glanced at her through his lashes in a look that was utterly charming. "But a kiss might help clear things up."

"Or make me even more confused," she countered.

A cool breeze swept across the patio, tousling Mel's hair and tugging on her skirt as if inviting her to come and play.

"I don't want to do that," Martinez said. "I want you to be sure."

His pocket chirped, and he pulled out his cell phone and checked the display. "Your uncle needs me."

Mel nodded, aware that she was disappointed that she wouldn't get to spend more time with him. She knew it was just as well. Things were complicated enough.

"Before I go, I have to tell you something," he said.

"Your first name?"

"No." He grinned. "You'll have to work for that. But I want to be sure that someone tells you tonight, because you certainly deserve to hear it. Melanie Cooper, you are the most beautiful woman I have ever seen."

Mel was caught in his black gaze for a moment, before she had the presence of mind to stammer, "Thank you."

"When you know what you want," he said. "Call me. I'll come running."

Mel stood stupidly watching him as he left to go back into the ballroom. She was incapable of speech and not a little giddy at the compliments he had paid her.

"Is this a great night or what?" Angie asked as she joined Mel.

Mel tore her gaze away from where Martinez had disappeared and studied her friend.

Angie's red lips were parted in a wide grin and her velvet brown eyes sparkled with undiluted joy. Mel glanced behind her, and asked, "Where's Tate?"

"He was a tad underdressed to stay for the event," she said. "So, we're going to meet up later at the Sugar Bowl."

At the mention of Mel's favorite ice cream shop, she felt her stomach growl. "Want to join us?" Angie asked. "Maybe we can invite Joe, too."

"Eh, I don't want to cramp your style," she said. "And I doubt Joe wants to spend any time with me right now."

"Oh, I don't know. I doubt he'd ever feel that way about you," Angie said. Her voice was soft, and Mel knew it had to be hard for her to watch a rift happening between her best friend and her brother.

"You and Tate need time on your own," Mel said.

"Oh, no. Just because Tate and I are . . . hmm, I don't really know what we are," Angie admitted. "But just because we are, does not mean things are going to change amongst the three of us. We're still going to do classic-movie night and hang out."

Mel smiled at her. She hated to admit how relieved Angie's words made her feel, but there it was.

"I thought I recognized the cupcakes in there," a voice said. "I might have known it was you two."

Mel and Angie turned to find a dark-haired woman in a clingy, satin sheath in deep purple approaching them. Mel frowned. She couldn't place the woman.

"Alma?" Angie asked. "Alma Rodriguez?"

"One and the same," Alma said and she gave them a tiny curtsey.

When Mel and Angie had met Alma the year before, she had looked like something that had crawled out of the city sewer, with her relentless black outfits and Addams Family makeup.

She'd had the snarky disposition to go with the look, and they had not started out on friendly terms at all. But when a murderer had almost taken Alma out, Mel had found her, saving her life and giving her another shot at her design career, which appeared to be flourishing.

"Is that one of yours?" Mel asked.

"That depends," Alma said. "Do you like it?"

"Are you kidding?" Mel asked. "It's not a dress; it's a work of art."

"Thanks." Alma smiled. Mel had seen her once or twice since her goth days, and it was good to see that she was becoming less the snarky, petulant designer she had once been, and a more a confident and gifted artist in her own right.

"So, what brings you to this shindig?" Angie asked.

"The same thing as every other designer in the Valley," Alma said. She turned away from them and scanned the room. "Everyone in the fashion industry is here to court the favor of her."

She gestured to a woman in a sea-foam green gown encrusted in crystals. Her raven hair was swept up in an elaborate do with long strands framing her face. When she turned around, they saw that it was Sylvia.

"Sylvia? Why Sylvia?" Angie asked.

"Because Sylvia Iozzi Porter Levin McKenna Lucci can make or break each and every one of our careers by giving us press in *SWS*," Alma said.

Angie laughed. "I can't believe you know all of her married names."

Mel frowned. There was something about the names that rang a bell with her, but it didn't immediately come to mind. She frowned.

"I heard she was at Bruno Casio's the other night being wined and dined," Mel said. "Probably you need to do something like that to get in her good graces."

Now Alma frowned. "I was at Bruno's the other night. I didn't see her."

"It may have been a different night," Mel said. "It was the beginning of the week, when we started the boot camp to make those cupcakes."

"No, it wasn't," Alma said. "Bruno always has a dinner party in his studio the same night of the week. It's what he's known for, because his designs sure aren't getting him any press."

"Are you absolutely sure?" Mel asked.

"Yes," Alma said.

Mel looked at Angie. "We need to tell Uncle Stan or Martinez."

"Mel, you can't be thinking what I think you're thinking," Angie said.

Mel widened her eyes in surprise. Of

course she was thinking what Angie thought she was thinking.

"Oh, excuse me," Alma said, obviously not listening to them. "I see an opportunity to schmooze."

Mel and Angie watched Alma strut away with her purple gown trailing behind her. She approached Sylvia, who greeted her with a smile and an air-kiss.

"There could be a million reasons why Sylvia said she was at Bruno's when she wasn't," Angie continued. "I really don't think it is as big a deal as you're thinking it is."

"Angie, she lied about her whereabouts on the night of a murder," Mel said. "That is a big deal."

"We don't know that she lied," Angie argued. "Maybe she and Alma just missed each other."

Mel glanced around the room and noticed that there was a bit of a hullabaloo at the entrance. Brigit and Hannigan had arrived together. There was a swarm of VIP-type people around them, and Mel looked for Martinez or Uncle Stan to be among them. No such luck.

"Is that the mayor?" Angie asked.

Mel squinted. It did look like him. Oh, boy.

"Come on," she said. "We need to talk to Brigit."

"Now?" Angie asked. "Can't it wait?"

At that moment, Brigit saw Mel through the throng on the patio, and she smiled. She turned and said something to Hannigan, and he nodded while she extricated herself from the group and approached Mel and Angie.

"Uh-oh, do you think she hates the display?" Angie asked.

"No," Mel said. "It's fabulous. If anything, she's coming to praise us to the skies."

Angie turned her head to look at her. "Do you really believe that?"

"No, but reality is highly overrated," Mel said.

"Agreed," Angie said.

They braced themselves for Brigit's opinion of the display. Much to their shock, Brigit grabbed their hands in hers and gushed. Yes, gushed.

"It is fantastic," Brigit said. "Our cupcakes look amazing in the cornucopia. It's brilliant, positively brilliant."

"Thank you," Mel said, her voice weak with relief.

Brigit laughed. "Were you worried I was going to trash it?"

"No," Mel and Angie said together, and

then they both added, "Yes."

Brigit let go of their hands and heaved a sigh. "I'm sorry if I've come across as an ogre."

"And an apology?" Mel asked. "Have you been drinking?"

Brigit glanced over her shoulder at Hannigan, who was watching her. Their eyes met, and it seemed as if the world fell away from them. Mel noticed that Brigit had to practically force herself to turn back around.

"Let's just say that I have hope that things might change for the better," she said.

"Cautiously optimistic," Mel said. "I like it."

A ruckus at the door caused them all to glance that way. Justin, in an impeccable suit, staggered back from someone, and Mel stood up on her tiptoes to see what was going on.

"What is it?" Angie asked. Even in her high heels, she was too short to see over the crowd. "What's happening?"

"Oh, no, not now," Brigit muttered.

"Amy Pierson," Mel said. "She's got Hannigan by the shirtfront."

Brigit made to storm forward, but Mel caught her arm and held her back. "Seeing you is not going to calm her down. Let Hannigan deal with it. He's a big boy."

Brigit looked as if she would argue, but one glance around the patio at the roll call of Phoenix's rich and famous and she nodded.

"This is supposed to be *my* magazine," Amy was screeching. "You promised!"

Hannigan barked something that sounded like a threat, but Amy was obviously beyond caring. Mel noticed that both Martinez and Uncle Stan had moved to the edge of the gathered crowd, as if prepping themselves to move in.

Amy's long brown hair was in a tangle, and the frothy, peach-colored gown she wore was sheer and low cut. Mel assumed it was supposed to be a mix of demure and slutty, but given that she looked three sheets to the wind, it really just looked slutty and sad.

Justin had hooked her about the waist and was trying to remove her forcibly from the patio.

"You said that if I got rid of Sam, you'd give me the magazine!" Amy continued to shriek. "I want it now. We had a deal. I took care of Sam, now give me my damn magazine and fire that old cow!"

THIRTY-ONE

As Justin hefted her into the air to haul her away, Amy pointed a sparkly polished finger at Brigit, who cast a stony glance in return.

The crowd parted, and Justin took the still shrieking and kicking Amy from the patio. Mel sort of hoped he would dump her in the pool to cool off, but given the expression on Uncle Stan's face, she was going right into a police car for questioning.

Martinez followed Justin and his armload of furious female while Uncle Stan spoke quietly but firmly to Hannigan, who cast a look, a worried look, at Brigit before he nodded and followed Uncle Stan through the doors.

Mel studied Brigit. Despite her emotionless appearance, Mel could see by the pallor of her face that Amy's accusation had rocked her.

Had Hannigan made a deal with Amy that if she got rid of Sam he would give her the magazine? Had his jealousy of his rival for Brigit been that great? It appeared so.

"Come on." Sylvia hurried over to join them on the patio. "Let's get you out of here."

"The dinner should be starting in fifteen minutes," Brigit protested. "I need to keep up appearances."

"Mel and Angie can hold down the fort while you take a few minutes to get yourself together," Sylvia assured her. "Follow me."

Brigit glanced at Mel and Angie. "Do you mind?"

Her usually strong voice sounded breathless, and Mel had no doubt that the scene with Amy had knocked the wind out of her.

"Of course we don't," Bonnie said as she joined their little group. "Go."

Sylvia led away Brigit, who to her credit managed to smile and wave at people as if nothing were amiss.

"Wow," Angie said. "You said all along you had a funky feeling about Amy."

"She's pathologically ambitious," Mel said. "But murder — that brings it to all-new levels."

"Come on," Bonnie said. "Let's start leading folks into the dining room. Brigit's a pro. She'll rally and get back here."

The three of them split up and, together

with the waitstaff, they managed to encourage the crowd, which had gossip moving through it with the heat and power of a wildfire, into the ballroom. Mel caught snippets of the rumors, most of which were that Amy had confessed to murdering Sam Kelleher at the behest of Ian Hannigan.

Mel was shaken, she had to admit it. She'd had a bad feeling about Amy, but the fact that she'd committed murder? It was a stunner.

To take another person's life was the worst crime a person could commit, and to do it for a career — it made Mel queasy to think that someone could be that much of a sociopath, and it was especially disturbing, since Amy had done it just outside of Mel's place of business.

The crowd took their seats as dinner was served. Mel kept glancing at the door to see if Brigit was on her way. Ten minutes passed and then fifteen. Mel wondered if Brigit had decided to abandon the party. She could hardly blame her. The crowd seemed to be buzzing with the same speculation.

"We need to do something," Bonnie whispered. "Justin, can you give the opening speech?"

"Me?" Justin glanced up from where he was pushing salad around his plate like it was a race between the lettuce and the croutons to lap the dish.

"You're higher up on the magazine than me," Bonnie said.

"It would be a good move," Angie said. "Just give them a short welcome address."

Justin glanced around the room and straightened his tie. "Fine, but could someone please go and see what is taking Brigit so long?"

"I'll go," Mel said.

"Hurry," Justin whispered, and Mel rose and hurried out the side door and back out to the patio.

She could hear Justin addressing the crowd from the podium as the door closed behind her. The night sky was pale purple with the oncoming night. Mel scanned the stone terrace but, other than a few of the waitstaff and a bartender, the patio was empty.

She really had no idea where Sylvia had taken Brigit. She'd been hoping to find them on their way back, but no. She hurried over to the bartender.

"What can I get for you, miss?" he asked. He was older, with thick gray hair and a neatly trimmed gray mustache.

"Is there a small meeting room around here where people could go to compose themselves?" His eyes narrowed in concern, and Mel said, "Oh, not for me, I'm fine. I'm looking for someone else."

He raised one eyebrow in a skeptical look, and Mel felt her stomach plunge into her feet. If his hair and mustache were black, he would be a ringer for Christopher Iozzi, one of the subjects of Sam's articles in *SWS*. *Iozzi!*

Mel felt her breath stall in her lungs. That was why Sylvia's name rang a bell. She had to be related to the Iozzi family.

What had happened to Iozzi? Mel banged on the top of the bar. She had read so many articles of Sam's that they had begun to blur in her head.

The doors to the ballroom opened, and Ian Hannigan strode out. He crossed over to Mel, and asked, "Where's Brigit?"

"What happened? I thought you were arrested," Mel said.

"No, I never told Amy to kill Sam." He rubbed a hand over his eyes. "I just encouraged her to get him to fall in love with her," he said. "She finally admitted as much, but the detectives are still questioning her over in some meeting room about his death."

"Iozzi," Mel said. "Who was he?"

"What? What are you talking about?" Hannigan asked. "I have to find Brigit. I have to explain."

"No!" Mel grabbed his arm. "I can't remember the story Sam wrote, but it's critical. What happened to Christopher Iozzi?"

Hannigan must have seen how serious she was, because he blew out a breath, and said, "Iozzi fancied himself an entrepreneur, but he was really a mobster. He got snagged in a drug bust, and Sam exposed his long association with the mob. It ruined him."

"Oh, no," Mel said. She remembered now. She closed her eyes and pictured the grainy snapshot of Iozzi coming out of the court-room, glaring at the photographer with his left eyebrow up in a contemptuous glance.

"He went to prison, where he was murdered in his cell by another mobster," she said.

"That's right," Hannigan said. "But what does that have to do with —"

"Sylvia Iozzi Porter Levin McKenna Lucci," Mel said.

Hannigan's mouth dropped open, and he braced himself on the bar.

"Sylvia took Brigit to freshen up," she said. "I don't know where they are."

"Are you two all right?" the bartender asked, looking worried.

"We need to find someone who just left

here," Hannigan said. His voice held a note of panic, and the bartender obviously heard it.

"Around the corner, there's a small room." He hooked his thumb in that direction. "It connects to the ballroom and is usually reserved for the bride when we have weddings."

"Thanks," Mel said.

Hannigan took off at a run, and Mel picked up her skirt and followed him around the corner of the stone building.

It could be coincidence, she told herself, but all of a sudden she remembered Alma saying that Sylvia hadn't been at Bruno Casio's house on the night of Sam's murder, and her stomach clenched with acid-churning fear.

A metal door painted to match the stone around it was set into the wall. Hannigan grabbed the handle and tried to wrench it open, but it was locked. Mel banged on the door with her fist.

"Sylvia, open the door!" she ordered. "I know what you're doing. You have to stop."

She could hear voices inside, but they were muted into indistinct mumbles. She exchanged a glance with Hannigan. He pushed her back and began to shove into the door with his shoulder.

"I'll get help," Mel said.

Suddenly the door swung in, and Hannigan stumbled forward, unable to stop his momentum. Mel followed and saw Sylvia strike Hannigan in the temple with an ornate candleholder that looked to be made of solid brass. He let out an *oomph* and slumped to the floor.

"No!" Brigit shouted, and she crawled forward to get to Hannigan.

Mel stepped back, planning to run for help, but Sylvia was too fast for her. She grabbed Mel's arm and yanked her into the room, then turned and slammed the door shut, trapping them.

Thirty-Two

"Sylvia," Mel panted. "You need to think about what you're doing."

"Oh, I can assure you I've thought about it," Sylvia said. She pointed the candle-holder at her and paced around them like a lioness sizing up a herd of antelope. "I've thought and I've planned. Really, you have no idea."

"Mel, we need help," Brigit said. "Ian's bleeding."

Mel looked, and sure enough the gash on his head was gushing crimson into the beige utilitarian carpet.

"There is no one to help you," Sylvia said. She glanced at Mel. "Sorry, but you're unfortunately what they call collateral damage."

Mel studied Sylvia's face. She could see the resemblance now in the nose and chin. Sylvia had to be Christopher's little sister.

"Your brother wouldn't want this," she

said. "Christopher didn't join the mob and earn a fortune so that you would end up with blood on your hands. He wanted better than that for you."

"Shut up!" Sylvia screeched, and pointed the candleholder at her like it was a gun. "You didn't know my brother. You don't know want he wanted for me."

"What are you talking about?" Brigit snapped. "Sylvia, what is wrong with you? You drag me in here, you curse at me and tell me I've ruined your life, and then you strike Ian. What the hell is going on?"

"Sylvia is an Iozzi," Mel said. "Related to Christopher Iozzi."

"Christopher Iozzi?" Brigit asked. "The drug-runner hiding under the veneer of a young entrepreneur? Sam wrote the article that exposed him."

"And got him killed!" Sylvia screeched. "You and your magazine cost me my brother."

Brigit rose, standing over Ian like a guardian angel. "Let Ian and Melanie go, they did nothing to you or your brother."

"Sorry, but no," Sylvia said. She picked up a jug of tiki-torch fluid and began to pour it on the floor. She looked at Mel and shook her head. "Wrong place, wrong time."

"You will not do this!" Brigit said, and

she lunged for Sylvia. Knowing that they were about to be barbecued, Mel jumped with her. Surely, two of them could overpower Sylvia.

Sylvia dropped the jug and swung her candleholder. It glanced off Brigit's shoulder and, before Mel could move, it slammed into her temple. The floor rose up to meet her, and everything went black.

It was the burn in her lungs that roused her. Mel felt as if her chest were on fire from the inside. She coughed and sucked in a breath, but it made it worse. She convulsed, feeling as if she were suffocating. Her eyes were filled with tears, and the smoke around her was as thick as fog, making it impossible to see.

She tried to remember where the door was, but she had no idea which way she'd been facing when she'd fallen. When she tried to crawl forward, she noticed through her tears that the room was surrounded by a ring of fire. A sob constricted her throat, but she choked it down. She had no time to cry. She had to get out of here.

She pulled her gown up past her knees so that she could crawl without getting stuck in her skirt. She inched forward until her hands touched the smooth fabric of a man's tuxedo jacket. She jumped back, and then realized it had to be Hannigan. She reached out and patted her way up the arm until she found his face. Through the tears that streamed from her eyes, she saw that he was still unconscious.

"Hannigan," she croaked. "We have to get out of here."

She shook his body. He didn't respond. She tried to drag him, but he was too heavy, and she couldn't get enough air into her lungs to give her the power to try. She couldn't leave him here to die. Adjusting her skirt to free her legs, she hunkered down on her knees and began to roll Hannigan in the direction that she hoped was the door. It was like trying to move a sack of cement.

Grief welled up from the center of her being. She was going to die. She would never see Joe again. She would never look into his chocolate brown eyes or feel his arms around her again. The pain this thought caused burnt hotter than the flames that licked and lapped at her skin, taunting her with her imminent demise.

No! Mel refused to give in. She refused to let go of her life so easily. She wanted to laugh with Angie and Tate again and cuddle Captain Jack. She wanted her mother to pester her with her silly worries, and she wanted to bake her cupcakes. She wasn't going to let go of all she held dear that easily.

Mel crouched beside Hannigan. She lowered her shoulder and used her body as leverage. She managed to move him once, then twice. She had rolled him about four times when there was a crash behind her. Terrified that the ceiling was coming down, she spun to see four burly firemen and another man coming towards her.

"Mel!" It was Martinez.

He snatched her up into his arms, leaving Hannigan to the firemen, and raced out of the room with her. As soon as they reached the patio, he set her down and put the oxygen mask he'd been wearing over her face.

Mel sucked in the sweet air while Martinez held her hand and checked her over. She immediately began to hack and cough as her body rejected the smoke that had gotten into her lungs.

Once the coughing fit stopped, she lifted her mask, and asked in a raspy voice, "Where's Brigit? Sylvia Lucci killed Sam, and she planned to kill Brigit, too."

"Mask on," Martinez ordered. He cupped her face and studied her eyes for a moment, as if reassuring himself that she was okay.

"I'll go see if they've found them."

An EMT arrived at Mel's side, but she didn't let go of Martinez's hand. She didn't like the idea of him going anywhere near the fire. He turned to look at her, gave her a slow smile, and leaned forward and kissed her head.

"Don't worry," he said. "I'll be careful."

Mel nodded and watched him go, feeling a surge of panic give her a case of the shakes, which in turn caused another bout of coughing. Damn, she hadn't even gotten his first name yet.

"I'm going to check you for signs of smoke inhalation," the EMT said. He was young, but he was very gentle as he tipped her head back and checked her eyes and then her nostrils with a light. "Are you nauseous?"

Mel thought about it for a second. Her lungs hurt as if she had bronchitis, and her skin felt hot. She had a scorching headache, but otherwise she felt okay.

"No," she said. "But my head hurts."

"You took a solid hit to the head," the EMT said. "You're very lucky, there's no sign of a concussion. Still, I want you to go to the hospital and get checked out."

She watched as Hannigan was strapped to a stretcher and carried to an ambulance. He hadn't even woken up yet. Across the patio, Mel could see that the police and fire departments had cleared the party out of the ballroom. As she squinted through the rescue personnel, she saw Uncle Stan escorting Angie through the crowd. They rushed to her side.

"Mel! What happened? Are you all right?" Angie looked frantic, and Mel had no doubt she was a sight.

Both Uncle Stan and Angie knelt down to hug her, and the feel of their arms about her made Mel's throat get tight with unshed tears. There was a shout and a crashing noise. Several firemen backed away from the building, and Mel felt her chest compress, and it had nothing to do with the smoke.

Where was Martinez? Had he gone back into the building after Brigit? Mel tried to stand, but Angie held her down.

"No. There's nothing you can do," she said.

They watched in horror as the firemen worked the hoses, trying to douse the flames before they spread to the bigger rooms. There was a shout, and then Martinez came out of the building, carrying Brigit MacLeod.

He collapsed onto his knees, a fireman catching Brigit before he dropped her. Moving faster than his bulky frame seemed capable of, Uncle Stan caught his partner before he hit the patio floor.

The EMT who'd been checking Mel raced over to the two men, helping Uncle Stan with Martinez. Mel watched with her heart in her throat. Finally, Uncle Stan looked up and caught her eye. He gave her a nod, signaling that Martinez was okay, and Mel slumped back against Angie.

"Can I take you to the hospital now?" Angie asked.

Mel fell into a coughing fit that left her weak and with a pounding head when it was over.

"Yes, please," she said.

Angie helped her up, putting Mel's arm over her shoulders to brace her. As the EMTs worked on Martinez, putting an oxygen mask on him and tending to his burns, he glanced up and met Mel's gaze. She gave him a small smile, and he winked at her in return.

"Take him to the hospital," Uncle Stan ordered, and the paramedics began to load Martinez onto a stretcher. Uncle Stan took Mel's other arm and helped Angie get her to a waiting squad car. "I'm going to have a squad drive you over to the hospital, and I'm calling your mother."

"No," Mel began to argue, but she started coughing. Angie stuffed her gown into the car after her and then climbed in herself.

A uniformed officer was at the wheel, and Uncle Stan gave him a nod. Before Mel could offer up any other protest, they were on their way.

Although Mel showed no signs of smoke inhalation, the doctors were worried about the knot on her head and admitted her for observation. Angie and Tate and her mother all hovered until the doctor noticed that Mel wasn't resting, and he shooed them all away.

Mel hated that she didn't know what had happened to Brigit and Hannigan. She wondered if they'd caught Sylvia and how Martinez was doing. She tried to find her cell phone, but she suspected her mother had taken it. When her doctor came to check on her again, he was unhappy to find her awake and had the nurse give her a sedative.

Before Mel could protest, she was zonked out in dreamland.

Mel awoke hours later. Her skin felt tight and her chest was still sore, but her head had stopped pounding and was now a tolerable ache. She wondered if that was the pain meds or if she was just feeling better.

She glanced around her room, surprised to find it was still dark outside. A snore brought her attention around to the chair by the window. Joe was asleep in a hunched-up position, being too tall for the chair. The sight of him made her heart flutter, just like always. She should have known he'd be here. That was so Joe.

The curtain that closed off her half of the room was pulled aside and to her surprise Martinez hobbled in on a pair of crutches. He looked as bad as she felt, and she gave him a wan smile.

"Are you okay?" she asked.

"I'm better now that I know you're all right," he said.

"You saved my life —" Mel paused and then smiled as she added, "Manolo."

Martinez gave her a full on grin. "You figured it out. How?"

"I badgered the nurse until she found out how Detective Martinez was doing," she said. "And she reported back that Detective Manolo Martinez was going to be just fine."

"Nice detective work," he said.

"Just lucky," she said with a shrug.

"Everyone calls me Manny," he said.

"Manny," she repeated. "The name suits you."

"I like hearing you say it," he said.

They stared at each other for a long moment. Mel got the feeling they had a lot to talk about, but Manny glanced at Joe asleep in his chair. It seemed to change his mind.

"So, do your lungs feel like they've been scraped with a cheese grater?" he asked as he looked back at her.

His voice was gravelly like hers, and Mel nodded, refusing to laugh for fear of another coughing fit. The doc could say it was good for her to cough it up, but it hurt like hell, and she was reluctant to feel that searing pain again.

"Yes. How about burns?" she asked. "I got a nice one on my leg that almost looks like a cupcake."

It was Manny's turn to squash a laugh. "I have a few," he said. "Not nearly as artsy as that, more like Rorschach splotches of pain, and I got a nice sprain trying to outrun the flames, thus the crutches."

A grunt from the chair made them both turn to look at Joe. He was sitting up and blinking. When he saw them looking at him, he shook his head as if to clear it and stood up. He crossed the room to the side of the bed and studied Mel with a worried look.

"Are you all right?"

She nodded. "I'm fine, thanks to Detective Martinez."

If Manny noticed that she'd reverted back to his professional name, he didn't show it.

"Stan told me what you did," Joe addressed Manny. "About how you went into the fire and got Mel out. I can't ever thank you enough."

He held out his hand, and Manny leaned on his crutch and shook it.

"No problem. It's all in a day's work." He looked back at Mel. "I'll let you get some rest."

"Thanks," she said, and then quickly added, "I really appreciate what you did, Manny."

Their eyes met for a moment, and he nodded and then turned and left. Mel couldn't help but feel there was much left unsaid between them.

Joe sighed and sat on the edge of Mel's bed very carefully, as if afraid any movement might cause her pain.

"How are you feeling really?" he asked.

"Fine," she said, which of course was a lie. "Do you know what happened to the others?"

"Ian Hannigan and Brigit MacLeod are both in critical," Joe said. "Sylvia Lucci did not fare as well. She died on the way to the hospital from smoke inhalation."

"She killed Sam," Mel said.

Joe nodded.

"She wanted to kill Brigit, too, for ruining her brother." Mel's voice was shaky, and Joe scooted up next to her and put an arm around her. Mel turned into him and let the tears fall down her face onto his chest.

"When I think that I could have lost you," he said. His voice was a low whisper. "I can't bear it."

"You didn't lose me," Mel said, leaning away from him and wiping the tears off of her cheeks. "I'm still here."

But she knew what he meant. The terror that had filled her in those few moments when she'd thought she and Hannigan were going to die. She never wanted to feel that desolate again. It had been the same feeling she'd felt when she lost her father.

It was then that Mel understood why she didn't want to marry Joe. Tate had been right. The reason she didn't want to get married was because she feared death. Not hers, but the death of the person she loved. If she married Joe, then one day she might lose him like her mother had lost her father, and Mel didn't think she would survive it. No, she didn't want to go through that ever again.

She realized Joe was talking, and she turned to face him.

"As soon as you get out of here," Joe said, "we're going to get you a ring and sit down with a calendar and pick a date. I don't ever want to feel like I did when Stan called to tell me you were missing in a fire. I want you to be my wife, Mel. I want to keep you safe."

"I'm sorry Joe," she said. "I just can't. I can't marry you."

THIRTY-THREE

Mel sat in her office, happy to have her space back. Brigit had sent an assistant over to clear out her things, and now that it wasn't being shared by the editor in chief of a major magazine, the small closet seemed almost roomy.

Brigit had recovered from the fire, as had Hannigan. Mel could tell from the way Brigit said his name when they talked that something was happening there that was more than professional. But maybe that was the result of surviving a life-threatening situation — it either brought people together or shoved them apart.

Mel hadn't spoken to Joe since her overnight in the hospital a week ago. She hadn't told anyone of their new status, mostly because she didn't really know what it was or wasn't. It seemed as if they were at a stalemate. Joe wanted marriage more than ever, but the very idea terrified her, and so they had retreated to their separate corners, at least for now.

She hadn't told her mother about "dear Joe" because she hated to disappointment her. And she didn't tell Uncle Stan, because she didn't want him to tell Manny and open herself up for something she wasn't ready to consider.

As for herself, she missed Joe. She dreamt about him and thought about him pretty much every second of every day. She supposed she could have choked down her fears, said yes, and married him, but —

The door to Mel's office burst open, and Marty dashed in as if his backside were on fire.

"I figured it out!" he cried. "I know who the spy is. I know who's been blabbing to Olivia!"

Mel's jaw dropped. "Who?"

"Me!" he cried, and clapped his hands onto his bald head as if trying to keep it attached to his body.

"No!" Mel cried.

"Yes!"

"What's going on in here?" Tate, Angie, and Oz all peeked around the door.

"Benedict Arnold here just confessed to being our spy," Mel said. She rose from behind her desk and shooed everyone out into the kitchen, where there was more space.

"Marty, how could you?" Angie cried.

"Dude," Oz said with a shake of his shaggy head.

"I know, I know," Marty said. "I was so stupid."

"Wait, back up. Let's hear the whole story," Tate said. "Hang on. I may need a cupcake to process this."

Tate disappeared into the walk-in cooler and came out with a tray full of cupcakes. He plopped it down on the table and everyone sat on a stool and chose the flavor that would help each of them swallow Marty's news.

"Okay, it's like this," Marty said. He paused and took a bite of his Tinkerbell, a lemon cupcake with raspberry buttercream, and once he'd swallowed, he continued.

"I've been trying to catch up to this millennium, you know, snorkel the 'net, twit on Tweeter, love on BF."

Oz choked on his organic vanilla cupcake, and Mel could tell he was trying not to laugh as he said, "You mean, surf the 'net, tweet on Twitter, and like on FB."

"Yeah, that's it," Marty said.

Angie nibbled her Death by Chocolate,

and said, "Welcome to the twenty-first century."

"Thanks," Marty said.

"So, I'm not making the Olivia connection," Tate said. "Did you link up with her online or something?

"No, I'm not stupid," Marty protested. "Okay, maybe I am a little slow on the whole cyber thing. But a few months ago, I decided I wanted to have a blog."

Mel lowered the Moonlight Madness cupcake she'd been about to devour. Given that it was chocolate with coconut, her absolute favorite, this said something about her state of alarm.

"What do you mean a blog?" she asked. "How do you even know what a blog is?"

"I sort of fell into one," Marty said. "And I liked it."

"Oh, my god," Angie groaned and put her head down. "Marty fell into a blog hole."

Tate had given up trying not to laugh and was doubled up, causing Oz to give up, too. Angie started to giggle, but Mel was too horrified to find anything funny about the situation.

"Marty, what did you blog about?" she asked.

"Stuff," he said.

"Stuff?" she repeated. "Define *stuff*!"

"Just, life, stuff," he said. Then he lowered his head, and his voice and added, "And you know, stories about the bakery."

"Ah!" Mel gasped. "You did not give out any of my recipes."

"No!" Marty protested. "I would never, but I may have blogged about an upcoming photo shoot, unintentionally giving certain people that information."

"What people?" Mel asked. "I want names."

The others, hearing the seriousness in her tone, stopped laughing, and all eyes focused on Marty, whose head had begun to glow red like an off-shore beacon.

"Well, her handle is Domicaketrix," Marty said.

Angie began to choke and splutter, and Tate thumped her on the back, and Oz just shook his head.

"Marty, how could you?" Mel asked.

"I was intrigued," he said, looking pained. "I'm only human, you know."

"You mean you're only a man," Angie retorted. "Please leave my gender out of it."

"Well, I didn't know it was her!" he argued. "I mean, who expected her to write such . . ."

His voice trailed off, and Mel crossed her arms over her chest and glowered.

"Write such what?" she asked.

"Hot stuff," he mumbled.

"Oh, man, it just keeps getting worse," Oz said. "Have a little dignity and try to save yourself."

"I can't," Marty said. "We're supposed to have a date and, well, she's here!"

"What?" Mel jumped up from her stool and hustled through the swinging doors into the bakery. She felt everyone follow behind her, and she snapped, "Stay here. I'll take care of this!"

She heard someone gulp behind her and figured it was Marty. The front door of the bakery was locked, but she twisted the dead bolt, shoved the door open, and stepped out onto the patio.

"You!" she cried. "Stay away from my staff."

Olivia was seated at one of the patio tables. She stood when Mel slammed out the door, and Mel stumbled. She had never seen Olivia in anything other than her bright blue chef coat with her gray corkscrew hair fastened in a ponytail on the crown of her head. That was not the Olivia who stood before her now.

"I can't stay away," Olivia said. "I have a date. Do we need to talk about this?"

Mel studied her. Olivia's hair was brushed

out and flowed in gentle gray waves to her shoulders. She wore just a trace of makeup, which accented her eyes and lips becomingly. Her sturdy frame was dressed in a muted print, georgette dress with a pleated skirt that stopped just above her knees. Her shoes were beige high heels. She looked lovely.

"Yes," Mel said. "I think we do."

Olivia gestured for Mel to sit at one of their iron patio tables. Mel did, and Olivia took the seat across from her, all very civilized.

"I started following Martin's blog —"

Olivia paused and glanced at the bakery window, where Tate, Angie, Oz, and Marty all had their faces pressed to the glass to see if Mel had put a smack-down on Olivia, no doubt. Olivia smiled and gave Marty a finger wave with her pretty pink nails. He grinned and waved back, causing Angie to cuff him upside the head.

"You were saying," Mel said.

"Oh, yes," Olivia said as she glanced back. "I started following Martin's blog to spy on you. I admit it."

"Uh-huh," Mel said.

"But who knew ButterMeUp would turn out to be such a hottie?" Olivia sighed.

Mel frowned.

"ButterMeUp is Martin's online name," Olivia said.

"I got that," Mel said. "I'm trying not to gag."

"Look, I know you're struggling in the romantic sense right now," Olivia said.

"He *told* you that?" Mel felt a pressure building behind her eye sockets that she feared was going to send her eyeballs popping out any second, the only upside being that they might hit Olivia.

"Well, he didn't know I was me," she said.

"You know, it's going to be really hard for you to have a date with a dead body," Mel said. She turned and glared at the window, and Marty jumped back as if her look had burnt him.

"Listen," Olivia said, "I don't get asked out on a lot of dates, and Martin, well, he's a real gentleman, you know?"

Mel sighed. "I know."

"Running a business is a twenty-four/ seven operation, as you know," Olivia said. "I've been alone for a long time."

"Your point?" Mel asked.

"I'm lonely, and I'm asking you to let Martin take me out without firing him or docking his pay or anything like that," Olivia said.

It sounded like every word had cost Olivia

a pint of blood, and Mel had to respect her for that.

She met Olivia's gaze, and they sized each other up. Mel arched an eyebrow, and Olivia mirrored her. They were still enemies — of that there was no doubt — but she couldn't deny Marty and Olivia the right to date without reprisals from her.

"Fine, but if I find out that you're after any of my recipes, I'm coming after you," Mel said. She hoped she'd channeled enough Jack Nicholson from *The Shining* to scare Olivia straight.

Olivia beamed at her, and Mel blinked. She would never have expected that Olivia could look so pretty.

"Marty, your date is waiting!" Mel called. She glanced at the window and saw them all looking at her in something akin to shock.

"Mel, can I offer you a bit of advice?" Olivia asked.

"Really?" Mel asked. "You're going to advise me now?"

"We're a lot alike," Olivia said.

"No, we're not," Mel argued. "You're crazy, for one thing."

"Don't you have to be to be a baker?" Olivia asked. "Listen, it's easy to be afraid of getting involved."

366

"I'm not —" Mel began to protest, but Olivia cut her off.

"Yes, you are. Marty told me that you used to be heavy and that your self-esteem isn't what it should be, considering what a lovely woman you've become."

"That's it!" Mel yelled, jumping up from her seat. "He's dead man walking!"

Mel was horrified that Olivia of all people knew of the most humiliating period of her life.

"Hey, I'm trying to help you out here," Olivia snapped, also rising to her feet. "Don't be threatening my date!"

"I don't need your help."

"Yes, you do," Olivia said. "Now shut up and listen. People don't love you back like your business does. They're unpredictable and demanding. Owning your own business is a beautiful thing, but it's not a life. Try to figure out how to have both before you're too old, like me."

Mel and Olivia stood a foot apart, both breathing heavy and looking like they wanted to take a swing at each other.

The door to the bakery opened, and Marty stepped out. Olivia stepped back from Mel and began to smooth her hair. Mel glanced between them. There was no denying it: when Marty and Olivia looked at each other, the air positively zapped with electricity. Wow!

"Do not talk about me," Mel said to Marty through gritted teeth. "Or the business or anyone else from the bakery. Clear?"

Marty nodded, but he only had eyes for Olivia.

"Come here, you saucy minx," he said.

ButterMeUp held out his arm, and Domicaketrix giggled when she took it. Mel watched them walk away, bemused by this sudden turn of events.

Oz, Tate, and Angie all came out of the bakery and stood on the front patio with her.

"I so did not see that coming," Oz said.

"Me, neither," Tate agreed.

"Are you sure this is a good idea?" Angie asked.

"No," Mel said. "But what could I say? It looks like they're smitten."

As they walked away, Marty put his arm around Olivia's waist and pulled her close. Their heads were pressed together as they shared a whispered conversation.

Mel felt a sharp stab of envy pierce her heart.

Was Olivia right? Was Mel doomed to wind up old and alone because she was too afraid of losing a man to let herself love him?

"I'm going to go do some paperwork," she said.

She closed the office door behind her and took a deep, steadying breath. Then she pulled out her phone and dialed.

"Hello," he answered on the second ring.

"So, I was wondering," Mel said. "Are you busy tonight?"

RECEIPES

PUMPKIN CUPCAKES WITH WHIPPED CREAM FROSTING

2 cups all-purpose flour
1 teaspoon baking soda
1 teaspoon baking powder
1 teaspoon coarse salt
1 teaspoon ground cinnamon
1 teaspoon ground ginger
1/4 teaspoon nutmeg
1 cup packed light-brown sugar
1 cup granulated sugar
2 sticks unsalted butter, melted
4 large eggs, lightly beaten
1 can (15 ounces) pumpkin puree

Preheat oven to 350 degrees. Line cupcake pan with paper liners. In a medium bowl, whisk together flour, baking soda, baking powder, salt, cinnamon, ginger, and nutmeg. In a large bowl, mix together brown sugar, granulated sugar, melted butter, and eggs.

Add dry ingredients, and mix until smooth. Lastly, mix in the pumpkin until thoroughly blended. Scoop the batter evenly into the cupcake liners. Bake 20 to 25 minutes until a toothpick inserted in the center comes out clean. Let cool before frosting. Makes 24.

Whipped Cream Frosting
1/2 cup heavy whipping cream, chilled
4 tablespoons powdered sugar

In a medium bowl, whip heavy cream on medium-high speed for 3 minutes. In a small bowl, sift powdered sugar. Add the sugar to the whipped cream mixture and mix on medium-high speed until stiff peaks form. Frosting should be able to stand on its own.

Garnish idea: Sprinkle with nutmeg or cinnamon.

GLUTEN-FREE CHOCOLATE CUPCAKES WITH GANACHE FROSTING
2 cups blanched almond flour
1/4 cup unsweetened cocoa powder
1/2 teaspoon salt
1/2 teaspoon baking soda

1 cup sugar
2 large eggs
1 tablespoon pure vanilla extract

Preheat oven to 350. Line cupcake pan with paper liners. In a large bowl, mix together almond flour, cocoa powder, salt, and baking soda. In a medium-sized bowl, combine sugar, eggs, and vanilla. Stir the wet ingredients into the dry mixture until thoroughly combined. Scoop the batter evenly into paper liners. Bake 20 to 25 minutes until a toothpick inserted in the center of the cupcake comes out clean. Let cool before frosting. Makes 24.

Ganache Frosting
3/4 cup heavy cream
8 ounces dark chocolate chips
1 teaspoon vanilla extract
Pinch of sea salt

In a medium saucepan, bring the cream to a boil then remove it from the heat. Stir in the chocolate until it is melted and smooth, then stir in the vanilla extract and salt. Let the ganache stand at room temperature for 5 minutes, then move to the refrigerator and chill until the ganache thickens and becomes shiny and spreadable. This could take anywhere from 15 to 30 minutes, depending on the temperature of your refrigerator.

Garnish idea: Pomegranate seeds or a chocolate dipped strawberry.

CORN CUPCAKES WITH A HONEY BROWN BUTTER FROSTING

1 1/4 cups flour
1/3 cup cornmeal
2 teaspoons baking powder
3/4 teaspoon kosher salt
3 tablespoons sour cream
1/2 cup canned whole corn kernel
1/2 cup unsalted butter, softened
1 1/4 cups sugar
3 large eggs
1 teaspoon vanilla extract

Preheat oven to 350. Line cupcake pan with paper liners. In a large bowl, whisk together flour, cornmeal, baking powder, and salt. In a medium bowl, mix together sour cream, corn, butter, sugar, eggs, and vanilla. Mix the wet ingredients into the dry mixture. Scoop the batter evenly into paper liners. Bake 20 to 25 minutes until a toothpick inserted in the center of the cupcake comes out clean. Let cool before frosting. Makes 12.

Honey Brown Butter Frosting

4 tablespoons butter, browned
1 cup sifted confectioners' sugar
1 teaspoon pure vanilla extract
1 to 2 tablespoons honey

In a small saucepan, melt butter over medium-high heat until nut brown in color. Remove pan from heat, and pour butter into a bowl, leaving any burned sediment behind. Once it has cooled completely, add sugar, vanilla, and 1 tablespoon honey. Stir until smooth. If the icing is too thick, add the remaining tablespoon of honey, a little at a time, until frosting is at the desired consistency.

Garnish idea: Sprinkle with 2–3 fresh corn kernels.

PISTACHIO CUPCAKES WITH CREAM CHEESE FIG FROSTING

2 1/4 cups flour
1 tablespoon baking powder
1/2 teaspoon salt
3 eggs
1 cup milk
1 stick butter, softened
1 1/4 cups sugar
1 teaspoon vanilla extract

1 teaspoon pistachio extract
1 cup ground pistachios

Preheat oven to 350. Line cupcake pan with paper liners. In a large bowl, sift together the flour, baking powder, and salt. In a medium bowl, beat together the eggs, milk, butter, sugar, vanilla, and pistachio extracts. Mix the wet ingredients into the dry ingredients until smooth. Stir in the ground pistachios. Scoop the batter evenly into paper liners. Bake 25 to 30 minutes until a toothpick inserted in the center of the cupcake comes out clean. Let cool before frosting. Makes 24.

Cream Cheese Frosting With Fig Garnish
8 ounces cream cheese, softened
1 stick unsalted butter, softened
1/2 teaspoon vanilla extract
3 cups powdered sugar
Fresh fig slices

Beat cream cheese, butter, and vanilla in large bowl until smooth. Gradually add powdered sugar and beat until frosting is smooth. Put frosting in a pastry bag and pipe onto cupcakes in thick swirls, using an open tip. Top with a slice of fresh fig.

ABOUT THE AUTHOR

Jenn McKinlay has baked and frosted cupcakes into the shapes of cats, mice, and outer space aliens, to name just a few. Writing a mystery series based on one of her favorite food groups (dessert) is as enjoyable as licking the beaters, and she can't wait to whip up the next one. She is also the author of the Library Lover's Mysteries. She lives in Scottsdale, Arizona, with her family. Visit her website at www.jenn mckinlay.com.

CPSIA information can be obtained
at www.ICGtesting.com
Printed in the USA
FFOW05n1344130114